I0587127

No Crime Intended

Steve Williamson

Copyright © [2025] by [Steve Williamson]

All rights reserved.

No portion of this book may be reproduced in any form without written permission from the publisher or author, except as permitted by U.S. copyright law.

Contents

Part 1

1

It's payday.

Rachel Carter stares at her phone, breath caught in her throat, as the red negative bank balance glares back, taunting her like a smug-faced emoji. She shudders. She can't even cover the mortgage payment this month. She presses her thumbs against her temples. This shouldn't be happening to a thirty-eight-year-old woman, in a good job, earning a decent salary.

The busy open-plan office hums and clatters around her. Fingers tap at keyboards, voices murmur into headsets, a photocopier spits out paper in rhythmic bursts. Somewhere, an abandoned phone shrills its infuriating ringtone. Every sound ratchets up her irritation levels until she wants to stand on her desk and scream, *shut the fuck up*. But that wouldn't be a good look for the tech service desk manager.

She escapes to the ground floor food-court, strides to the espresso bar and orders her usual double-shot latte. She stirs in half a sachet of sugar, dusts it with cinnamon powder and mentally calculates how much she could save if she were to break her two-coffees-a-day habit. Not enough. Not even close.

She finds a corner table, away from the grinding of beans and clatter of cups. She knows exactly where her money's going.

Living close to the edge is nothing new. In university, she would often scrape through the final weeks of term, surviving on budget meals and cheap cider. Back then, a quick call to Mum and Dad would fix things if she became really stuck. She can't do that now. They're modest-living retirees. This problem is hers to solve and she'll start with her husband.

She unlocks her phone, opens LinkedIn, and navigates to her saved jobs list. Two roles:

Social Media Marketing Guru

Digital Media Manager

Both London-based, decent salary. She forwards them to Richard.

She remembers when he first went freelance. Every time he gained a new client, they'd celebrate by going for a meal. That's when they were close. Now, three years on, he has more clients than ever yet seems to earn less. She enjoys being the higher earner, but he needs to pay his share. It's been months since he paid anything towards the mortgage.

Her thoughts drift to the interview she has tomorrow, in the cyber security team. A full grade promotion and more money. She feels ready for the step up and has spent all week preparing by reading up on the latest cyber security risks in the pharma industry. She would love to get back to being hands-on technical again. Her love for programming began in high school where she was a member of the computing club. Her project – a language translation app that converted English to French and vice versa – was a prize winner. Nowadays, that sort of thing would be called artificial intelligence. She's always been technically curious, and this job would be the perfect career move. She needs this more than ever.

Her phone pings:

Richard: Stop sending me crap. These are low grade jobs. not worth getting out of bed for!

Well, that was expected. He enjoys his self-employed lifestyle too much. No, she will not stop sending him jobs. They'll talk tonight.

She sits and gazes at people she doesn't know walking by. Her company – Synaptonica Pharmaceuticals – is one of four organisations occupying this central London office. Still a fledgling company, trying to carve out their niche in an industry dominated by big pharma corporations. They've invested millions into their research programme: a big bet on a new drug to treat dementia. If it gets through clinical trials, it could be transformational for patients and a blockbuster revenue generator for the company.

Back at her desk, her workday follows the usual dreary routine: unnecessary meetings, verbose emails and well-intended interruptions from colleagues. Lionel, her deputy, saunters over for his daily drama. Today's crisis involves a new app that has gone live with no user acceptance testing. It's supposed to simplify the work of research scientists by capturing results of their experiments. But support calls are surging and stress levels in the team are rising because users are shouting at them. She indulges his crisis for twenty minutes before reassuring him she will be recruiting a new team member. Appeased, he wanders back to his desk, exchanging fist-bumps with a few colleagues on the way. She's still thinking of a polite way to tell him that jet-black dyed hair, on a man approaching fifty, is not a good look.

Rachel spent most of her lunchtime on the phone to the mortgage company. After navigating an overly complex numbered menu system, she finally spoke to a genuine person, and explained her husband was between jobs and had a short-term cash-flow problem. Could they skip a couple of payments? They put her on hold, kept her hanging on for ten minutes, before offering her a six-month repayment holiday. She was close to tears at that point. A lifeline.

It's 5.30 p.m. Most staff are heading home, but Rachel is in the all-gender restroom, standing in front of the mirror. She smooths the front of her skirt, checks the collar of her blouse and reapplies a touch of concealer beneath her eyes. It's been a stressful day, but she's determined not to let it show for her meeting with Jonathan Winstanley, her leadership mentor. Few people get a chance to meet with the chief financial officer, and she will not waste this opportunity.

She polishes her thick-rimmed glasses, angles them to catch the light, then wipes grime from her shoes with a leather wipe. One last check. Her blonde hair, cut into an asymmetric bob, sits just right. Yes, she looks professional. *Hold your composure, girl.*

Jonathan's not much older than her, but his career path seems to have been supercharged. She wonders what he's got that she hasn't. When they last spoke, he told her she was a 'rough diamond,' which sounded like a compliment. There's a lot she wants to discuss, but with only thirty minutes available, she'll stick to two topics: her counter-proposal to the outsourcing initiative, then his advice for her interview tomorrow.

She steps out of the lift and makes her way to his office. Her heart is racing, and she feels the nerves stir inside. But there's something else. Belief in herself.

She takes a seat in his twelfth-floor executive office, gazing out at the darkened skyline, mesmerised by the glass skyscrapers, which resemble misshapen LEGO towers. Her eyes find The Shard. It always draws her in. Richard proposed there, in the cocktail bar on the fifty-second floor, where he went down on one knee in front of a room of strangers. That was six years ago. They always said they'd go back. They never did.

Jonathan reclines in his high-backed leather chair and tugs his tie loose. A framed magazine spread, hanging on his wall, catches her eye. His photo dominates the page alongside a bold headline about visionary leadership.

He swivels to face her. 'Good to see you again, Rachel. How's your day been?'

She takes a breath, 'Hectic. Impatient users demanding immediate service, stressed team members. We had this call—'

He points to her notebook. 'So, what would you like to discuss?'

Don't waffle. She takes a breath. 'Can we start with the outsourcing proposal?'

He shrugs. 'Sure.'

She outlines her alternative to the outsourcing plans. One where she keeps most of her team. It involves upskilling and shifting towards a more proactive model, providing a better-quality service for no extra cost. As she talks, she notices him clicking his mouse, looking at his monitor. She falters.

He turns back to face her. 'What you need to think about, Rachel, is how to deliver more with less. We can get the same number of service desk agents in India for less than half the cost of London. It's a no-brainer,' he says.

Her pen is poised above a blank page, but she writes nothing down. 'I'm also thinking of the people impact.'

He smiles. 'Empathy is a nice leadership trait. Good for the company image. But...'

'Business first,' she finishes his sentence.

He nods. 'Let me tell you about my career journey.'

He launches into a self-promoting monologue. She's heard it before: a start in professional services, a stint with two of the big-four and a transfer to New York. An executive search firm brought him back to London, as CFO, who would deliver greater shareholder value by more efficient cost management.

Rachel nods, feigning admiration. She's still thinking about her team. The team she doesn't want to see being made redundant, but he's as good as closed down that discussion. When he stops talking, she tells him about her planned interview tomorrow, for a role in the cyber security team, working for Ray Dunlop.

His smile drops. 'Ray Dunlop works for me.'

'I know.'

He leans forward on his desk. 'How important is this job to you?' he asks with a smirk.

She takes a breath. 'It just seems like the perfect next-step.'

He nods. 'He's interviewing external candidates. You're up against tough competition.'

'And I have a lot to offer.'

He stares at her for a moment, smiling. Then he stands, comes out from behind his desk and crouches down beside her chair. His hand drops onto her shoulder. Too close.

'Listen,' he says, voice low, 'I could just tell Dunlop to appoint you? Cut out the interview charade.' He leans in, inches from her face, eyes sweeping over her body as he massages her shoulder.

Rachel stiffens. She knows what's coming. Abruptly, she rises, shaking her head, one hand raised in warning – keep your distance. He ignores it, steps in and grabs her waist.

He smiles. 'Have you ever done it on an office desk before?' He leans in for a kiss. The sour edge of coffee clings to his breath. Rage burns inside her. He has no right to touch her.

'No!' she shouts as she turns her face, shoving him back. Her eyes dart to the window, but there is no line-of-sight into the office, no witnesses. She moves for the door, but he shadows her. Her legs tremble, her heart pounds like it wants to leap out of her chest. She wants to hit him, but he'll easily overpower her, and they are alone and now she's scared.

'Jonathan, this is inappropriate.' She forces the words out, steadying her tone, hiding her fear and fury.

He blocks the door, arms folded, entitled smile plastered on his face. 'How about this? If you get the job, we'll celebrate. Dinner. Just the two of us.'

Dinner with him will never happen. But this is her chance to escape. She fakes a smile. 'Okay.'

He steps aside. Her trembling hand snatches the handle. She pushes the door open and rushes out, though not quickly enough to stop his hand brushing down the back of her skirt. She strides down the corridor, steps into the lift and stabs the door-close button again and again. When the doors finally shut, she exhales a shuddering breath. Relief, laced with disgust.

This isn't the first time someone's hit on her at work. She can handle smutty remarks and juvenile flirting. But this was different. Threatening. A meeting in his office after hours. He'd planned this.

She steps out into the ground-floor lobby and spots a woman in a security uniform. They nod to each other. Two younger men with backpacks are chatting, oblivious to her harassed appearance. She pushes through the revolving door, glancing behind as she walks out into the night-time bustle. Buses rumble past, horns sound, shop fronts dazzle. The cold air hits her face. She should be safe now. Just another city worker making her way home. But she's still trembling. And angry. She had prepared for that meeting thinking he would see her as a future leader. Someone worth mentoring. She shouldn't have been so naïve.

Dim yellow street lights cast long shadows as Rachel walks the cracked pavement back to her North London home. Her eyes scan the ground so she can avoid the uneven slabs warped by tree roots. Her mind is still looping through the encounter with Jonathan. The company has policies against that kind of behaviour. He's probably done it before and got away with it. Her inner rage is still simmering. She used to look up to him, but now she just thinks he's an entitled prick. She could report him using the integrity helpline, but it's her word against his and whistleblowing a senior executive, without witnesses, could backfire in a way she doesn't need right now.

She reaches her mid-terrace house, unlocks her front door and exhales as she enters. Richard is out, as usual. They're like ships that pass in the night these days. He works from home during the day; she's in the office. He heads out around 6.30 p.m., shortly before she arrives home. It's Wednesday, so he'll be at his pickleball club, coaching the improvers group and preparing for whatever tournament they have on at the weekend.

Wednesday used to be date night. Dinner, cinema or just down the pub. They took turns choosing, but he would give himself the power to veto her choice. She still remembers the night she chose to see *No Hard Feelings* at the cinema – an easy-watching comedy. She asked him to get the tickets. He did, but not for her choice. They watched *The Hunger Games* instead.

Date night faded. She doesn't miss it.

She walks into her narrow L-shaped kitchen, reaches for the Bombay Sapphire, pours herself a large one, drops in some ice cubes, tops it up with tonic and gives it a swirl. The sound of the clinking against the glass is helping her wind down. She opens the fridge. Her shelves – the top two – are stacked with Tupperware boxes, containing various homemade meals and leftovers. His shelves are stocked with convenience foods. She's not in the mood for cooking tonight, so retrieves a portion of bread-and-no-butter pudding, warms it slightly, and spoons Greek yoghurt on top. She's proud of how she can turn leftovers into a satisfactory meal. She checks her windowsill garden: basil, thyme, spring onion, pak-choi and spinach are all thriving. A large jar of Kombucha is fermenting in the corner.

As she eats, her mind shifts to her money problem, and a feeling of frustration takes over as she thinks about the conversation she needs to have with Richard. It has a certain inevitability about it. She'll tell him they're running out of money and will ask when he's next getting paid; he'll say he can't predict when his next viral video hit will be, but that's when the money will come in. She'll suggest part-time work; he'll accuse her of stifling his creativity. And then they'll shout at each other, with no compromise. She can't let it go that way tonight. This is too important. She needs him to work out for himself that this crisis is his problem as much as hers.

She moves to the lounge, places her glass on the pine coffee table and closes the curtains before sinking into the sofa. Her head buzzes and her neck and shoulders are stiff. She needs to unwind, to calm herself before Richard gets home. As a married couple, they should be able to talk properly and openly. But too often, their conversations spiral into bickering and end in stalemate or silence. It's the big things that weigh heaviest.

Like children. For Rachel, the thought of having a family is impossible to quieten. But whenever she mentions it, he fires back the same line. 'We agreed before we married that we would remain child-free.' Yes, that is correct. But she feels differently now. He should at least talk to her about what she is feeling instead of closing the subject and making her feel guilty.

At just after nine, the front door rattles open. There's a dull thud as his sports bag hits the floorboards.

He sticks his head into the lounge. 'Hi.'

'Hi,' she replies. No kiss.

He points to her drink. 'Tough day on the helpdesk?' He smirks.

She glares at him.

'Oops, sorry. I mean the tech service desk,' he says with a laugh.

'Why don't you grab a beer and come in and talk to me.' She keeps her tone light.

He disappears into the kitchen, returns a minute later, and drops into the chair opposite. Gangly, relaxed. Carefree. He's wearing long cotton sports shorts. Rachel watches him as he takes a long drink from a bottle of Moretti. She starts calmly. Tells him she had to arrange a mortgage repayment holiday, but it's only temporary – six months.

He nods. 'Loads of people are in the same boat. Cheap Covid mortgages, then they re-mortgage, and find they are paying double.'

She stares at him. *Yes, everything's gone up, except our joint income*.

'What do you think we should do?' she says.

He takes another swig, shrugs. 'I don't know. What do you think?' he says, as if the crisis is happening to someone else.

She bites her lip. 'If I get this promotion, that will help. But that's not enough. I'm worried we'll go bankrupt.'

He laughs, then leans forward in his chair. 'Show me your bank statement.'

She freezes. She hadn't planned for this. 'Trust me. I've been through everything.'

'It's on your phone.' He holds out his hand, jiggling his fingers. 'Let me look.'

Her hand grips tightly around her phone. If he sees her account statement, he'll notice the regular monthly payment she's making to her brother, Tony. She needs to deflect.

'I need you to contribute more,' she says, her voice stern.

He shakes his head. 'Have you any idea what it's like being self-employed?'

'No, but I know what it's like being married to someone who is.'

And that was the detonator. He stands, raising his voice. She matches him. They shout and talk over each other. He storms out, kicks his sports bag and stomps upstairs.

Rachel exhales hard, slumps into the cushions and drains the rest of her drink. She tried. She said nothing about getting another job and this is how it ends. At least he didn't see her bank statement, and the payments to Tony. She can't afford to subsidise him anymore, but she can't just stop supporting him either. He needs her, and she owes him.

It's past midnight and Rachel lies awake while Richard sleeps beside her, breathing heavily, not quite snoring. The thick duvet between them forms a soft, silent divide, like a peace wall. If bad days came with ratings, today would be on the scale of a multi-car pile-up: the debt, the incident with Jonathan and a husband who's found a new level of obstinacy.

Theirs has always been a volatile relationship. Trivial stuff like forgetting to put the bins out would flare into a fight, then pass like a sudden storm, smoothed over with make-up sex. Not anymore. Now, the void between them only widens. Their lives are diverging. She goes to the gym; he plays pickleball. She maps out her next career move; he makes viral videos that rarely go viral.

But it's not just about money or children. It's the way he takes pleasure from making her angry: laughing at her leftover meal creations, mocking her job as a manager. Belittling her achievements as if it were a sport. She's thought about couples' therapy but can imagine him turning it into a point-scoring contest, triumphantly listing her flaws and failings.

She tries to recall the last time they had sex. Six months, maybe more. In their early days, they were insatiable, and she remembers the excitement of buying their first sex toy together. Now she owns three, which are hidden with the *Mother & Baby* magazines at the bottom of her wardrobe. But toys don't provide intimacy. She wants to be desired, but he doesn't even initiate sex anymore. Maybe he fears she'll *accidentally* get pregnant.

2

Ray Dunlop, chief information security officer at Synaptonica, sits in his private office, nestled at the corner of the cyber operations centre – a secure zone, separated from the hubbub of the open-plan office zones used by most of the workforce. Three triple-monitor workstations face a video wall where a real-time network map pulses with colour-coded alerts. On the opposite wall, a framed portrait of Alan Turing hangs with quiet authority. *Code Breaker*, the caption reads. The centrepiece of the room is a large circular table, which is used for the daily huddle.

This is his space, reflective of his high standards of neatness and order: clear-desk policy, coats and bags out of sight in a cupboard. The potted plants and cylindrical air purifier help create the serenity necessary for the cyber security operations team. The thought of working in the cramped open-plan work zones unnerves him. The chatter, the clutter and the food smells would agitate him too much, and he'd end up shouting at people. He fought hard for this space. No one else below executive level has their own office. But Ray's work – stopping cyber-attacks and investigating digital misconduct – requires a high level of privacy. The auditors agreed, and he won his case.

Sitting on his desk are two clear plastic evidence bags, one containing a laptop computer, the other a mobile phone. Juliette from human resources sits opposite. She gently places her corporate-branded mug on the leather coaster. She understands his rules and knows when to bend them. The familiar flicker of shared humour passes between them.

He taps the laptop bag with his index finger. 'You were right. He wiped most of his files, but we did a forensics job on the hard drive. The main evidence is a twenty-minute sex video, shot in the basement changing room – the one used by runners and cyclists.' He smirks and passes her a USB thumb-drive. 'It's all on here – a clone of his hard drive.'

She shakes her head. 'Just give me a potted summary.'

Ray runs through it. 'The sex was consensual, but the filming of it wasn't. The original video was hazy, which explains why he transferred it to his laptop for editing.'

Juliette takes a sip of her tea. 'Creep. Can you tell me if he shared it?'

Ray explains, with some pride, how they extracted the event logs from the computer, which record every single action and event. Through these digital fingerprints, they discovered he had uploaded it to a cloud storage account. Beyond that, it was untraceable, but it is safe to assume it is being shared.

He watches her hands glide across the notebook. As she writes, he thinks back to when they were lovers. Ten years ago, both coming out of toxic marriages. They were both vulnerable and needed each other. It didn't last, but they remain friends and confidantes.

'What caused her to self-report? Did someone find out?' asks Ray.

Juliette looks up. 'A few days after the event, her manager nudged up beside her and said, "my trouser snake would love to meet your python." A tattoo reference, I believe?'

Ray shifts in his seat. He shouldn't be enjoying this as much as he is. 'It's actually a cobra,' he points to his stomach, 'starts here, then it winds its way down. Quite artistic, if you like that sort of thing.'

She grimaces. 'I don't.'

'I know.'

She smiles. 'That's when she realised there must be a video, and he had seen it.'

'Well, he's committed a criminal offence, so she could report it to the police,' says Ray.

Juliette sighs and tells him how the woman broke down in tears, terrified her husband would find out. Also, there is the company image to think of, so everyone just wants to keep it in-house. The likely outcome is going to be that she keeps her job, with a warning. Video man and her manager will both have to exit the company – through a mutual consent arrangement.

'I can guarantee you won't keep this one quiet. It wouldn't surprise me if someone affixed a commemorative plaque to that changing room door,' says Ray.

She shakes her head. 'They should've got a hotel room.'

'At London prices?'

'Fair point. And when needs must...'

'At least we knew how to be discreet,' says Ray.

'And we didn't carry mobile video cameras back then.'

A beat of silence stretches between them, not uncomfortable – almost nostalgic. Ray glances at the photo of his wife, Kirsty, and feels a sudden nudge of guilt.

'Shall we finish the paperwork?' says Juliette.

Ray signs and time stamps the chain-of-custody form, slides it into a clear folder and passes it across the desk. They've spoken for an hour. Long enough for any meeting, but he's enjoying her company, and she seems happy to hang around.

'How's the world of HR? Any more juicy investigations in the pipeline?' asks Ray.

Juliette sighs, then runs through her investigation workload: Bullying complaints, suspected bribery, misconduct, yet another sexual harassment case and the perennial whinging about unequal pay and home-working privileges.

'What about the Winstanley misconduct investigation?' he asks.

She sighs. 'Case closed, unsubstantiated.'

Ray slaps his hand on the desk. 'That's pathetic.'

She holds her hands up. 'I know, but Harriett told me it was in everyone's interest to close the case.'

Ray feels a rage building in his gut. Jonathan Winstanley. His boss. From their very first meeting, when he told Ray he would help him streamline his operations, he knew they wouldn't get along. His pathetic attempt to imitate Ray's Scottish accent added further insult. They barely have a civil conversation nowadays. He points to Juliette's large folder. 'Do you still have the case evidence?'

She pauses, glances from side-to-side, then retrieves a stapled document from her folder and slides it across the desk. Ray whisks it into his drawer.

Juliette checks her watch. 'Anything else, workwise?'

Ray's enjoying her company and thinks about something else to talk about, just to keep her here. He tells her about the latest briefing from the National Cyber Security Centre, where they spoke about fake employees: state-sponsored threat actors from North Korea and other countries of concern are infiltrating companies, especially those with valuable intellectual property. They apply for jobs using normal channels – fabricated

CV, fake references. Once onboarded, they're issued a laptop and access credentials, then help themselves to company secrets and conduct digital reconnaissance.

'Can't you detect that sort of thing?' says Juliette.

Ray shakes his head. 'Not if we let them in the front door and give them credentials.'

She raises her eyebrows. 'How can HR help?'

'We need to strengthen the pre-employment screening procedures.'

She flips a page in her notepad and scribbles another note. 'Speaking of recruitment, have you found a deputy yet?'

Ray smiles. 'I hope to make an appointment by tomorrow.'

She raises her eyebrows. 'Tell me more.'

Ray tells her about the interviews he's conducted. Twelve so far, all of them falling short of the mark: AI-generated CVs full of techno-speak and exaggerated work experience. Some candidates insisting they work from home four days a week. Two promising candidates remain. The first he's already interviewed, a trans woman who designs encryption algorithms in her spare time. The second is an internal candidate, who he is interviewing this afternoon – Rachel Carter. The tech service desk manager.

'I know her. I think your boss is her leadership mentor.'

'I'm not holding that against her.'

'Has he mentioned her?'

Ray snorts and shakes his computer mouse. His monitor flickers to life and he opens an email. 'He sent me this,' he says, swivelling the screen so she can read.

Ray,

You're interviewing Rachel Carter today. She is the best candidate for the role and will add tremendous value to your team. So I want you to appoint her. This is my direction.

Best,

Jonathan Winstanley, CFO.

He stabs his finger towards the screen. 'That jumped-up prat will not tell me who to hire.'

Juliette grimaces. 'It puts you in an awkward position, though.'

He smiles. 'Do you think there's something going on between them?'

Juliette shrugs. 'No idea,' she closes her notebook and stands to leave. 'Tread carefully, Ray. He holds grudges.'

They both stand, hesitate as if considering a hug, but hold themselves back.

Ray adjusts the knot in his tie until it sits exactly at the centre of his collar. At the sink, he runs his hand under the cold-water tap, brushes damp fingers through his wavy brown hair, then adjusts his pocket square so it peeks at just the right angle from his breast pocket. He strides back to his office and scans the printed CV sitting on his desk, mentally thinking through his questions. She wouldn't be the first candidate to look good on paper, then turn out to be a dud.

There's a knock at the door. He looks, and a woman steps in. She's wearing a red jacket, matching skirt and has neatly styled hair.

'Hi, I'm Rachel Carter.'

Ray crosses the room, extending his hand. 'Ray Dunlop.'

Her grip is firm, her posture upright and she gives off an air of confidence. So far so good.

'It's quiet round this side of the building,' she says, eyes glancing to the outer room.

'This is a secure zone. Most of our work is sensitive – security incident investigations, digital forensics. Can't really have chattering staff looking over our shoulders.'

She smiles. 'Makes sense.'

Ray catches the accent. Yorkshire perhaps. He and Kirsty enjoy walking holidays up in the Dales.

After some small talk, he steers them into the interview proper. She handles the questions well, admitting when she doesn't know something. She then talks about the difficult people she must diplomatically deal with on the service desk, such as the senior manager insisting on shorter passwords so he wouldn't keep forgetting it. Another asked for the anti-virus to be uninstalled because his laptop was running slow.

Ray is mentally ticking the boxes: technical skills, communication skills, knows when to stand her ground. Attended a cyber security conference recently. Everything he's looking for. He can already picture her dealing with the clueless auditors who waste his time with their pointless questions. He's going to probe a little deeper.

'What do you think is the biggest cyber risk to a company like ours?'

She smiles, eyes flickering with thought. 'Intellectual property theft and the threat of ransomware that could bring our supply chain to a standstill.'

Ray nods. Textbook answer. 'Can you expand on that?'

'The company's greatest asset is its intellectual property – the years of scientific research, which could deliver the next generation of treatments for neurological disorders, like Alzheimer's. That data is like our crown jewels. That makes us a target for state-sponsored threat actors and e-crime groups specialising in extortion. So, we need multiple layers of defence, such as access controls, firewalls and encryption.'

Ray smiles. Good answer. One more test. 'The rest of my team – mostly security analysts – are all male. How do you feel about fitting in?' says Ray.

Rachel raises an eyebrow. 'That's fine. But how come there aren't any women?'

He shrugs. 'Not enough qualified female applicants. It's an industry-wide issue.'

He can see from her face that he's pressed a button. She launches into a critique about biased job descriptions, women with imposter syndrome and macho male images on job adverts, such as the one with a young male, wearing a hoodie, sitting at a computer in a darkened room. She mentions a global community for Women in Cyber, which she's part of.

'The problem is not with women, but with biased recruitment processes,' she states.

Ray lifts a hand. 'Point taken.'

She pauses. 'Sorry if I'm being too direct. I've worked as a programmer in male-dominated teams. Some of them couldn't even code a recursive algorithm.'

After an hour, he wraps things up. Another handshake and a mutual wish for smooth train journeys home.

He reclines in his chair. Few candidates last the full hour with him. She's good and would fit in well. He liked how she contradicted him. He enjoys a bit of verbal sparring, always has. It reminds him of his university debating society days, when he'd argue the least popular side just to keep things interesting. Kirsty has said he sometimes comes across as aggressive, but that may just be the Scottish burr. Rachel stood her ground.

He swivels in his chair and thinks back to the other good candidate – mild-mannered Sydney. She has deeper technical skills and is an expert threat hunter. He wants both but knows he can only have one. He'll sleep on it. Either way, it'll be *his* decision, not Winstanley's.

At 5.30 p.m. Ray begins his end-of-day ritual. Desk drawers locked, key in the safe. Waste bin by the door. A squish of antibacterial spray over the keyboard. Microfiber cloth for the monitor. He shuffles some books on his shelf, so the unread ones are on the top, running from left-to-right by relevance. All surfaces clear. He no longer leaves notes for the cleaners. They do an adequate job.

3

Rachel squeezes her hands into the stiff leather boxing gloves. Adam – her sparring partner – stands opposite, raising the pads, bracing himself.

'Power behind those punches,' yells the instructor. 'Picture a person who's really pissed you off.'

That'll be easy. She unleashes a flurry of jabs, Adam's arms recoiling with each blow. The smack of leather against leather is raw and satisfying. She switches to uppercuts. Her wrists ache and her shoulders are burning, but she keeps going, remembering how much she wanted to hit Richard last night.

The conversation with Ray Dunlop replays in her mind. She thought he was about to offer her the job, but he'd chosen someone else. He called to say she had so much to offer and wished her luck. It's not the first time she's missed out in a promotion, but this one hurts. Every Friday, after work, is pub night with the team – drinks, banter and funny stories about callers to the service desk. It's normally the highlight of her week, but she left early last night and headed straight home. She'd already messaged Richard. He must have known how upset she was when she stepped through the door. But there was no hug, not even a 'sorry, that sucks.' Just a smirk of satisfaction.

The whistle shrills. Time to swap. She takes the pads and Adam starts his set. As always, he punches with neat, steady movement and focus, unlike her full-on fury. Sweat trickles down her spine; her muscles burn, and her rage simmers.

Another whistle. Next station: medicine ball. She hoists the twelve-pounder above her head and slams it to the floor. Again, again, again. Her grunting draws glances, but she doesn't care.

A long, drawn-out blast of the whistle signals the end of class. 'Great workout,' instructor Andrew calls out. He catches Rachel's eye and gives her a salute. Her body aches in a way that feels earned, reminding her of her rugby days back at university, when she would launch herself into every tackle. She feels better for that workout.

She slaps Adam's shoulder, leaning on him slightly. He's soaked with sweat too. 'Coffee?'

He nods. 'See you in ten.' They high-five and head to their respective changing rooms.

Rachel bags their usual table in the coffee area, tucked in a corner. The air is humid, tinged with a chlorine smell from the swimming pool. Music pulses faintly from the spin studio. The regulars are here: chatty yoga ladies with roll-up mats, tattooed twenty-somethings and the cappuccino couple, sharing a slice of carrot cake, their heads leaning in close. They used to be married to other people. She remembers when their partnership started, always at the same class, coordinated arriving and leaving timings. Gym buddies turned partners.

Richard's smug reaction from last night still stings. It never used to be like this. It started two years ago, when she got promoted to manager, which meant a pay rise, new responsibilities and her own team. She was buzzing with excitement and booked a spa weekend at a country hotel to celebrate.

Just the two of them. He ruined that weekend. 'I could never do a job like yours,' he said, shaking his head, 'you're just corporate puppet-dancing to someone else's tune.' His ridicule hurt. For a while, she thought it was jealousy but concluded that he's too invested in his own delusional dream of becoming a big name on social media that he recognises nothing good in her job.

Adam appears, fresh from the showers, well-groomed as usual: hair blow-dried, beard neatly trimmed. The single black hooped earring in his left ear is new. She's not sold on that accessory, but he still looks good. He deserves to have a nice woman in his life.

'I'll call off the search party,' she says with a smile.

'Sorry, queue for the showers.' He sinks into the chair opposite, stretches his long legs out and groans as he rolls his shoulder.

'You okay?' she asks.

'Muscle strain, probably from your uppercuts,' he says with a smile.

Rachel laughs, stands and steps behind him. 'Let me sort you out.' Her fingers press into his shoulder, searching clumsily for knots. She isn't sure she's doing it right, but his contented sigh tells her enough. She lingers a moment longer than necessary. He smells good. New aftershave, fresh and clean. There's a warmth between them, something subtle, under the surface, waiting to slip free.

She sits back down, rummages in her kit bag and pulls out a Tupperware box. She lays two homemade flapjacks on napkins and slides them to the centre of the table.

He picks up his flapjack. 'You spoil me.'

As he bites into it, she tells him about the failed promotion and how disappointed she was because the interview had seemed to go really well.

Adam frowns. 'I'm sorry for you. What did your husband say?'

She smiles. 'Put it this way, he's lucky I didn't hit him.'

Their eyes meet. She remembers the first time they met, six months ago. Body pump class. He helped her set up the barbell. Now they're gym buddies. Some people may even think they're together, a bit like the cappuccino couple. She suppresses that thought.

'What's your plan for the weekend?' she asks.

He leans back. 'Kids are with their mum. Snooker this afternoon. Then... a date tonight.'

Something sinks inside her. She keeps her face neutral, but her hand curls around her glass.

'I hope it goes well.'

She doesn't, really. But that's what you say when you're trying to be nice to a good friend. Even when you feel something else entirely. She knows he likes her too, but he's never made a move. Probably telling himself not to get involved with a married woman. Maybe he's right. Rachel has thought about it, but she hasn't prepared herself to cross that line.

'How about you?' he asks.

'As Richard's out all day, I've arranged for my brother and his daughter to come round. It will be the first time she's been to the house. I'm a bit nervous,' she says.

They gather their things. As they step outside into the cool afternoon air, she loops her arm through his. Her pulse quickens.

'Good luck for this afternoon,' he says.

'Thanks. And good luck with your date.'

She rises onto her toes and plants a light kiss on his cheek. 'See you Thursday for spin class.'

4

Rachel sits on a crowded train, feeling alone, as it trundles north to south, stopping at every station on the line. The carriage is buzzing with chatter and strewn with discarded newspapers. The bins overflow with takeaway coffee cups and sandwich wrappers. As she watches the blur of terraced houses and narrow gardens backing on to the railway line, she thinks about the afternoon ahead. This week has been one disappointment after another and now she's nervous because, despite her planning, so much can go wrong.

She disembarks at London Bridge and makes her way towards the arched entrance of a converted Victorian fire station. The restaurant has kept its character – exposed brick walls, fire brigade memorabilia and black and white photos of fire crews. The open kitchen echoes with clattering pans and crockery. Plates pile up on the collection counter as kitchen staff and servers shout instructions to each other.

She really can't afford this meal, but today's special. She orders a Diet Coke and a main course of grilled hake and side salad, then gazes blankly at the street outside, watching slow-moving traffic and smiling tourists ambling by. She wishes her life was less complicated.

Half an hour later, she finishes eating and spots Tony through the kitchen hatch. He hasn't seen her yet. She grins and taps out a message on her phone:

Rachel: Service is rubbish in this place. Hake tasted like decaying shoe leather. If I were in charge, I'd sack the chef.

She drains her drink and waits for a response.

A few minutes later, a familiar voice comes over her shoulder, 'I thought we'd banned you from here?'

She turns to face Tony, standing there in a white chef's jacket. Clean shaven for once, which makes the fading scar on his jawline more visible. The misshapen nose and half-missing ear tell their own story – the aftermath of a prison fight. To a stranger, he would look like a ruffian and someone to be avoided. But to her, he will always be her little brother. She jumps up, hugs him tight, feeling herself trembling with relief. 'Good to see you, Tony.'

Six months ago, he would have been in a cell or sleeping rough. Now, he's sober and training to be a chef in a real kitchen. 'This place is busy.'

'Over two hundred covers since breakfast, and I'm training up a new guy who's never used a tin opener before.' He glances at his watch. 'All okay for the visit?'

She gives the thumbs up. 'Sorted.'

'Give me ten minutes to finish up out back.'

He strides back to the kitchen with a confidence she hasn't seen in years. He was always vulnerable, and she was a crap big sister. She still remembers the night fifteen years ago when he phoned, asking if he could stay with her. He was drunk; she told him to sort his life out. Their dad had told him the same. He couldn't. He was only nineteen. She won't abandon him again. Paying his rent has been a price worth paying to see this new man.

Later, they sit side-by-side on Rachel's brown leather sofa, cradling mismatched mugs of weak tea made from reused tea bags. They continuously glance up at the front bay window, eyes fixed on the tree-lined road, crammed with parked cars. If Rachel were in the least bit religious, she would say a prayer at this point. She closes her eyes. *Please let this go well.*

They see the black Volkswagen Golf pull up; they both jump up and head to the door. Sarah walks up the path. Rachel hasn't seen her for over two years. She's still gothic-looking and has a new eyebrow piercing. If life had taken a different route, they would be sisters-in-law. Maybe even friends. But Rachel's eyes go straight to the child clasping her mum's hand. Curly blonde hair, wide, curious eyes. Florence. Five years old. Tony's daughter. Her niece.

Sarah fixes her gaze on Tony. 'What's your plan for this afternoon?'

'We'll mostly be here. If it stays dry, we'll go to the park.'

She turns to Rachel. 'Can you guarantee you'll be with them the whole time?'

'Absolutely,' Rachel says with a smile, 'I'm really looking forward to this.'

Sarah nods slowly. 'I'll be back at six.'

Florence drops her mum's hand and reaches for her dad. Tony lifts her, and she wraps herself around him, clinging tightly. It's been a month since they last saw each other. Two years since they spent time alone. First time in this house.

Rachel watches, imagining a day when her full family can reunite. Her mum and dad would love to see their granddaughter. But Tony still won't talk to them. One step at a time, she tells herself.

Rachel rummages in her bag – the one that usually holds her laptop and study notes – and pulls out a LEGO set. 'Who wants to build a Disney castle?'

They sit on the floor together, sorting through the 300-plus pieces. Tony flips through the pages of a thirty-page instruction book. The box says *Ages 12+*.

'I think we might need a LEGO architect for this,' he says with a laugh.

Florence takes charge, arranging bricks by colour into tidy piles. Then they all take turns fixing them together, without reference to the instructions, which seem overly complicated for an adult, never mind a child. Within an hour, they have something resembling a castle and many pieces left over. Florence is bored by this time and announces she is hungry. Tony suggests pancakes.

Rachel shows Tony the kitchen layout, then dashes out to the Co-op. As she queues behind six people, holding a jar of Nutella and a tub of cream, her heart pounds. She's technically breaking the supervised contact order, which means she is the named adult who must be present at all times with Florence and her dad. If Sarah finds out, she could cease the arrangement. That court order was unnecessary. She is eventually served and sprints back home.

The three of them squeeze around a tiny table in her kitchen, layering chocolate spread and squirting cream onto warm pancakes. Rachel watches father and daughter laughing together. It's a precious moment, and warmth settles inside her. She loves being Aunty Rachel. It's a glimpse of motherhood, which she hopes will come to her someday.

Her thoughts drift to her finances. She can't continue to subsidise Tony anymore, but he doesn't earn much. If he doesn't pay child support, he loses access. If he doesn't pay rent, he could end up homeless. At least he's trying to earn a living, not like Richard.

Sarah returns at five-to-six, and Rachel invites her in. They chat politely in the kitchen while Rachel makes tea. There's a dusting of flour on the floor and smears of chocolate spread on the kitchen table and a pile of crockery sits in the sink. Sarah asks to use the bathroom. Rachel suspects she's checking the place over. That's fine. She has a nice house, and other than the aftermath of pancake chaos, she'll find nothing to complain about.

They sit in the lounge and sip tea while Florence drinks orange squash. The atmosphere is calm, and everyone seems happy. It couldn't have gone better.

Rachel clears her throat. 'Sarah, I was thinking... Maybe next time, Florence could stay overnight. We have a spare room.'

Sarah's smile fades. Her eyes dart towards Florence, then back. 'Would your husband be okay with that?'

He'll hate it. Rachel waves a hand. 'Oh yes, Richard will be fine.'

Sarah hesitates. 'Let's give it a bit more time, if that's okay.'

She's about to protest but stops herself. *Small steps.* 'Of course. Let's chat next time.'

They say goodbye at the door. Florence looks back, smiles and waves her little hand. Rachel waves back. She pictures herself tucking her into bed, reading stories, then waking up to her giggles in the morning. Richard will object, especially if it involves Tony. But she'll take that fight. This is her family.

They sit together, drinking tea. Tony checks his watch. 'When's Richard back?'

She snorts. 'Not till late. He's in Leicester for a pickleball tournament.'

He sniggers. 'Is he still campaigning for it to be an Olympic sport?'

She rolls her eyes. 'It's only a matter of time, apparently.'

They both laugh, a moment of silence, then he speaks. 'Can we talk about money, Sis?'

'Of course.'

He leans forward. 'My rent has gone up by 200, and I'm still on minimum wage and don't always get full-time hours. I want to pay my way, but...' He holds out his arms, as if pleading. 'I hate to ask. I just need a bit more help. Until I qualify, then I can get a job as a hotel chef, full-time.'

Her heart sinks. There must be another way. Could she ask Sarah to give him some leeway? But she doesn't want her thinking he can't pay his way. The smile drops from his face. His confidence has evaporated. She now sees the younger, more vulnerable Tony. The one whose next action would be to reach for a drink. It's happened before. She can't let him slip, again. Not now.

She nods. 'Okay. I can cover you.'

He wraps his arms around her. 'Thank you.'

She smiles. 'I'm sure you'd do the same for me, if I was stuck.'

He laughs. 'Unlikely. Your life's well sorted.'

If only he knew.

After he leaves, she does a sweep of the house, picking up Florence's Barbie cup, the sticker book and a couple of forgotten LEGO bricks. She boxes them up and slides the container into the bottom of her wardrobe, where Richard will never look – beneath the box of sex toys and the stash of *Mother & Baby* magazines.

In the evening, she sits alone with a gin and tonic, ice clicking softly as she swirls the glass. A television game show provides background noise, but she's not following it because her mind is too busy. She sinks back into the cushions and replays Tony's words: *your life's well sorted*. Not said unkindly, more with admiration. And maybe, from the outside, it looks that way – married, good job, own house. Her gaze drifts to the photo montage on the wall: wedding and holiday snapshots of a happy couple. A facade concealing the stresses and strains of her real life, which is dominated by an out-of-control debt pile and a miserable marriage. She guesses others, who seem well sorted from the outside, are hiding their life stresses too. Adam, for instance. He seems happy in his life, though he grimaces at any mention of his ex-wife. He's out on a date tonight and she wonders how that's going. Badly, she hopes.

Then there's money. That will not fix itself and she can't rely on Richard contributing much anytime soon. If he finds out she's subsidising Tony, he'll throw a tantrum. He hates Tony. It goes back to his stag night when Tony started a fight with Richard's best man. It didn't seem like a big deal to Rachel. That's the sort of thing blokes do on stag nights, isn't it? But he hasn't let it go.

She needs to re-think her finances. Two days ago, she had a plan: get promoted, convince Richard to get a job and reduce Tony's payments. Two out of three would have worked. But now? As Mike Tyson once said, *everyone has a plan until they get punched in the mouth*. She feels like she's taken a triple jab.

She glances at her phone. A couple of messages have come through – a huge thank you and hug emoji from Tony, then one from her single friend

Cathy, asking if she'd like to meet up during the week. Yes, she would. Nothing from Richard. There was a time when they would always message, little check-ins to say they were thinking about each other. Not anymore.

She drains her glass, pours another and pulls a patchwork throw over her legs. If she and Richard split, who would move out? Not her. Too much of her personality is in this house: the colour scheme, the up-light floor lamps, the curtains, handmade by her mother, and her herb garden. She visualises it as a family home, but that's not an image she shares with her husband. Where does that leave her? She can already hear his retort: the only reason they have this house is because his parents gifted them the deposit.

Thoughts keep swirling inside her head. Maybe this is just her life now, and she just needs to be content with it. But why should she go through life unhappy? She feels the need to draw a decision tree to impose some logic onto her chaotic thinking, but she fears the logical outcome.

She takes another long sip of gin. Warmth spreads through her, making her feel bold. An idea surfaces. It may be reckless. She grabs her phone and scrolls through her WhatsApp history until she finds him, the man from the cyber security conference. Tall, quiet, Eastern European, she thinks. Not flashy sales, nor smooth corporate, just someone who slipped in and out of conversational groups, listening to everything but saying little. His interest was piqued when she mentioned her company. *Your skills could be useful to my business*, he'd said. *Let's stay in touch*.

Aleks. Yes, that was his name.

Before she thinks too hard, she taps out a message, and hits send. Her heart skips as the screen confirms it's gone. She's made the first move. Her heart races with exhilaration, waiting for his response.

5

Another day, another train into the city. Her anxiety levels continue to rise as she walks across the concourse at Victoria and steps outside. The rain has stopped but the pavement still glistens. She pauses at the crossing to check her phone map. Five minutes' walk. She's already having second thoughts and considers turning back.

A young man with a dog on a lead catches her eye. She turns away, hoping he'll keep walking.

'Can you help me out?' His voice is meek.

Rachel glances back at him. He is in his early twenties, scratched face, long, unkempt hair tucked behind his ears. His stained and ripped clothes hang off his skinny frame. She looks down at the dog. It might be a Labrador cross. She crouches down to pat its head. His tail rises in hope.

'What's his name?'

'Bowie.'

'Hard to get work, I guess. With a dog.'

He nods. 'Not everywhere wants a dog hanging around. But he won't go with anyone else. I just need to buy food for both of us and find somewhere to sleep.'

She doesn't normally carry cash but reaches for her purse and finds a forgotten ten-pound note and hands it to him. He thanks her and quickly walks away. That's money she can't afford to give away. But it's easy to judge when you have a home and a job. Who knows what his background is? Tony probably had to beg on the streets like that, getting ignored or rejected. She heads back to the crossing and follows her map to the Victoria Park Plaza with no further hesitation.

The hotel lobby looks like a holding zone for suitcases and carry-bags. She navigates around them and weaves her way through a group of Asian tourists towards the lounge area and finds a quiet corner close to the bar. She drops into a cushioned armchair. Soft background music plays. She browses the table menu – teas, pastries and alcohol, at what her father would describe as thieving rip-off prices. She never feels comfortable in places like this. Back home, a treat is a trip to Betty's Tea Room in Harrogate for a large pot of tea and a plate of sandwiches.

She's early and is thinking about how to start the conversation. It's difficult to pitch herself when she knows so little about him. There's no website, not even a LinkedIn profile. What self-respecting professional isn't on LinkedIn? Maybe she should just cut to the chase and come out with it: I don't know what you do – it's probably something dodgy and I don't need to know the details – but I'm looking to earn a bit extra. Is there anything I can help with?

Then she spots him, emerging from the lift, and waves. He walks over. Her heart is kicking against her ribs. He's just as she remembered: tall, composed, gold-rimmed glasses giving him that intellectual look. His black crew neck and tailored trousers say style, without trying too hard.

She stands. He reaches out to hug her, but Rachel thrusts out her arm and they shake hands.

'Nice to see you, Aleks.'

He smiles. 'The pleasure is all mine.'

They both sit. He places two iPhones on the table, screen-side down. 'How's life at Synaptonica?'

She shrugs. 'It has its ups and downs but still hanging in there. How's business with you?'

'Never been busier.'

They continue with the small talk, polite smiles and carefully curated replies. It feels like an awkward first date. Despite subtle probing, she learns nothing about what he actually does. She breaks the conversational rhythm. 'When we met at the conference, you seemed interested in my job and said you could always use someone with my background, so...'

He nods. 'I remember.'

'Back then, I was full-on with work commitments. But things have changed. So if you still need someone like me, then...' She laughs. 'I'd love to find out more.'

Aleks raises a hand towards the bar and a young bow-tie-wearing waiter with slicked-back hair promptly appears. Aleks orders two gin & tonics. She hopes he's paying – it's fourteen pounds a shot. *I can prepare three good meals for that.*

'Are you still the helpdesk manager?' he asks.

'We're called the technology service desk these days.' She launches into an explanation, describing everything they do: password resets, software installs, recovery from backups, server reboots and access provisioning. A lot more than a help desk. He doesn't need to know all this, but this is what she does when she's nervous. Talks. It always helps.

'You must have a high level of access to do all that?'

She nods. 'We all have privileged access. We couldn't do our jobs otherwise.'

He raises his eyebrows, showing interest. She keeps talking and tells him about the promotional opportunity she missed out on.

'That's bad luck. Do you know who got the job?'

She shakes her head. 'An outsider.'

He nods slowly. 'That must cause you to question your loyalties.'

Loyalty. She has to think about that one. Yes, she's always been a good corporate citizen because Synaptonica care about their staff. At least they used to. But the outsourcing plan for her team is causing her to question her commitment. Her workplace used to feel like an extended family, with people looking out for one another, doing what it takes to get the job done. Now everyone stresses about the new performance metrics: ticket volume, resolution times. Never mind customer satisfaction, it's all about delivering a service at the lowest possible cost. Next week, she needs to prepare the dreaded staff league table and tell two perfectly good team members they are underperforming.

'A lot has happened recently that's causing me to think differently about the company,' she says.

He nods. 'Sounds like they don't value your skills.'

She's not sure where he's going with these probing questions and decides to turn the conversation around. 'Can you tell me a bit about what you do, exactly?'

He interlaces his fingers and pauses for a moment. 'We have a portfolio of clients. Some use us for competitor intelligence. Others need cyber security services.' He smiles. 'For example, system security testing.'

'Well, I've got my ethical hacking certification,' she says.

He smiles, a little too patronisingly, she feels. The waiter returns and places two gin glasses on the table. Aleks signs the bill.

'Cheers,' they say as they clink glasses.

'Do you have access to the R&D network,' he asks, almost casually, 'or their databases?'

The penny drops. Competitor intelligence. He's thinking about their medical research – the intellectual property that is so tightly safeguarded. Yes, Synaptonica has a lot of that, and he wants to get his hands on it. She feels uncomfortable. Bending a few rules is one thing, but stealing trade secrets? Never. She's not that desperate, *Not yet*.

She shakes her head. 'The research databases are behind a firewall, with multiple layers of protection. Only authorised research scientists can access it.'

She takes a sip of her drink, letting the ice click softly. If this were a date, she'd be planning her escape. Something like, *Is that the time. Early start tomorrow, Lovely to meet you.* Then a polite smile, a kiss on the cheek, and she'd be gone.

Aleks leans back, studying her reaction as if he's testing how far he can go. 'Do you have any vacancies in your team?'

She hesitates, wary. 'I'm recruiting for a new service desk analyst.'

His expression brightens. He sets his drink down and points towards her, the gesture smooth and deliberate. 'Then I have the perfect person for you.'

'What?'

'Her name's Izabela. You should hire her.'

She lets out a faint sigh. 'That would be tricky. We have strict recruitment procedures.'

He clasps his hands together, tilting his head just slightly. 'We will compensate you, of course.'

Rachel breath catches. *Compensate.* The word seems to reverberate inside her. She badly needs money, more than she'd ever admit. He must sense that because his smile widens almost imperceptibly.

'How does twenty-five grand sound?' he says, his voice calm and confident.

Her mouth drops open at the thought of an instantly disappearing debt problem. *How could he possibly know that?* She picks up the plastic stirrer and stabs the ice in her drink. Her hands are trembling. 'What's her background?'

He shrugs. 'What are you looking for?'

Rachel describes the role – a mix of technical troubleshooting, debugging, software installs, a bit of everything. She starts to think of the recruitment process. The forms, the approvals. It takes weeks, but there is a fast-track process. She could justify it as an *urgent operational need*. People do that all the time just to bypass the bureaucracy of recruitment.

'I'll need a CV, evidence of qualifications and previous employment references,' she says, clinging to some semblance of professionalism.

Aleks laughs softly. 'Not a problem.'

A silence stretches between them. She can feel him watching her, patiently waiting for her conscience to bend. Her pulse pounds in her throat. *What if I get caught?* But she knows others who've done this. Senior managers slipping their friends in through this recruitment back-door. Yes, she can do this too.

'Okay,' she says quietly, 'but she'll have to start as a junior analyst.'

Aleks extends his hand. 'Deal?'

Rachel hesitates, arm hovering. 'If I get caught, I lose my job.'

'We're always discreet.'

She reaches for his hand. They shake. his grip is firm, almost reassuring.

'I think you and Izabela will make a good team,' he says, smiling like a man who's just won big on a lottery scratch card.

She finishes the watery remains of her drink, the lemon bitter on her tongue. She's not sure what she's agreed to, only that something has shifted, as if she's just forked off her familiar path and entered perilous new territory. And there's no going back. *Easy money,* she tells herself. Just a one-off. *For Tony. For Florence. For her future.*

Back home, she installs the apps Aleks recommended – Telegram for messaging and a crypto wallet for payments. She's dabbled with cryptocurrency in the past – buying and selling Bitcoin, Solana and Ethereum, mostly for curiosity. This is taking her into a whole new league. She'll set up a charade interview for tomorrow and use the fast-track recruitment process, then Izabela can start on Tuesday. She should feel guilty. Instead, exhilaration is rising within her. Has she really just sorted out her financial crisis in a single afternoon? It almost seems too easy.

She sinks back into the sofa with a growing sense of confidence. Upstairs, she can hear Richard moving around. They still aren't talking. Voices and music come from his computer. She smirks. Maybe he's having one of his creative moments.

6

Rachel thinks back to the last time she was sat in this office, only last week. He touched her. Assaulted her. He was obscene. She escaped, but the rage still burns inside. And here she is again, face-to-face with Jonathan Winstanley. Alone.

He swivels lazily in his leather chair, basking in the power that comes with high office. She doesn't feel scared, though. Unlike last time, there are people milling around outside. She would love to call him out and let everyone know he's a lecherous sex pest. But she can't. Not today. Because he's probably the only one who can help her right now, which means she'll have to play the game.

She tilts her head and forces a smile. 'I enjoyed your speech in the all-staff broadcast on Friday. You're a great presenter.'

He pushes his shoulders back. 'Leadership is about setting high standards, Rachel.'

Hypocrite. She takes a breath. 'It was inspiring, Jonathan.'

His grin widens. 'I'm glad you came to see me, because I feel I need to apologise.'

This had better be good – not that she'll ever forgive him.

'I gave Dunlop a clear instruction to appoint you to the cyber team.' He hits his fist on the desk in a hammer-like motion. 'He went against me and there will be consequences.'

Now she wants to slap him. She shrugs. 'Win some, lose some. I've moved on from that. Running the service desk is keeping me busy.'

'I just don't like to see you unhappy.'

'I'll tell you what makes me unhappy – the bureaucracy in this place. But not even you can fix that.'

He snorts. 'What do you mean?'

'I'm trying to recruit a new team member. I've found the perfect candidate, but HR has frozen my headcount.'

He chuckles. 'I can fix that in two minutes. But why are you recruiting? We're outsourcing.'

'That will take at least three months. This is temporary. I need another head to raise my performance metrics.'

He leans across his desk. 'I know how you can raise your performance metrics.'

His leer makes her skin crawl, but once again, she forces a smile and lightens her tone. 'There's a time and a place for that, Jonathan.'

He nods agreeably, then points to the plastic folder she's holding. 'Is the recruitment form in there?'

Rachel pulls out a stapled document and hands it over. So much depends on his signing this form. If he doesn't, she can't onboard Izabela, and she'll be back at square one with no money and no obvious way out. There's Tony and Florence to think about. She watches him pick up his fountain pen. He pauses, glances back at her. She gives him a tilt of her head again and a promising smile. The performance continues.

He signs slowly then holds the form out, but doesn't let go. 'We still need to arrange dinner, don't we?'

She was expecting this. 'Yes... sometime.'

'Tomorrow?'

'I can't this week. My mum and dad are staying.'

He holds her gaze, fingers still clamped to the form.

'Let's chat next week,' she says, 'we'll fix something up.'

A long pause, a smile, then finally he lets go. 'Next week.'

Rachel darts out of his office, form in hand. Her charade worked, but she hates herself for it. This is not the first time in her life she's had to play the impressionable bimbo, but that was back in her university days and mostly for comedy value. This is different. She's desperate and feels powerless. She now needs to conjure up an excuse to avoid dinner with him next week. It needs to be good. He's persistent.

The recruitment and onboarding process had consumed most of Rachel's previous day. Today, as agreed, Izabela arrived at 8 a.m. with her passport and work visa. It normally takes three days for a computer account to be set up, but Rachel escalated the service ticket to high priority. By 9 a.m., Izabela had her building pass and had logged on to her laptop computer. It's amazing what an executive signature on a fast-track recruitment form can achieve.

She glances across to Izabela, sitting in front of her laptop, with Lionel hovering over her in full mansplaining mode, pointing out the various icons on the start-up screen. His face lit up when Rachel asked him to be Izabela's new-starter buddy. Izabela is a few years younger than Rachel. Attractive, dark eyes and long, glossy hair that turns heads every time she walks past. She's only been here a few hours and seems to have made friends already, confidently introducing herself to anyone who casts a glance in her direction.

Rachel's phone pings. It's a notification from her crypto wallet: 0.12 Bitcoin received from an unidentifiable source. The first payment. Ten grand in real money. She's never made so much for doing so little. But she reminds herself what she had to do to earn that, and the dishonesty weighs on her. Izabela, officially, has to play the part of a junior support analyst, but Rachel's still not sure how it's going to play out. She clearly has an ulterior motive, and the more she thinks about it the more anxious she becomes. She feels like she's playing a part in a stage play, without a script. One thing she can be sure of: if she gets caught, she'll lose her job.

She turns back to her screen and tries to refocus on the management drudgery that fills her day. Unread emails, requests for performance metrics, staff surveys, expense reports, compliance training overdue notifications and a sinister-looking reminder about completing the performance league table for her team. Then, top of her inbox, is the one email she's been dreading. It has the subject line: *Proposals for Streamlining Service Desk Operations.*

In her mind, this is the cheap labour deal. She opens the two attached files – the usual slick PDFs, with stock images of smiling tech workers in some Indian city. Both laced with management speak and trendy phrases like *centre of excellence* and *innovation hub*. They want her to evaluate each one and provide feedback by the end of the week. She's already given her opinion and a counterproposal, which wasn't even acknowledged, so she may as well flip a coin as the endgame will be the same – most of her team get made redundant. She glances across the work zone, at her colleagues. The team who brings in cake for birthdays, samosas for Diwali and then they all go to the pub on a Friday, after work. It feels like she's being asked to choose their executioner.

'Rachel, you need to sort out my access.' A sharp voice cuts through her thoughts.

Izabela stands over her, arms crossed, eyes sharp. Lionel follows a few paces behind, like someone chasing a runaway puppy.

'I've told her she needs to complete the training first,' says Lionel.

Rachel nods and keeps her tone managerial. 'We have procedures, Izabela. The training's online. Once you complete it and pass the assessment quiz, I get a notification. Then I can grant you the access you need.'

She leans in, planting both hands on Rachel's desk. 'And I need to install some software,' she says in a sharp whisper.

Rachel holds her gaze. Izabela folds her arms, testing boundaries.

Lionel gestures hesitantly. 'You can just shadow me in the meantime.'

Izabela turns and they both make their way back to her desk, but not before glancing back. As if giving Rachel a warning. Rachel exhales and watches them go. Lionel will have to keep her on a short leash. Play your part, Izabela. *That was the deal.*

It's mid-morning and her workday is already full of stress. At least she has something to look forward to tonight.

Rachel and Cathy sit tucked into a corner table of a Cantonese restaurant in Chinatown, a table barely big enough for their spread of crispy duck, noodles, brightly coloured sweet and sour dishes and dim sum in a bamboo basket. A red lantern glows above them while Mandarin string music plays in the background. Two days ago, this meal would have been unaffordable, but her first payment from Aleks dropped just in time. She has no intention of being reckless with her windfall; this is just an overdue catch-up with her close friend, Cathy.

They both joined Synaptonica as programmers around five years ago and hit it off from day one. Similar age, both studied computer science at university, then found themselves as the only women in a team of twelve. They were a formidable force back then. Even when assigned to different projects, they would still test each other's code and share ideas. Cathy left after a year because she was tired of her boss claiming the credit for her work. She's now thriving at a big pharma company. The two of them remain friends. Cathy, unmarried by choice, is glowing.

'It's only been six weeks,' she says coyly, 'but it feels like we've been together for months.'

Rachel leans forward, smiling. 'Have you got a picture?'

Cathy scrolls through her phone and hands it across. 'His name's Derek. That was us on the South Downs last week.'

Rachel studies the image of Derek, a tall man in a flat cap with his arm slung protectively around petite Cathy. Both in walking gear, carefree. 'Nice smile,' she says.

'He's quite introverted socially, but when it's just us, we can talk for hours.' Cathy can't stop grinning.

Rachel spoons some egg-fried rice onto her plate. 'How did you meet?'

'On a SAP project. He's a system integrator, I'm lead developer.'

Rachel lets out a laugh. 'How romantic.'

Cathy fiddles with her chopsticks. 'We've got a rule: no work talk outside office hours, unless it's gossip.'

'I'm really happy for you.' Rachel raises her glass, genuinely pleased for her friend.

Cathy continues to talk excitedly about her new man. Rachel imagines her getting married. It brings back memories of when she and Richard first got together. They would go away for weekends and were happy with each other's company. Then sports, work, diverging social lives eroded the bond that once made them inseparable. She stops herself from dwelling on her disintegrating marriage. She hopes this is the real deal for Cathy. Her friend deserves to find happiness. Then she imagines Cathy pregnant and becoming a mother before she does. That thought gives her a sudden surge of urgency.

It's been a while since they had a proper catch-up, and Cathy asks about Rachel as if probing at something she knows is there but needs coaxing out. Rachel talks about her niece Florence and her brother Tony – how being a dad has changed him and he's now getting his act together, and she is hopeful he will reconcile with Mum and Dad soon. She shows her pictures on her phone.

'And how's Richard?' asks Cathy.

The question hits Rachel like bad wine on the taste buds. Her smile drops. 'He's fine. Still a self-employed digital media consultant.' She shrugs.

'Still doing your date nights?'

Rachel smirks. 'No, thankfully.'

The silence that follows tells its own story.

Cathy leans in, lowering her voice. 'You don't seem yourself. Do you want to talk?'

Rachel slides her plate aside, cradles her glass and lets the words pour out: his stubborn insistence on working as a low-earning freelancer, the priority he gives to his pickleball pastime, how she feels happiest when he's out of the house. And then her irrepressible desire for children, the one thing they can't even have a proper conversation on.

She falters as a waiter whisks away their dishes. 'So I'm in a quandary.'

Cathy's expression softens. 'Do you think you can get back to loving each other?'

Rachel shrugs. 'Maybe, if we both tried.'

'And children?'

Rachel exhales, eyes dropping to the table. 'That's the trouble. I don't even see him as the father of my children.' Her fingers twist the stem of her glass. 'Which makes me wonder if I already know what comes next.'

Cathy nods slowly. 'It sounds like you're at a crossroads. One path has an uncertain future, but one you control. The other, you stay, make the most of it, but live with regrets.'

The waiter reappears and brusquely asks if they want more wine. They shake their heads, wave him away and continue their conversation. He returns one minute later with the bill and two fortune cookies, which he drops onto the table. The ladies linger for ten minutes longer, split the bill as always, pull on their coats and step out into the crisp night air. They say goodnight, hugging tightly before parting ways.

Rachel walks beneath the glowing Chinatown arches on Gerrard Street and heads towards the Tube station. Her mind is clearer now. Cathy hadn't told her what to do. She didn't need to. Deep down, she already knew.

7

The morning walk from Kings Cross to Charing Cross is Rachel's favourite part of the day. Thirty-five minutes of movement without interruption or distraction. A space where she can untangle her thoughts and drift into her own daydreams. Today, Florence is the first thing on her mind. Richard is heading to a pickleball tournament in Germany in a few weeks, which makes that weekend an ideal opportunity for Florence to sleepover. Just one night. The idea makes her smile, though she'll have to persuade Sarah first.

The warmth fades as other thoughts creep in. Her marriage. Her own yearning for children, not yet an obsession, but an ever-present desire. At least Cathy helped her sort out some of her muddles and confusions, but clarity brings its own weight. She knows what she wants and what she must do, but not how to get there.

By the time she reaches the office, she's counting the minutes until she leaves again. She's going to the gym tonight and Adam will be there. She squeezes into the elevator, wedging herself between strangers, bracing herself for the dramas of the day ahead: Izabela with her constant demands for elevated access and dubious software, then Lionel, ready to press the panic button whenever there's a call spike.

Stepping into the open-plan zone, she glances at the wall display: ticket volumes rising, response times slipping and service levels sinking. Everything flashing red. Not exactly surprising with one team member on maternity leave and another long-term sick because of work-related stress. But, sure. Let's all get behind the genius company mantra – *Do more with less*.

She slumps into her chair and powers up her laptop. She opens her email and watches her inbox flood with junk: surveys, newsletters and salespeople wanting to meet with her to demo their AI-enabled miracle apps. One email hits her like a smack in the face. The subject line: *Service Desk Outsourcing – next steps*. Her head sinks. She exhales, opens it and reads. It's exactly as she expected. An execution notice dressed up with professional politeness. Thanks to all stakeholders for their input... a partner has been selected... working through the contract... official announcement within the next three weeks...

She glances across the office to her team. They don't deserve to be treated like this. Some have given many years of loyal service and have families. Part of her wants to stand up and announce it straight: *Team, in exchange for your many years of dedicated service, the company is going to shaft you.* She thinks that sounds quite good, and after a few drinks in the pub, she'll probably blurt it out.

To Rachel, this is just another signal of the toxic culture created by the new leadership, in particular, Jonathan sleazebag Winstanley and his buddy Mike Chester. Both strutting onto the stage for the all-staff broadcast last week, congratulating each other for hitting milestones, parroting the usual corporate buzzwords, then declaring that staff are the biggest asset to the company. After work that day, Chester gate-crashed their gathering at the pub. He put his corporate credit card behind the bar, ordered drinks and within half an hour, had his arm around one woman, explaining how, if he mentored her, he could accelerate her career development. It looked almost comical. Him, an overweight fifty-year-old, his thinning hair greased back, trying to seduce a woman at least twenty years his junior. How do people with such low self-awareness get into such senior positions?

She recalls when she became team leader, two years ago. Her first managerial role. She brought in new software, streamlined processes and raised all performance metrics – all the things a manager should do. Now, she's reduced to following the directives of men who've never taken a service desk call in their life. Maybe Richard is right and she is just a corporate puppet, dancing to someone else's tune. She has never felt more despondent in her job.

The voice of Billy Idol blares from the ceiling speakers – 'Rebel Yell' at full blast. The trapped heat of fourteen bodies pedalling on power cycles has turned this cramped fitness studio into a hothouse. *Open the bloody fire doors, someone.* Rachel has quickened her pedalling cadence, legs burning as she pushes past 210 watts output. Her eyes flick to Adam's display. He's on 230, but full-out and dripping with sweat.

'Give me more, more, more,' yells the instructor.

Rachel grits her teeth, dials up the resistance and increases the pace, hitting 300 watts, and holds it. The bike whirs and the reflection in the mirrored wall is a flushed, determined blur of her glowing red.

Thirty seconds later, the music cuts, the bikes whirr to a stop and gasps of relief fill the studio. Instructor Andrew congratulates the class as everyone dismounts and starts stretching their aching muscles. Rachel and Adam high five. She sneaks a glance at his finishing stats and smiles. She's edged him. She'll keep her banter dry for later.

'Fancy a cooldown jog?' says Rachel, trying to sound casual.

Adam runs a hand through his sweaty hair. 'Sounds good.'

They jog out together, turning onto a gravel path that snakes through unkempt park land. A lingering whiff of weed drifts from the nearby skateboard park. Not a route she would take alone at night, but she is confident with Adam. Their arms brush. He doesn't pull away. That's a good sign. They jog past two dog walkers wearing high-viz arm bands, then they are alone again. This would be a good moment.

'How was your weekend?' she asks.

'I won the snooker challenge. So that was an easy fifty quid.'

'What about your date?'

He hesitates. 'Better than expected. She's separated; shares childcare, so a lot in common.' He gives a slight smile, the kind that shows he's not revealing everything.

She feels the hit in her chest. That wasn't what she was hoping to hear. They continue their slow jog.

'What about you?' he asks.

She smiles. He won fifty pounds. Nothing compared to her windfall and what she had to do to earn it, but she can't tell him that.

'I've made a big decision.'

He glances at her. 'Sounds serious.'

'I'm going to separate from Richard.'

His mouth drops open. That clearly wasn't what he was expecting to hear. She hadn't planned to spit it out quite like that, but sometimes you just have to say things. She tells him they've been living separate lives for so long now – they don't eat together, have different social lives. Tension and arguments are part of their shared life, and they haven't had sex in over six months. Maybe she's over-sharing now. Bottom line, she can't see a future together. She hasn't quite summoned the courage to start that conversation, but she will. Soon.

'I'm sorry,' he says, but he doesn't show shock or surprise. His face seems to light up with a smile of curious anticipation.

'I've known for a while it's not working. It's the right decision.'

His gaze drops to her hand. 'I noticed earlier, you're not wearing your wedding ring.'

Well spotted, Adam. And here we are, jogging alone together. What more of an invitation do you need? He goes silent. Maybe he's thinking about making a move. She won't say no. They continue their slow jog back to the gym, then talk a bit more in the car park.

'Separation can be rough,' he says, with the tone of someone who's been through the painful experience. 'I'm here if you want to talk...'

'Thank you.'

They linger in the car park until their sweat and perspiration chills them, then say their goodbyes. That will do, for now.

'Only me,' she shouts, walking through the front door.

No response. No surprise – they've hardly spoken all week.

Faint laughter and muffled voices drift down from upstairs. She remembers, he'll be recording his weekly podcast, *The Pickleball Show*. Him and a few other paddle devotees, unable to go more than a few days without discussing their dinking drills or spin techniques. She used to admire his passion for the sport, and there's no denying he's one of the top coaches in the country. But that doesn't pay the bills, and neither does his freelance gig. Reality will hit him soon. Fast and hard, like a pickleball slam, if there is such a shot.

She heads into the kitchen, throws her damp kit into the washing machine and assembles a quick dinner, comprising her homemade goat's cheese and potato quiche with salad leaves snipped from her window garden, then drizzled with her own honey-mustard dressing. She inherited her love of wholesome, home-prepared meals from her mother. Simple, nutritious and tastier than ready meals. Something else Richard doesn't appreciate.

She sets up her laptop on the kitchen table, mouse in one hand, fork in the other. A few clicks take her to the London Women's Clinic website. She browses through the *Fertility Services* section: it covers IVF, surrogacy and more. She navigates to *Egg Freezing* and reads through it carefully: hormone injections, scans, egg harvesting, then freezing, and there's a decent success rate of women becoming pregnant in later life by thawing their eggs. The procedure seems straightforward.

She closes her eyes for a moment and pictures herself pregnant. That Richard isn't part of that picture doesn't unsettle her as much as it should. She's rationalised that her marriage has reached its conclusion. Yet, there is an underlying doubt, lingering deep inside. Is there something more she's failed to consider?

It's not just about children. The fact is, she doesn't love him anymore and can't see they can ever rediscover the passion they once had for each other. A lump forms in her throat. She never thought she'd be joining the ranks of separated friends and acquaintances. Perhaps others saw it coming before she did. Tonight, she told Adam what she was going to do. He's been through divorce. They have a connection. Maybe this will bring them together. She really likes him. But it's too early to think like that. She hardly knows him. Not really.

Her concentration switches back to the clinic's website. Egg freezing feels like insurance. An option that means she's not racing against time. She scrolls to the pricing – £3,500 for one cycle. Then there are the added costs of thawing, fertilisation and transfer. She studies the treatment packages. The costs add up: ovarian stimulation, egg retrieval, freezing, thawing, fertilisation and transfer. At her age, she'll need multiple cycles to improve her chances of becoming pregnant. The full package: £14,000.

Her heart drops. She's just about to clear her debts. She couldn't possibly borrow more.

8

It's Sydney's first week in the cyber operations team. Ray deliberated long and hard over whether to select Rachel or Sydney. In the end, he decided he needed a cyber threat hunter more than he needed a deputy, and Sydney has that expertise. Winstanley was furious. 'You'll regret going against my direct instruction,' he'd said. Ray told him to report it to the Ethics and Compliance department, as he seems to have friends there, always willing to do favours. Ray found it hard to suppress his satisfaction. He knows he mustn't push his luck, though. He's won this time, but Winstanley plays dirty.

Ray, Aidan – a long-time member of his team – and Sydney gather round the centre table for their morning huddle. They glance at the video wall, which is flashing with alerts and scrolling text, as normal.

Ray, dressed in his trademark three-piece suit, places his phone in the middle of the table. Aidan, six feet four, hair tied back in a man-bun, lounges in a patchwork shirt that looks like a hand-me-down from a summer solstice festival. Ray often imagines him fitting in with the Hare Krishna chanting band who parade through Leicester Square in the evenings. Sydney, who turned up on her first day wearing a trouser suit, has now settled for black jeans and a multi-coloured crew neck. They each have a takeaway coffee.

Ray slides a leather coaster towards Sydney. 'For your coffee.'

She glances at Aidan. He gives a small nod, as if to say *just go with it*.

Ray starts the timer on his phone. 'Aidan. You're first. Anything to report?'

Aidan sips his coffee. 'Four indicators of compromise yesterday. Two were attempts to breach our Citrix gateway, one was a false positive, another originated internally, by someone running *Metasploit* from an anonymous server account. Looks like network reconnaissance: port scans and misconfiguration probes. It was no one from our team.'

Ray tilts his head. 'Do we know who?'

Aidan scoffs. 'What part of "anonymous" don't you understand?'

Ray leans forward. 'Have you checked the logs, traced the host IP address, pulled the access control lists?'

'No, but our security analysts have, and they're pretty good at their jobs.'

And they're off. Ray and Aidan volley technical jargon and counter arguments like seasoned rivals on a ping-pong table. Aidan matches him, as always. That's what makes him valuable. Sydney watches, open-mouthed, hesitating to jump in – first-week caution maybe, or just not comfortable sparring with her new boss. Ray's not arguing just for the sake of it. He wants to challenge their thinking. Synaptonica are a big target for e-crime and nation state threat actors, always looking to get their hands on the innovative medical research stored in the digital vault. He needs diligence.

Ten minutes later, they land on the most likely explanation. Someone in the network engineering team is preparing for the next patching cycle. Not malicious. Just careless. Ray takes an action to speak to the team lead to remind them to stop using non-identifiable accounts. He'll likely upset someone; he normally does. But feathers need ruffling sometimes.

Ray turns to Sydney. 'Feel free to jump in with a counter-opinion. We enjoy a good debate here.'

She smiles. 'As you ask, I think you were too quick to dismiss it as non-malicious. Nowadays, bad actors are pretty good at gaining a foothold in the network and remaining below the radar. I've also noticed the current stack doesn't ingest the full endpoint telemetry. That gives us a blind spot'

Ray nods and glances at the video wall. Alerts flash continuously. Mostly day-to-day blips on the network, nothing worth investigating. But that makes him nervous. Sydney's right. It would be easy for someone to dwell without detection.

'If we upgraded the SIEM and do better correlations, we'll increase the signal-to-noise ratio, which means wasting less time on meaningless alerts,' says Sydney.

'Agreed, but our technically illiterate chief financial officer thinks that's an unnecessary expense.'

'Would a business case help?'

Ray shakes his head. 'Don't waste your time. He's a halfwit who doesn't know a SIEM from a sewing machine.'

Ray wants to go further. Tell her that Winstanley is an untrustworthy rogue, who creates rules for others to follow, but he ignores. But he holds back for fear of creating a toxic culture image during her first week. Ray likes Sydney. He made the right choice. Not only does she fit in well, but she's already spotting flaws and has some good ideas. He hopes this place treats her well. Some people might look twice. The broad shoulders, large hands, a voice that doesn't quite hit the high notes. None of that matters to Ray. What matters is whether she gets one step ahead of the hackers.

Sydney checks her watch. 'I've got the new-starter induction in five minutes.'

'Okay, let's wrap up.' Ray stops his phone timer. 'Don't forget, we're going to the pub tonight – a welcome drink for Sydney.'

Sydney heads out, Aidan returns to his triple monitor workstation and Ray retreats into his office. Sydney is right about the ageing technology stack. But Winstanley won't budge. A bit of Ray wishes there was a genuine cyber-attack. Nothing major, just something to scare him, which he could point to and say *I told you so*. He glances out at the large monitor, flashing red with alerts. So much data, not enough information.

It's been one week since Izabela joined the company, and it's been a stressful settling-in period for Rachel. New starters are normally compliant and respectful to their manager. On day two, Izabela demanded elevated access privileges, enough to give her access across the entire network. Rachel refused, telling her cyber security perform continuous monitoring of all privileged access, which isn't entirely true. She already knows the cyber team just don't have the bandwidth to do that. But granting her entitlement to anything higher than what a service desk analyst needs is a risk she will not take. The two of them are still testing each other's boundaries.

Rachel enrolled Izabela on the new-staff induction training, which she is attending today, reluctantly. 'I'll just skip it,' she had said. Rachel told her she must go and make a good impression as a grateful and committed new employee. 'I always do,' she replied sulkily.

Aleks kept his side of the bargain and the second payment landed in her crypto wallet this morning, which means Rachel is now debt free. The mortgage repayment holiday gives her enough margin to continue supporting Tony. Hopefully, by the time payments recommence, he will be working as a chef full time and earning good money. She feels relieved.

She should stop now. Just accept her bounty and fade into the background. But she can't. Not yet.

Aleks asked to meet up with her. She's can guess why, and it has given her an idea.

Rachel leaves the office early, her coat drawn tightly against the cool afternoon air. It's a brisk ten-minute walk from her office in Charing Cross Road to the British Museum. She quickens her pace, weaving through satchel-swinging school kids and wayward cyclists mounting pavements and running red lights without so much as a ping of their bell. Hazards everywhere. The next one might be of her own making.

She arrives at the entrance to the British Museum and enters through the wrought-iron gates. Despite walking past this iconic landmark every workday, this is the first time she's stepped inside. She places her bag in the hard plastic tray at the security checkpoint. Her heart thuds harder than it should. She breathes slow and steady through her nose until the machine gives a soft beep, and she's waved through by security. She enters the main hall, heels tapping on the stone floor as she makes her way to the Egyptian wing.

She spots Aleks immediately, admiring a bronze statue of a cat goddess. Even in his flat cap and silk scarf, he's unmistakable – slender frame, fitting in effortlessly. To anyone else, he could be an academic historian or a cultured tourist.

She draws up beside him. 'Hello, Aleks.'

He turns, offers a thin smile. 'Nice to see you again, Rachel.'

They shake hands; his grip is firm. Hers feels faintly clammy by comparison.

He lowers his cap slightly. 'How's Iza settling in?'

Rachel exhales sharply. 'She's still too conspicuous. Barges into management meetings, ignores procedures and has no respect for the organisational hierarchy. Our deal was discretion.'

He chuckles. 'Are you happy with your compensation?'

She glances briefly around then nods. 'Yes. Just as we agreed.'

They walk towards the centrepiece exhibit, the Rosetta Stone. Aleks gazes into the protective glass case. 'I love museums. Exhibits like this bring to life the most fascinating stories, don't you think?'

Rachel wonders how long it will take for him to get to the point. He wanted to meet, and Rachel suggested here for a reason. 'Is there something more you want from me, Aleks?'

He faces Rachel face-on, his wide eyes like lasers focussed on her face. 'Iza feels a bit... constrained. Access restrictions, Policies and such like.'

Rachel shrugs. 'As I mentioned before, our security is tight.'

He smiles. 'If you could elevate her access, just temporarily, then—'

Rachel shakes her head. 'If she's caught, it comes back to me, and I have too much to lose.'

He exhales impatiently. 'We will compensate you further.'

They slowly circle the Rosetta Stone. That was exactly what she was expecting him to say and he's playing right into her hands. 'Are you open to a counter-proposal?'

Aleks shoots her a look. 'Such as?'

Rachel peers at the inscriptions on the ancient stone. 'Does the name Peter Higgs ring any bells with you?' she asks.

He shakes his head.

'You'll like this one.'

Rachel tells him about Dr Peter Higgs. A museum curator, trusted and respected at the British Museum, who, over a ten-year period, stole hundreds of artefacts and sold them on eBay. About 1,800 objects went missing from the museum strongroom: gems, medals and jewellery. Because of his position, he had privileges that ordinary staff would not have. Museum procedure for visiting the strongroom requires two people to be present, but approved persons such as Dr Higgs could go in without an escort. The museum had records of the people who turned off the alarm to the strongroom. He did, but they failed to act on it.

Aleks listens, without comment or interruption, but Rachel notes the narrowing of his eyes. He's interested.

She continues the story, explaining that an antiquities dealer, who bought some items, became suspicious, did some investigating and discovered a link between a fake eBay seller account and Peter Higgs. He notified the museum multiple times. They did a cursory investigation but gave him the brush-off. Eventually, he reported it to the press, who exposed the theft and the negligence of the British Museum to investigate.

'Using eBay was his mistake,' he says with a wry smile. 'There are alternative marketplaces which offer... discretion.'

She smiles. 'My point is, the biggest threat to any organisation is not the outsider trying to break in, but the *trusted insider* who already has access to pretty much everything.'

'And who is beyond suspicion,' he adds with an understanding nod.

They wander towards the museum's central foyer. The light from the glass roof falls in geometric patterns between them.

'Are you still in the competitor intelligence business?' she asks.

He smiles. 'We have clients who are eager to learn what their competitors are working on, especially in pharmaceutical research.'

'Interesting.'

They walk towards the exit in silence. Rachel knows she has his attention. Her heart is pounding. She feels like an actor, playing a character that is so far removed from her true self. She's confident. Over-confident, perhaps.

'There's something I'm looking to do. It's personal and will cost about fifteen grand.'

Aleks smiles. 'If you want to share some... intelligence then we can continue our partnership.'

Rachel smiles. 'Only I can do this. Izabela can't be involved.'

He smiles. 'I'll send you a link to a Dropbox account. It will be safe and secure for file storage.'

After a brisk thirty-minute walk from the office, Ray, Aidan and Sydney reach the Engineers Arms. Ray's choice. Aidan moaned. Something about passing a perfectly good Wetherspoons, but Ray wanted somewhere that resembled a proper pub. Quieter, so they could talk.

Sydney eyes the line-up of hand-pumps on the bar. 'I don't recognise any of those.'

'All cask ales,' says Ray, 'traditionally made.'

'This better be worth the walk,' Aidan mutters.

Ray grins. 'Trust me.'

Ray orders three pints of IPA. The barman takes payment and offers to bring them over. Ray asks for three beer mats.

They settle into a booth with high-back wooden panelling and cushioned benches. The pub is half full – a mixture of lone drinkers, hunched over phones and small groups, likely decompressing from a day at work. A brass wall sconce above their table casts a warm amber glow over the scarred oak-wood table. The faint murmur of conversation and the low hum of background music give the place just enough life. Ray slides the mats into place. He senses Sydney, while outwardly confident, hasn't quite settled in yet. But after tonight, he hopes she'll feel more part of the family.

The barman, tray in hand, approaches. He places them carefully on the beer mats, then darts back.

Ray raises his glass. 'Welcome to the team, Sydney.'

They clink glasses. 'Cheers,' they say in unison.

The conversation drifts naturally into shop talk. They hypothesise on tactics used by hacker groups in recent ransomware campaigns and swap ideas on how to improve their own security.

'How was the new-starter training?' asks Ray.

Sydney smiles. 'Worthwhile and informative, if I'm being polite.'

Aidan smirks. 'Don't feel you need to be polite with us.'

She takes a large drink, places her pint glass back down. 'Well, it started fine. Ten of us. Team-building exercise, then diversity and inclusion presentation. But it went downhill from there, to be honest.'

Ray raises an eyebrow. 'How come?'

Sydney's smile drops. 'Three other women, around my age, started planning a "girly shopping trip" for the evening: Oxford Street and Regent Street. But they didn't invite me. I interjected, reminding them I'm a girl too. They laughed and said *of course you can come*, but I could tell they didn't really want me tagging along. I felt excluded.'

Ray's expression tightens. 'I'm sorry that happened to you, Sydney.'

Aidan shakes his head. 'That's not okay.'

'Not the first time. Still stings, though,' she says with a shrug.

The mood drops, and the three of them fall silent for a moment.

'It wasn't a total disaster, though. I made one friend. A lady from the tech service desk who started last week. Her name's Izabela. She's studying cyber security part-time, so we had lots to talk about.'

Ray feels better. For a moment he thought she might have second thoughts about joining.

'I offered to give her a tour of the cyber operations centre. She's really keen to see how we work. Would that be okay?'

Ray nods. 'Absolutely. So long as you're with her.'

Aidan, who has already drained his pint, sets his glass down. 'She can shadow us tomorrow while we set up that new honeypot.'

9

Most staff have gone home and the open-plan zone, which was a buzz of activity an hour ago, now resembles the aftermath of a party no one enjoyed. The cleaners have arrived. One runs a vacuum in slow arcs across the carpet, the other collects desk clutter: crisp packets, lost charging cables, abandoned coffee mugs and empty cake boxes left over from someone's birthday celebration.

Rachel scans the office space and decides it is now safe. Four of her team are still at their desks, probably trying to close out service tickets. She gives them a wave before slipping into an empty meeting room, shutting the door behind her. They are likely chasing their performance targets and will probably forget she's even here.

She starts her laptop and watches it go through a protracted boot-up sequence. She had planned to phone Sarah tonight, to build up some goodwill for allowing Florence to sleepover in a few weeks' time. But that will involve a long chat, so another time. She'd sent a message to Adam earlier, teasing him about his sub-par effort at spinning class last night. 'Payback at circuits on Saturday,' he'd replied. Lots of smiley face emojis between them. No love hearts yet.

She pulls out her notebook and glances at the flowchart she'd sketched out earlier. The logic is sound – on paper, at least. Five steps. Five hacks. Will it work?

Hack one: get past the firewall. No one other than research scientists and a few authorised technical staff can access the research network because it's protected by a firewall. For anyone working outside the research labs, the only way in is via the jump server. Rachel had temporary access granted six months ago because she was working on a special assignment. These accounts should be time-bound, but it looks like someone's neglected to set an account expiry date. She double clicks the icon for the jump server and types in her credentials. There's a flicker on the screen, cryptic status messages appear, then a new window, with a black background and a white flashing cursor appears. Success. She's through the firewall and now has a foothold on the protected research network. That almost seemed too easy. But she still has more to do. She glances out towards the open-plan zone. The cleaners are sitting, chatting and her four team members still have their heads buried in their laptop monitors.

She scrolls the server list and finds the icon for the digital research vault, the primary store of all research files: target molecules, lab results, scientific papers. Competitor intelligence, as Aleks refers to it. But there's another login screen which ensures only authorised research scientists can get in. Another locked door.

Hack two: obtain user passwords. She switches windows and opens the Service Desk app – the one she uses every day. She navigates to the management screen and clicks on the *View Audit Logs* button. A long list of system event records floods the screen. In the two years she's done this job, she has never had reason to review these log records. They mostly contain unintelligible details such as user IDs, IP addresses and timestamps.

Lionel once described it as a 'useless data dump.' He's right. Except for one column: *New Password*. Every time a user resets their password, the system creates an event record and logs an *encrypted* version of the new password – a hash value of sixty meaningless characters of no use to anyone. Unless they have the right software tool.

She opens *Hashcrack* – a password cracking tool. It's on the banned software list for the company, but the next security scan isn't until two weeks' time. She'll be finished by then. She selects a record at random, copies the ciphertext password, pastes it into *Hashcrack, hits* enter and waits. Five minutes pass. It times out. She picks another. Same outcome. Those passwords are too long or too complex, which makes a brute-force hack impracticable. She chooses a third. Copy, paste, enter. Thirty seconds later, as if by magic, the eight-character plaintext password appears. Success. Rachel knows passwords are often compromised by hackers – through phishing emails and network sniffing. The service desk even send out guidance on how to best protect passwords. This is the first time she has ever attempted to crack a password and it wasn't even difficult. She looks up the user ID. It's a junior research scientist, Julie Watson. No one she knows.

Hack three: get into the digital research vault. She double-clicks the icon and the Welcome Page appears, with a login prompt. She enters Julie Watson's user ID and password. A few seconds watching the whirling mouse pointer, and she's in. She reclines in her chair and exhales. Another step closer.

She navigates the menu, tries a random search but finds Julie only has access to one folder, relating to some pre-clinical research project. She scrolls the list of twenty files, spreadsheets and Word documents . She opens some and scans through to find what looks like lab results and scientific write-ups she doesn't understand. It's all very specialised and she has no way to determine their significance. She may as well be looking at artefacts in the British Museum archive, attempting to guess their provenance and value.

Hack four: remove files from the digital vault. This is where it gets tricky. She browses the file list again, selects a spreadsheet at random and clicks the download icon. A prompt appears, asking her to select a location to save to. She selects her laptop drive under a newly created folder, *shopping*. Presses *save* and it's downloaded. No warning alerts appeared. She now has it on her laptop. She closes down the Digital Vault app and logs out of the jump server. Did that action trigger a network event record? She has no way of knowing.

Hack five: transfer files outside of the company. She logs out of her laptop and logs in again using Julie Watson's user ID and password. The laptop churns with background processing, then a new screen appears. She opens up Outlook, and Julie's inbox appears. She only wants this for one thing. She clicks on *new message*, attaches the file from her laptop, enters the address of the test Dropbox account she set up earlier, then clicks *send*. It sits there for a few of seconds, then it's gone. She goes into the *sent* folder and deletes it, then to the deleted items folder and deletes it from there too just to be sure there is no trace. She logs out and closes down her laptop.

Job done. Five layers of security breached. But tonight was only a test. Proof that her plan works. A warm thrill rises through her, sharp and exhilarating, like standing on a summit after threading a path through a snake-infested river. *Izabela could never have done this.* The thought tastes of triumph.

The office goes suddenly dark. She waves her arms, and the motion sensitive lights flickers back on. She glances around the office. The cleaners have left. A few people remain. It's late. Perhaps they're lingering by choice to avoid their unhappy home life. Rachel packs up her laptop and makes her way out.

On the train, she sits alone, headphones clamped to her head, contemplating her next steps. Recruiting Izabela was bending the rules, hacking passwords and leaking research is blatant theft. Her mind calculates the failure points in her plan: system logging and data loss prevention alerts going to the cyber team. But that's why she didn't use her own email account to transfer the files.

If no-one finds out, would that be a crime? The more she thinks about it, the more wrong it feels. A bit like having an extra-marital affair and not getting caught. The guilt remains long after the thrill has gone.

The train clatters over points and slows. She thinks of smooth talking Aleks. He promised discretion. Can she trust him and who are his clients who are going to pay for these files? Consequences flash though her mind: dismissal, reputation ruined and a criminal record that will follow her with every new job application. By the time the train pulls into her station, her head is pounding with a slow incessant worry.

She lifts her laptop bag, steps off the train and walks towards the ticket barrier as her hesitation grows.

Dishonest. Stupid. Stop now.

10

Rachel has been hiding in the ladies' room for half an hour, reading emails, tapping messages, scrolling social media. She checks the time. It's just past six. Another fifteen minutes and she should be safe. Yesterday, she was here for forty-five minutes, all to avoid Jonathan Winstanley.

She ignores his Teams messages, but now he prowls the open-plan offices like an alpha tomcat marking his territory. He chats to people he cares little for, then zeroes in on her desk, always with the same murmured question, 'When are we going to dinner?' With colleagues around, she can fend him off. End of day, when the space is more sparse, he returns. That's why she grabs her coat, clears her desk and escapes to the ladies' room. Just so it looks like she's left with everyone else. Except she hasn't. She has things to do after hours. Things she promised herself she would not do.

This isn't the first time someone's stalked her at work. A few years ago, a young analyst kept 'coincidentally' choosing the desk opposite. He admitted he was following her and said he wanted to try and woo her. She smiled and told him he had six hours to work his magic. He filled that time with a string of tongue-tied compliments and a desperate invitation to dinner. He was persistent, but harmless. Winstanley is different. He's more threatening, and she fears being alone with him. Even last week, after he signed that recruitment form, she was trembling as she fled his office.

Normally, she would face up to bullies, but he seems to have some sort of power of intimidation over her, which she cannot overcome right now.

She flips back to Facebook. Sarah has posted a photo of Florence in her school uniform, holding up a *Special Helper* certificate with a giant gold star. Rachel smiles. They spoke on the phone the other night and Sarah put her on. Rachel asked if she would like to sleep over; she said she would, and Sarah agreed. It's all arranged for two weeks from now, when Richard's away. A warm, loving feeling passes through her. Having Florence in her life only strengthens her yearning for children of her own.

Rachel returns to her usual after-hours meeting room. It's been one week since she tested her hacking plan, and she has been here every night since. Monday was password-harvesting night – she only needed four or five but ended up with forty. Tuesday she logged in and out of the digital research vault using different credentials, browsing folders, trying to make sense of the contents. She couldn't. Conveniently, each file carries a sensitivity label, so she focused on those marked *Highly Confidential*. Now, 200 files sit on her laptop. Her haul. Some seem more significant than others, such as those authored by Dr James Craig, a senior clinical scientist.

She shouldn't be doing this. Her pulse quickens as she stares at the file list glowing on her screen. *How much would someone pay for this?* The thought makes her stomach twist. She's never stolen anything in her life before. It feels like she's walked out of a shop with stolen goods, unchallenged, and can't bring herself to go back. Last night's dream still clings to her: police lights flashing outside her house, a search team combing through her belongings. Laptop seized and name on the news. Ridiculous. Paranoid.

Yet the fear sits heavy in her gut because she knows, no matter how she justifies it, this is theft.

Twelve files. That's all she agreed to. No more. After tonight, it's over. She'll email them using other people's accounts, cover her tracks, erase every trace. Her plan is meticulous. Almost foolproof. Still, as she grips the mouse and moves the pointer towards *send*, her hand trembles. A voice in her head whispers, *you're being watched*.

A gentle tap at her door jolts her upright. She quickly locks her screen, breath caught in her throat.

The door swings open and Deirdre, the cleaner, pokes her head through. 'Cup of tea, Rachel, love?'

'Thank you,' she says, waving her to come in.

Deirdre has befriended Rachel this last week. Every night, she makes her a mug of tea and sits down for a chat. She used to work in Sainsbury's but gave that up so she could look after her grandson during the day and clean in the evenings. She talks about her partner of eight years who still won't marry her, and her son of twenty-three, who can't hold down a job for more than a week and is always asking her for money. She thinks she's about to hit the menopause because of her night sweats, but she can't get an appointment with a doctor.

When they finish their tea, Deirdre collects the mugs and smiles. 'Thanks for listening, Rachel. I feel better now.'

Deirdre provides a convenient distraction. The two of them casually chatting like this removes the surreptitiousness of her extracurricular activities. It's also a nice diversion from everything else going on in her life. She reminds Rachel of Aunt Brenda. Not a real aunt; a friend of the family whom she's always called Aunt. She too is an open book. Lives on her own and craves company. Rachel can have conversations with her that she can't have with her mum and dad, such as talking about Tony and how he's trying to rebuild his life. Rachel fears he will relapse, but Aunt Brenda doesn't think so because having Florence gives him a sense of responsibility he's never had before. Rachel clings to that.

She turns back to her computer, refocuses her mind and methodically logs in and out of the other peoples accounts, opening their emails and transferring the files one-by-one to the Dropbox account Aleks set up. The remaining files will stay on her computer. She wonders who his client is. Perhaps it's best she knows as little as possible. Her job is done and now she can move on with her life.

Her phone vibrates on her desk, making her jump. She glances at the screen and smiles when she sees who the caller is.

She accepts the FaceTime call and Adam's face fills the screen. 'Hello, muscle man.'

'Hello, studious one,' he says.

'What have you been up to?'

'Just got back from the gym. You said you'd be in the office revising, so thought it would be safe to call.'

They had lunch together on Saturday and have spoken every night this week. Their conversation slips into easy banter as she reminds him, she's still fastest on the spin bike, and – adjusting for body weight – she can lift heavier weights. After a few more laughs and lingering smiles, they say their goodbyes.

Rachel sets the phone down, leans back in her chair as a rush of affection passes through her, creating the sort of high that occurs with a new boyfriend. She's going to his house for dinner on Friday. He had offered to take her out to a restaurant, but she suggested he cook as there would be less chance of them being spotted. Coffee and chat after a gym workout is innocent enough, but what looks like a romantic dinner for two on a Friday night will surely set tongues wagging if they bumped into someone they knew – fellow gym-goers or even worse, someone from Richard's pickleball club.

It's 8 p.m., yet it doesn't feel late. Her job is complete, but curiosity still lingers within her. She has all those passwords and some of them belong to interesting people. Like Mike Chester. Another undeserving board director, just like Winstanley. He must have some interesting material in his inbox. She would love to know more about what they talk about – big business deals, new strategies. The sort of stuff people at Rachel's level would never be privy to.

She logs into her laptop using his ID and password, then opens his email. Her inner voice is back, subliminally reminding her she is violating company policy, and any form of hacking is grounds for dismissal. She fights with her own conscience, telling herself she's not stealing anything. She's just browsing.

Mike Chester has 1,500 unread emails in his inbox, some going back months. It's mostly day-to-day management stuff – expenses for approval, meeting minutes, project updates. The sort of stuff Rachel deals with. At least she reads her messages. She keeps scrolling but finds nothing of interest. She switches to Teams. More clutter amongst a series of random message threads: pub quiz photos, birthday memes, a blurry shot of him with his arm around a reluctant younger woman. *Does this man do any proper work?* Then one thread catches her eye – Jonathan Winstanley. This might be interesting. Her stomach tightens. She clicks open the message thread:

Mike: Just been told to attend the extraordinary board meeting on Monday. What's happening?

Jonathan: Don't know, but there's been an uptick in share-buying activity

Mike: Possible takeover bid?

Jonathan: Good for our stock options if it is.

Rachel takes a breath then reads it again, allowing it to sink in, thinking about the significance of this news. Who would buy Synaptonica? It can only be one of the big pharma companies: AstraZeneca, GSK, Pfizer. Some big-league player looking to swallow up Synaptonica. It's the research they're after. That's where the value is. She suddenly feels unsettled. Those would be good companies to work for, but a takeover could mean office closures and job losses – not in the research labs, but head office. This is worse than outsourcing. She scrolls down, hoping to find out more, but there's nothing. A new message thread between them starts the following day. She clicks it open:

Jonathan: How are you getting on with the new girl?

Mike: 8 out of 10.

Jonathan: An improvement on the last one, then.

Mike: How about you and your mentee – Rachel?

Jonathan: Work in progress

Mike: Banged her yet?

Jonathan: You'll be the first to know.

Mike: I'm not handing over that 500 until I see proof

Jonathan: What do you want, a selfie in the sack?

Mike: Ha, ha. No mate, just her underwear :-)

Rachel freezes. Her jaw drops. Suddenly, she is back in his twelfth-floor office, alone, fighting him off. She reads it again. Rage doesn't come, not immediately. More a feeling of enlightenment. She's no stranger to misogynistic language, mostly schoolboy stuff. But this scrapes the dregs of the sewer. It's the hypocrisy that really grates her. She shakes her head as she recalls the all-staff broadcast the other week, where they reeled off their oft-used mantra: *We are proud of our culture and our shared values of integrity and respect.* It didn't sound sincere.

She picks up her phone and snaps a picture of the screen. She's not sure what she'll do with it, though. Reporting it would be like walking into a police station carrying stolen goods. But she'll not let this go.

She's startled when her phone vibrates in her hand, then sighs when she sees the caller.

She taps *Accept.* 'Hi,' she says flatly.

'Just checking to see when you're coming home,' says Richard.

She meets his eyes through the screen. 'Makes a change from me waiting on you.'

A pause. 'I just find it strange that you need to be in the office every night to study.'

She stands up, holds the phone away, so he has a full view of the office. 'More study resources here.'

They have a few more single sentence exchanges then finish the call.

He's checking up on her. Not surprising, given her change in routine and behaviour over this last week. The conversation she promised herself she would have with him is overdue. There's just so much happening in her life and she's struggling to juggle all these stress balls. But she can't avoid it for much longer though. She already told him she'll be staying over at a friend's tomorrow night – Izabela, the new girl. He didn't seem convinced.

She turns back to her computer. Ten more minutes, then she'll head home. Big night tomorrow and she wants to get a decent night's sleep, for once. A flashing message box appears on screen.

John: Hi Mike. How come you're logged on? Working late?
John: Got 5 mins for a chat?

Her heart jumps as she realises others can see he's online. She panics. Thinks about replying, pretending to be Mike. Starts typing, then stops herself. That would be reckless as he would see it in the morning. The dots on screen tell her John is typing again. She hurriedly closes the app and his email and logs out. She's just been incredibly stupid. She slips her laptop into her bag, slides into her coat and makes for the exit. No more. She must stop what she's doing now.

11

Rachel sinks into her seat and opens her laptop. The morning at the clinic has buoyed her: a warm conversation with a friendly nurse and screening results that came back as normal. A step towards the future she longs for. But the fear of being discovered as the person who hacked into Mike Chester's account has muted her excitement. She barely slept last night as she imagined the chain of events unfolding. He notices someone logged in with his account, so he reports it. The service desk reset his password, then they pass it to the cyber team – as standard procedure. They will investigate and inspect the authentication logs, which will identify the specific laptop used. Her laptop. The only one she uses.

She logs into the Service Desk management console and browses the morning tickets. Nothing from Mike Chester. Not yet. But it's early, and if he's buried in morning meetings, he might not even know.

She glances across the work zone. It's dress-down Friday. Jeans and jumpers replace business attire as the whole office carries the chilled Friday vibe. Most of her team wear headsets, voices raised in cheerful rhythm as they guide users through fixes and workarounds. Lionel hovers over Izabela, offering help she almost certainly doesn't need. A tray of iced cupcakes sits on a spare desk. It's probably someone's birthday or it may just be a random act of generosity. They also celebrate births and pregnancies.

She smiles. It's a great team, and most weeks she'd join them in the pub to kick off the weekend. But not tonight. Tonight, she's heading straight to Adam's. The thought settles her. She's been looking forward to this all week.

She turns back to her computer, opens her e-mail and watches the usual junk mail tumble in. One subject line jumps out, marked important: *Action required: Notification of HR Recruitment Audit*. Her stomach knots. Audit. A word designed to induce panic. It normally involves someone poking into her work and challenging her competency to do her job. She clicks it open. HR audit is reviewing all staff onboarded through the fast-track recruitment process. Her heart sinks. Typical. The one time she's used fast-track – for Izabela. Why now?

Attached is a multi-page form demanding details of prior employment, periods of study or extended leave and home addresses going back ten years. She needs to deflect this somehow. Maybe she can stall until after the outsourcing announcement. Then it becomes irrelevant, doesn't it?

She spots an empty meeting room.

'Izabela,' she calls out.

Izabela looks up.

'Five minutes,' Rachel says, gesturing to a vacant office.

Izabela strides in a moment later, carrying two chocolate cupcakes. In keeping with the Friday theme, she's wearing a baseball cap and an open checked shirt over a black *Star Trek* T-shirt. Carefree and smug. Enough to further raise Rachel's irritation levels.

'Happy Friday, Rachel.' Izabela slides a cupcake across the table. 'I hear you've been busy.'

Rachel forces her a tight smile. 'Three weeks ago, I fast-tracked you into the company.'

Izabela nods. 'Three weeks ago, you were desperate for cash.'

Her retort stings. She swallows it, still wondering what exactly she's doing. Lionel said she's on laptop restores and software installs. But what else?

Rachel remains straight-faced. 'We have a bit of a situation to deal with.' She slides the multi-page form across the desk. 'HR have asked you to complete this, by next week.'

Izabela reads it, while licking frosting from her finger. 'What happens if I don't?'

Rachel smiles. 'They'll probably terminate your employment.'

Izabela brushes cake crumbs off her lap and shrugs. 'Don't worry, I've completed everything I need to do.'

She speaks with the confidence of a chess master who's just calculated their winning move. Calm and superior. But if she's finished, perhaps she will leave? That would be good news. She's had enough of her demands and hates the way she manipulates people: acting naïve, feigning gratitude for help, especially from men who fall for it. Rachel would be glad to see her gone. Today, preferably.

Izabela stands, heads to the door, pauses and looks back. 'If there's anything you want help with, Rachel...'

Rachel matches her smile. 'I've done everything I need to do, thank you.'

At least she can be certain of one thing: Izabela hasn't got into the research network. She can't have, because Aleks is paying Rachel for that. Izabela's not smart enough.

Rachel slips into the lunchtime commotion of the food court. Cutlery clatters, trays bang, people chatter as they dart between counters and tables with their meal deals. She finds a high table, settles onto a stool and prises open her Tupperware box of honey-glazed salmon, puy lentils and salad, garnished with the spring onions she'd snipped this morning.

Her mind drifts to tonight. Adam's house. She pictures a typical single-bloke pad with bare walls, no plants, a lounge filled with exercise equipment and a bathroom crammed with grooming products. The thought makes her smile.

'Hello, Rachel.'

A voice cuts through her thoughts. Jonathan Winstanley casually drops onto the stool opposite, smiling like an old friend. Her chest tightens as fury rises inside her.

'Hello, Jonathan,' she says evenly.

He snatches a plastic fork from the dispenser and spears a piece of her salmon. 'Have you been avoiding me?'

'Have you been stalking me?' Her eyes lock on to his as she recalls the message exchange she saw between him and Mike Chester last night. She can't believe she once respected this man. Now, she just sees a gormless looking sex-pest.

He grins. 'We have a date to arrange, remember? Thought I'd see how you're fixed over the next few days.'

She wants to slap him, right here in front of everyone. She looks from side-to-side. This place is bustling. Slapping him would silence the hubbub and create one hell of a scene. She would just say he tried to grope her.

'Well?' he presses, leaning closer.

She snaps the lid shut on her lunchbox, gripping it tight. One... two...

A tray clatters onto the table.

'Rachel, you didn't tell me you were coming down here,' says Izabela, swinging onto the next stool. She thrusts out her hand to Jonathan Winstanley. 'Hi, I'm Izabela. I'm in Rachel's team.'

He looks her up and down, smile widening. 'Jonathan Winstanley.' He takes her hand.

'What do you do, Jonathan?'

He chuckles. 'I'm CFO.'

'That's cool.' She bites into her panini, pours green smoothie into a glass.

He watches, curiously. 'How are you finding it here?' he asks.

She chews, swallows and wipes her mouth. 'The bureaucracy is awful. I can't believe we still have Windows 10. But the people are really nice. It's sociable.'

Rachel smirks. The company will have Windows 10 for a while because Winstanley won't pay for what he considers to be unnecessary software upgrades. S*weat the asset* is another one of his dim-witted mantras.

Izabela keeps talking while his eyes wander between her face and her breasts. Rachel watches, intrigued. Amused as Izabela tries to reel him in. What a great distraction. After a few minutes, he stands to leave, looking bored. He gives Izabela a smile then fixes his gaze on Rachel and holds it for a second. It's a look that says they have unfinished business. He turns and walks away.

'He's an important dude, right?' says Izabela.

Rachel laughs. 'Oh, yes. Sits at the top of the house.'

She smiles. 'I must get to know him better.'

A lunch trays lands in the spot where Winstanley had been sitting. 'May I join you lovely ladies?' Lionel asks, hauling himself onto the stool.

Rachel smiles. 'Sorry, I've got stuff to do. I'll leave you two to chat.' She grabs her lunchbox, climbs off her stool and strides back to the work zone, pulse still racing.

Ray, Aidan and Sydney gather around the table for their daily huddle in the cyber operations room. Dress-down Friday has no relevance here. Ray still wears a suit. Aidan and Sydney stick to their everyday office gear. A phone sits in the centre of the table, timer counting down, showing fifteen minutes remaining for their meeting.

'I think we should switch off our data loss prevention solution,' says Ray.

Aidan and Sydney exchange a glance.

'Our biggest risk is intellectual property theft, and you want to kill the one system designed to detect that?' says Aidan.

Ray shrugs his shoulders. 'It's like a firehose. Five terabytes of data a day. It alerts us to trivia like users sending their CVs to recruitment companies, and the rest is unintelligible noise. The analysts are suffering alert fatigue.'

'We should start doing some correlations,' says Sydney, flipping to a blank page in her notebook. She sketches a flow diagram, then slides it over. 'If we corelate the DLP alerts with other signals, such as unusual login times, strange device activity, we'll get fewer false positives and genuine alerts worth investigating.'

Aidan leans in. 'If we can't upgrade our SIEM, then we'll build our own correlation engine,' he says with pride.

The conversation ramps up and ideas flow, Sydney's pen sketching and Aidan's hands moving as they visualise a solution. Ray watches in silence as they brainstorm, until a piercing chime interrupts their flow when the timer hits zero. Thirty minutes is up, conversation stops, and the meeting ends, as it must.

Ray stands and grabs his phone. Aidan and Sydney move to the whiteboard and recommence their conversation about data sources and logic trees. Ray has no intention of switching off DLP. He just wanted to provoke them into thinking harder about a solution to their big data problem. One of his frustrations is their inability to do any meaningful analysis of the systems logs that get generated – millions of records an hour capturing every network event, all flowing into a database, which, at the moment, is an infinite sink. He knows that somewhere amongst that torrent of data might be a critical signal they've missed. Staff sharing passwords, insiders stealing sensitive data, users browsing the dark web all hint to a bad actor inside the company. The alerts they receive only skim the surface and they need to do better. A new Security Incident and Event Management system would help. Something else Winstanley refuses to pay for.

He strolls back into his office, and his thoughts switch to next week's holiday in the Yorkshire Dales. Long walks and pub lunches with Kirsty. No emails or work interruptions. He's told them not to disturb him. 'Can't imagine what we'd need you for,' was Aidan's response. He glances back at the two of them, deep in conversation, markers squeaking as they flowchart and scribble. He quickly pokes his head back into the meeting area.

'I'd like a working prototype by Wednesday,' says Ray.

Sydney looks up. 'I thought you weren't back until the week after?'

Ray smiles. 'I'd still like it working before I get back.'

'Friday, then,' Aidan mutters, without turning round.

12

Rachel never imagined that calm could settle over her so quickly. The moment she sinks into the deep cushions of Adam's leather sofa, a generous gin and tonic cradled in her hand, the tensions of the day begin to ebb away, dissolving like bath salts in warm water. She can breathe easy now. Her last act at work was checking to see if Mike Chester had reported his account being used. She had a headache worrying about it. To her immense relief, nothing yet. Another bullet dodged. She's never been so ready for a drink as she is now. Her shoulders drop as she stretches her legs out, the cool ice clinking in her glass and helping her unwind.

She had been wrong about Adam's house. She'd pictured a bare bachelor pad with dumbbells in the lounge. Instead, she finds pictures on the wall and a simply furnished place but with a warm, lived-in feel. It was the bathroom that startled her most. Two shelves crammed with aftershaves, a line of twenty ornate bottles of every conceivable shape and size. She only uses one scent – Chanel No. 5 – and has done for years and can't think of a single friend who keeps a perfume collection, let alone a man. She laughs quietly to herself. It's nice getting to know someone's quirks. And an obsession with smelling nice? Well, she can live with that.

She watches him moving around the kitchen, opening cupboards and clattering pans. His brow furrows in concentration as he reads a recipe he printed from the internet. She would love a house with an open-plan layout like this. The kitchen is her favourite place to be and having it as part of the lounge, like this, with large windows on to a patio, is a dream.

'Are you sure you don't want any help?' she calls out.

He looks over his shoulder and smiles. 'I'm not great at kitchen team-work. Best you sit there and be princess-like.'

'I can do that,' she says with a smirk.

She places her drink on the side table and walks over to the record player, its vintage wood casing and old-school dials catching her eye the moment she walked in. She unclips the record box and flips through his vinyl collection – Arctic Monkeys, Manic Street Preachers, Foo Fighters, David Bowie, Oasis, Coldplay. She could listen to any of them except Coldplay. She and Richard went to see them at Wembley once and she doesn't need that memory tonight. She enjoys live music but hasn't been to a concert for a while. Perhaps Adam can take her sometime. Bryan Adams is touring right now, and she'd love to see him live. She selects an album by Dire Straits, *Brothers in Arms*. She slides it out of its sleeve, slots it onto the turntable, turns a dial and watches the needle arm raise itself and drop onto the vinyl with satisfying precision. The soft string notes of 'So Far Away' fills the room with a feeling of warmth and nostalgia.

'Good choice,' Adam says, glancing over.

'I used to listen to them at uni,' she says.

He chuckles. 'They're a London band?'

'I don't hold that against them.'

He slices something on a wooden board, glances up again. 'They chose their name because they were broke, living hand-to-mouth.'

She settles back on the sofa, sips her drink. The lighting is soft and the air warm. Her eyes fall on the large canvas photo of Adam and his children that hangs on the wall. He talks often about his children – a girl and a boy, fifteen and twelve. The same age gap as her and Tony. She imagines him to be a great dad. A thought rises from her subconscious: *Would he consider having more children?* She pushes it down. This is early-stage relationship, a time to just enjoy each other.

The next track comes on, 'Money for Nothing'. She laughs, before reminding herself that her secret side-hustle is not something to be proud of.

He sets the table, lights the centre candle and pours red wine into broad glasses and sets two plates down. The food presentation may not be perfect, but the meal of sea bass with baby potatoes, asparagus and mushrooms looks amazing. The last time someone cooked a decent meal for her was her mum, when she last visited her parents.

'Why Worry?', plays. She listens: *But baby, just when this world seems mean and cold. Our love comes shining red and gold.* The lyrics wrap around her, setting a romantic mood, just as she had hoped. He's doing a lot to make her feel special tonight.

After their meal, he busies himself with the dishwasher while Rachel drifts towards the record player and selects another album – *The Last Ship*, by Sting. She likes the tactility of the vinyl and the mechanics of placing the record on the turntable then watching the arm lift and drop. When the music starts, she returns to the sofa.

Their heads lean together and they fall into a natural kiss. Tentative at first, almost cautious, as if testing boundaries. Then it deepens. His hands find her waist, and she lets herself be pulled closer. Her heart is racing. It's been so long since she felt this desired by someone. Someone she cares for. She realises how much she's missed this closeness.

All week she's told herself this will be the night. She'd dreamed about it on her morning walk from the train station to the office. It was a pleasant distraction during some of those tedious management meetings. The thought had excited and unsettled her, because she knows she is cheating. Something she's never done before. But her marriage is already dead in the water and there hasn't been intimacy there for many months, a fact that helps suppress the nagging guilt.

Now, with her body pressed against his, the hesitation she once harboured has gone and she is ready for the full experience. She doesn't just want it; she needs it. She wants to feel alive again.

'Shall we move this somewhere more comfortable?' she murmurs.

He smiles, takes her hand. She follows as he leads her upstairs, leaving behind two unfinished glasses of wine, a spinning record and a flickering candle.

The soft glow of the bedroom light wraps the room in warmth, creating a tranquil ambiance that feels worlds away from the nerve-racking chaos of the office. His fingers fumble with the clasp of her bra, jeans are unbuttoned, and clothes drop to the floor. His gaze moves over her and lingers on the two elephants tattooed across her breasts – a warm reminder of her solo journey through India after university. For a moment, she feels exposed, almost shy – a side of herself she hasn't revealed in years. Then he smiles, and the tension eases. She exhales, letting herself feel safe

They collapse onto the bed, limbs wrapped around each other. She wants to draw out the pleasure, savour the experience. But in a moment, he's above her. When he moves inside, she clings to him, eyes closing, submitting to the rhythm. It's quick, but she doesn't mind. The look of satisfaction on his face as he collapses beside her makes her feel special in a way she has missed for so long.

They talk quietly, laughing about how they've both imagined this night many times, then they drift into a contented silence. His breathing steadies; his eyelids lower. But she isn't finished. She moves her fingers over him, teasing him back to life until he hardens again. Now she feels the thrill of power and is ready to take control. She shifts on top, guiding him, telling him what she wants, moving at her own pace. Her confidence surprises even herself as she lets out a sharp cry. This isn't just making love; she's reclaiming a part of herself that's been asleep for too long.

Later, they lie tangled, the sheets warm and damp between them. Adam drifts off again, a faint smile still on his face. She stays awake, enjoying the afterglow, wanting more, and she'll have it in the morning.

As she stares into the darkness, her thoughts drift to the moment they first met, six months ago. There had been a spark. But it was the events of the last three weeks that fanned the fire. That heart-to-heart with Cathy was a moment of enlightenment. The moment she admitted to herself that she had to take control of her future. She's forked off from her old life and stepped onto a new path. Who knows where it leads, but she's certain she doesn't want to turn back.

Adam knows nothing about her darker exploits at work, except for her frustrations about an obstinate new staff member she hopes will quit soon. That part of her life feels like another world, one she tells herself is nearly over. Maybe this is the start of something more honest. She closes her eyes, leaving fate to be determined.

Hot water sprays over her skin as she stands under Adam's rain-shower the next morning. The marble-tiled wet room gleams and steam curls upwards as water seeps through a central drain in the middle of the floor. Last night had been everything she had hoped for, and this morning, even more. They'd slept soundly. She had woken early and stirred him from his sleep. It was so easy to arouse him. Then they made love again. So natural, as though her bodies had been waiting for it.

For a moment, she imagines him slipping in behind her, arms around her waist, lips on her shoulder. Instead, she remembers his words: *You're amazing in bed*. Yes, she's good at sex – with the right partner. She makes a mental note to get a wax-job for next time.

Still, reality is descending on her once again. When she had picked up her phone this morning, there were two messages from Richard. One late last night, to say good night – he's never done that before. Another this morning asking when she's getting back. She hasn't replied to either. It's a reminder that the conversation with Richard – the one she's been avoiding – must happen soon as she's now crossed a line. It's not that she feels guilty about what is technically cheating, but she needs to stop lying. And he needs to be allowed to get on with his life.

She pats herself dry and steps back into the bedroom just as he returns with two mugs of milky espresso-based coffee. He's still smiling. That's good. They climb back into bed, sit propped up, chatting casually as the radio murmurs in the background.

She leans into Adam's shoulder. 'There's one thing we should probably sort out.'

Adam tenses slightly. 'Oh?'

She sips her coffee. 'We forgot to use protection last night.'

He chuckles. 'We got lost in the moment, I guess.'

She nods. 'We should probably think about that next time, you know, just in case.' Her tone is playful, but the words carry a sense of importance.

He grins, rests a warm hand on her thigh. 'I wouldn't worry about that.'

She frowns. 'What do you mean?'

He laughs. Holds up two fingers and makes a snipping motion. 'Snip-snip. Had it done a few years ago.'

Rachel's smile drops and the breath catches in her throat.

Adam slurps his coffee. 'No chance of me getting you pregnant,' he adds cheerfully.

13

Rachel's breath comes in hard bursts, her face streaked with a mix of sweat and drizzle as she jogs the final stretch towards home. The trees that line her street wear the colours of autumn – muted gold and russet brown, and scatter their leaves with every gust of wind. She reaches her front door, stoops to untie her laces and thwacks the soles of her muddy Nikes together, each satisfying smack releasing mud and grit from the park. Her chest is still rising and falling as she feels a resolution emerging.

Yesterday – Saturday – had been a stressful day. Not from arguments or disagreements at home – they kept out of each other's way for most of the time – but from the anxiety that came from lying and deceiving. Where she'd spent Friday night, slipping out of the house on a flimsy excuse just so she could chat to Adam. Sharing a bed with Richard only intensified the need to escape from self-induced torment. Even in their king-size, with a safe stretch of no man's land between them, she felt trapped, her body rigid with guilt. Lying awake, she ran through every deception, each one weighing her down. She's not sure how much longer she can bear it.

But exercise always clears her head and five miles of pounding through parkland released enough endorphins to allow the accumulation of stress, worry and unanswered questions to evaporate like the sweat on warm skin.

Now, she has the clarity of mind and mental strength to face up to those difficult conversations.

She's falling for Adam. That much is certain. Their night together had been perfect; the warmth of his bed and his arms wrapped around her body has stayed with her.

Later, at home, she googled *vasectomy reversal*, an act of hope. She quickly learned that success rates are good – ninety per cent if performed in the three years from the original procedure. That's all she needs to know. She has no intention of raising the topic, not at this stage in their relationship. She just needs to know that they can unbolt that door in the future. Right now, it's about building on what they have.

In the kitchen, she fills a glass with water and gulps it down then lets out a long sigh. Upstairs, she hears Richard moving around. Footsteps, running water from the bathroom. She had warned him earlier that they need to talk, and it has to be tonight, Sunday. The only evening their lives overlap in the same space. This might get ugly, but she's ready for it.

She hears him descend the stairs, and her heart gives a warning thump. She tells herself to stay strong. It's going to be okay. She's rehearsed different versions of this talk during her run, over and over. She flips the kettle on and grabs two mugs from the draining board. She reminds herself to keep it civil. No shouting.

Richard enters the kitchen, looking unusually well-presented for a Sunday: clean shaven, smart jeans and grey crew neck.

'Tea?' asks Rachel.

He takes a seat, stretches his legs out. 'Yes. Thank you.'

Rachel pours boiling water into the two mugs, using one teabag for both, then stirs in the milk. She sets them down on the table, then sits opposite. She can't remember how she was going to start, so she just dives straight in.

'I think we should separate,' she says.

He exhales sharply, looks from side to side. 'Are you having a bad day?'

She hesitates, then remembers what she rehearsed earlier. 'We've drifted apart. We live separate lives, there's constant tension between us, and... I'm sorry, but I don't love you anymore.'

He drops his gaze, then lifts his eyes to meet hers again. 'You're the one who's changed.'

That's true, as is normal when people grow older. What she wants to say is, *You haven't changed, and that's part of the problem*, but holds back. 'I would like us to separate civilly. Give each other some space and make plans to move on.'

She picks up her mug with a trembling hand, takes a sip of tea. Silence.

He nods. 'I know you've found someone else.'

Rachel glances sideways as she swallows a lump in her throat.

'The bloke from the gym.' He glares at her

She shudders, turns away, struggling to find a convincing response. She should have thought of this. It's not as though she and Adam are discreet when they're at the gym. They're always together and probably look like a couple to any onlooker. So he knows, but it changes nothing, and he can't just put the blame on her for where they are. She could go through a litany of marital issues that have led to this. Then he would do likewise. No, they just need to move on, peacefully.

'I don't want to separate,' he says, leaning forward on the table. 'We should try to rebuild our relationship.'

He looks as though he means what he is saying. She feels a pang of guilt but tells herself to stand firm. She shakes her head. 'It's too late for that.'

He takes a sip of tea. 'I'm thinking about cancelling my trip to Germany next weekend. I don't really need to be at that tournament. We could spend time together. Just to chat.'

Rachel gasps. 'No, don't do that.'

He folds his arms. 'Why? Do you have other plans?'

She realises that her secrets and lies are stacking up, and fears they're going to come collapsing down on top of her any minute. It's time to unburden herself and tell the truth. She takes a breath and tells him about Tony and Florence. How she has arranged for them both to stay over next weekend. She describes how Tony is rebuilding his life, training to be a chef, and how committed he is to being a proper father to his gorgeous daughter. And they were here the other week.

She waits for an outburst that doesn't come. Judging by the look on his face, that was the last thing he was expecting. She reaches for her phone, taps on the photos app and swipes until she finds what she's looking for, Tony and Florence sitting on the floor together.

She shows him her phone. 'This was us a couple of weeks ago.'

She flips to another photo of Florence playing with LEGO. She swipes through a few more and lands on one where Florence is holding on to her with her arms around her neck. She won't mention the court supervision order that requires her to be continually present. He doesn't need to know that.

He sighs. 'Well, that's something else you're hiding from me.'

'They're my family,' she says firmly.

The quick-fire questions come: how often have they been here? Why did she not think she could talk to him about it? What else is she hiding from him? Rachel keeps calm. There is much she can say in reply, but she sticks to her script: we need to recognise and accept that we have grown apart. It's now time to move on, but we can still at least be friends. Their conversation runs its course. Emotionally exhausted, they retreat to their parts of the house. Richard to his work study and Rachel to the lounge.

Rachel weighs out 500 grams of wholemeal flour and tips it into the bread pan. Salt, sugar, oil and water are each added in turn, with a spoonful of yeast on top. She sets the timer on the machine and imagines the slow sequence of kneading, rising and baking that will occur through the night, then the satisfaction of waking up to the aroma of freshly baked bread. On the wooden chopping board, a pumpkin rests, the first of the season she picked up at the greengrocer yesterday. She plans to make curry for mid-week dinners and roast some for her lunchtime salads.

A sense of relief has settled within her after the talk with Richard today. She hadn't meant to mention Tony and Florence but letting that slip is one less secret to hold on to and the weight of deception feels lighter. She feels she's taken a big step towards creating a new future for herself.

And yet, unease flickers. Richard hadn't reacted the way she expected. He seemed hurt and genuinely shocked and doesn't even want to separate. Maybe he doesn't see how dysfunctional their relationship is and is content with this status quo: his low-earning freelance gig, the pickleball club. Perhaps for him, marital conflict is just a sport with a perpetual point-scoring leaderboard. But doesn't he miss sex? She can't imagine going through the rest of her life without it. Friday night reminded her of that. The thrill of being desired. The unbridled intimacy. She has wondered if he's getting it elsewhere and at one time that thought would have cut her up. Now, strangely, she thinks it would be a relief as it would make their separation simpler. But no. She would know.

Her mind inevitably drifts to Adam. Richard never mentioned his name and maybe he just guessed. Those long absences when she goes to the gym for a one-hour class. Enough to spark doubt. Luckily, the Tony and Florence revelation derailed his train of thought before he could probe further. Still, that risk gnaws at her. The last thing she wants is Adam to be pulled into this mess as he has complications of his own, mainly battles with his ex-wife over money and childcare. He doesn't need more stress in his life.

She waters her pots of herbs and salads on the windowsill. She's decided she'll sleep in the spare room tonight. That will help create boundaries, even in this small house. He'll likely resist, and it will take time to establish a new normal, but he must accept it sooner or later. At least she's convinced him to go to his pickleball tournament in Germany next week, giving her a free weekend with Tony and Florence. A reminder of the nice things she has in life and a future to look forward to. Simple and free.

14

Day Zero

Ray climbs out of the rolltop bath and wraps himself in a large, fluffy towel. He hoists the sash window open and listens for a moment. No traffic or rumble of trains. Just the sound of blackbirds cawing and leaves rustling in the wind.

'Are you joining me today or are you and that bathtub forming a relationship?' shouts Kirsty.

He sticks his head round the door. She's already pulled on her all-weather outfit and is lacing up her walking boots. An Ordnance Survey map lies open on the bed.

'I'll be ten minutes, love,' says Ray.

He lines up his products on the windowsill: face wash, shaving soap and brush, aftershave balm, deodorant bottles, all evenly spaced like soldiers on parade. His phone is ringing in the bedroom. He jumps, then reminds himself this is a no-work-interruptions holiday. Kirsty told him that on their last trip away he was so mentally at work that she could have had more meaningful conversations with the Highland cattle that were grazing in a nearby field. He finds it difficult to switch off sometimes. There's always some problem that needs his input. But, after just two days in the Dales, he feels relaxed and last night enjoyed his best sleep in weeks. No laptop, which feels like leaving the house without underpants. Kirsty will get his undivided companionship for the rest of the week.

He brushes up a lather into his stubble and tries to recall the meticulously planned itinerary for the day: a climb to some famous summit, the name of which he can't remember, a waterfall trail then a rest stop at an out-of-the way village, which has little more than a pub, a post office and corner shop. He will need his walking poles for today's ten-miler; his hips, knees and ankles are aching, and they have four more days remaining.

He hears his ringtone from the bedroom. It's 8.24 a.m. They're persistent.

'Shall I answer that for you?' shouts Kirsty.

'Please. And if it's work, say I'll get back to them next week.'

A moment later, she kicks open the bathroom door. 'It's Aidan.'

He drops his razor into the lathering sink water, turns his head. 'Tell him I'm worshiping the rising sun.'

Kirsty backs out of the bathroom. A few seconds later, she barges back in. 'Raymond, you need to take this. He's shouting and swearing,' she says, thrusting the phone towards him.

Ray grabs the phone. 'Okay, who's died?'

'Don't start having a hissy fit. You need to hear this,' says Aidan.

'Go on.'

'We've got an in-progress malware attack. Two hundred server outages already. The ERP system is down – one manufacturing site has lost connectivity completely and the head office users can't log on.'

Ray jolts upright. 'Switch to video,' he shouts.

The cyber operations room appears on his screen. Sydney is at her work-station, her head darting between the monitors in front of her, while she types furiously. The video wall shows the network graph, covered in red dots and continuous alerts scrolling from the bottom.

Ray's holds his phone closer to his face with a trembling hand. 'Have you stopped inbound internet traffic?'

'The malware is coming from inside,' shouts Sydney, without taking her eyes of the monitors in front of her.

'It's spreading. We need to activate the kill switch,' says Aidan.

Ray drops his head onto the bathroom door. 'Are you sure it's a malware attack?'

'We're certain,' shouts Sydney, turning round from her monitor.

Ray looks at the video wall, then the server availability dashboard. It's never been this red before. He hasn't got time to ponder this decision.

He takes a breath. 'I authorise the kill switch.'

'Can you repeat?' says Aidan.

'I authorise the kill switch.'

Sydney types furiously. Aidan stands over her, reading through scrolling text on the monitor. They have practised this many times.

'VPN deactivated,' says Aidan.

Ray glances into the bedroom and sees Kirsty sitting on top of the bed, holding her roll-up cagoule. His grip tightens on the phone, and a cold unease builds in his chest. He checks his watch and wonders if he can handle this from here and still salvage his holiday.

'Firewall rules modified,' says Sydney.

Ray lets out a sigh of relief as that should at least protect the digital research vault.

'Authentication tokens invalidated,' shouts Aidan.

One more step.

'DHCP server disabled,' shouts Sydney.

He sees the graphics fade from the video wall. The scrolling text on their workstation monitors has stopped. Aidan and Sydney stand facing the camera, looking at Ray, like foot soldiers addressing their commanding officer, awaiting their next order.

He's shut everything down and prevented anyone from reconnecting to the network. As he should, because that's what their containment protocol is for. And now the chaos begins.

'Our critical incident plan says we should send a SMS message to all staff,' says Aidan.

Ray nods. 'Yes. Do that.'

He steps out of the bathroom and into the bedroom, unshaven and undressed. Kirsty has her suitcase on the bed and is removing garments from the wardrobe.

'I understood little of that conversation, but you need to get back, don't you?' She looks at him, not angrily, just upset.

'I'm sorry,' says Ray.

She jolts her head towards him. 'I'll drive.'

He thinks of what he can do to make it up to her. But there is nothing. Their holiday is over. Every holiday and every weekend break is the same. There's always a work issue to deal with. She refused to go on holiday with him again, but he promised this time to disconnect from work. It had all started so well. Now he has a *genuine* work crisis and a wife who has been let down once too often.

Rachel weaves through the ambling tourists and coffee-clutching commuters preparing to start a new workweek. The temperature has dropped but this walk to the office feels like a meditative ritual, where she can unpack her stresses and gear up for whatever Monday will bring.

This morning's exchange with Richard was civil. He'd talked about his new project involving some social media influencer. She'd smiled, kept her scepticism to herself and wished him luck. They're both treading carefully, neither wanting to provoke an argument. Then he uttered words she never thought would ever come out of his mouth: 'I'm going to apply for a couple of jobs.'

She and Adam pinged their usual good morning messages, with love heart emojis tacked on. She's looking forward to seeing him at the gym tomorrow, then perhaps to his place afterwards. Her mind skips to Florence and the sleepover next weekend. *Note to self: buy storybooks and a new age-appropriate, LEGO set.* Not having to hide that from Richard anymore is one less burden on her mind. Yet a thin unease lingers. A feeling that some unannounced curveball will come her way and ruin her weekend plans.

She inhales deeply as she forces herself to focus on work. Monday is busy for the service desk, and she has the added worry of responding to the HR audit by getting Izabela to comply and complete the forms. But like an aching tooth, it's Jonathan Winstanley who is also forefront of her mind. She knows he's going to plague her again today. She can see him staring down at her, thinking she owes him. *Stop being intimidated by him*, she tells herself. Anger rises within her as she thinks about other women he's harassed and the way he and Mike Chester treat the office as their hunting ground, keeping score of their conquests. She feels her fists clenching. They don't deserve to hold the jobs they do, and she wants to expose them for the sleazebags they are. She'll think of something. But it will have to be something that doesn't involve logging into other people's accounts after hours because she still has that nagging fear of being discovered as a password cracker. The cyber team monitor the logs. One reckless move, and it's all over.

Her phone rings. It's Lionel. A bit early for his daily drama so she lets it go to voicemail.

A gathering of well-dressed evangelicals crowd the pavement ahead. One of them is preaching enlightenment while others hand out leaflets. A young, well-dressed man from the group steps into her path and thrusts a leaflet into her hand. 'Jesus loves you,' he says. She slips it into her pocket. If that's true, then he'll make sure Izabela leaves and never darkens her desk again. She veers towards the crossing, pulls out her phone and quickly returns Lionel's call.

He answers instantly. 'Are you on your way in?'

'I'll be ten minutes.'

'We have a crisis,' he says in a tone even more ominous than usual.

She tries to hide a laugh. 'Okay. Tell me about it?'

'The network is *dead* and people are turning up here in person asking us to fix their laptops.'

Rachel exhales. 'Sounds like Microsoft have pushed out another dodgy software update.'

'No, it looks more like a cyber-attack.'

Rachel stops walking. A sensation passes through her, from head to toe, like an electric charge. 'I'll be right in.'

She ends the call and at that moment, her phone pings with a text message:

Corporate Alert: We are experiencing a major IT outage. We are working urgently to fix this issue and will provide a further update as soon as possible.

She picks up her pace, her heart pounding. This is no coincidence. It must be Izabela. She arrives at the glass doors of the building, rushes into the reception area and squeezes through the closing lift doors. The only other occupant is a man she recognises – mid-forties, smart suit, chewing gum, as always.

He nods towards her. 'You manage the help desk, don't you?'

She glares back. 'It's the tech service desk, actually.'

He laughs. 'I wouldn't want your job today.'

The lift stops, the doors ping open, and she darts out.

'Good luck,' he calls after her.

She pushes open the door to the open-plan zone and steps into chaos and confusion. Her team, huddled in groups, are browsing their phones and chatting. Laptops lie open but the monitors are blank or frozen on a log-on screen. Lionel is talking to some staff, using lots of hand gestures. She walks up behind him, drops a hand onto his shoulder. 'What's the latest?'

He turns. 'Confirmed cyber-attack. I've just spoken to that hippy bloke from the cyber team. They've hit the kill switch.'

'I didn't know we had such a thing.'

He shrugs. 'Well, we do and it's nuked the network. Laptops can't even get an IP address.'

A woman she doesn't recognise cuts in. 'The other companies in this building are fine, and look.' She points towards the window that overlooks a multi-coloured office across the street. 'Google are working normally.'

Rachel nods to Lionel. 'Let's invoke the crisis plan.'

She soon finds herself encircled, familiar and unfamiliar faces all looking for explanations and guidance she cannot provide. Then she spots her, sitting on her own, browsing her phone.

She pushes through the cluster of staff and grabs Izabela by the arm.

'What the fuck?' she hisses.

Izabela stands to face her, eyes wide open. 'Back off, Rachel.'

'You need to stop this, right now.'

Izabela leans in close, voice low. 'Go back to your job.' She smiles. 'We're in charge now.'

Rachel glares at her for a moment then turns away.

Rachel finds an empty meeting room, collapses into a seat and buries her face in her hands. Her heart is pounding, her legs tremble and she feels sick. Her thoughts spiral as she thinks of the impact this is having. They are a workforce of 10,000 people: head office, production plants making medicines and research scientists in labs. If that's all come to a standstill, it could cost millions.

She peers out of the window into the open-plan zone, watching the clusters of staff chatting, shrugging shoulders and wondering if they should just go home. The word is out that it's a cyber-attack.

This is my fault.

Her immediate thought is to come clean. She could go round to the cyber security centre, march into Ray Dunlop's office and tell him everything. Then they will have Izabela. Even if she refuses to talk, they can take her laptop and trace everything she's done and stop further carnage. That would be the right thing to do. The company can then recover and get back to some sort of normality. But there will be consequences for her. An image of her crypto-wallet flashes through her mind, the numbers ticking up with the second-by-second price change. How could she claim she didn't know what was going to happen? Then she thinks of her own hacking exploits – the research documents. So far, no one knows, and she has to keep it that way.

She closes her eyes and thinks. She's in too deep. It's not just her job she could lose. This could make her criminally liable.

Ray spent most of the drive bouncing between calls from the most senior people in the organisation: his boss, Jonathan Winstanley, Catherine Davenport, the CEO, and others who rarely find five minutes to talk to him. They all want answers: is it a cyber-attack or a technology outage? That one he could answer. Who's responsible? How long until we're back online? Any other company affected? Why did our cyber defence software not stop it? Those questions, he could not. The only saving grace from the car journey was the fact that Kirsty could tell this was a genuine crisis and not just an over-dramatised issue.

He learned there was a board meeting scheduled for the afternoon. Davenport was furious that it had to be cancelled. He spoke further with Aidan and Sydney. They have identified the malware files and can kill it. But, at this stage, that's like discovering a vaccine after half the population has died.

Four hours after departing the holiday cottage in Yorkshire, Ray strides into the cyber operations centre and finds it crawling with people who have no business being there. Some offering unsolicited advice, others just sticking their nose in.

'This is a secure zone,' he announces. 'If you're not part of the cyber team, please leave now.'

Most of them scatter at his uncompromising tone. One doesn't. A tall, balding man whom he recognises as working in finance, stands his ground. One of Winstanley's puppets.

'Are you deaf?' snaps Ray.

The man smirks, making a show of looking at his watch. 'Finally showed up, have you? Must be nice waltzing in while the rest of us sort out your mess.'

Ray closes the distance between them. 'Piss off, spreadsheet man. Nothing you do is that important.'

'At least I know how to do my job,' he says, folding his arms.

Ray clenches his fists and looks up at this man, who is at least four inches taller. 'Bean- counting's not complicated.'

Finance man takes a step back. 'You're out of line, Dunlop. I'm going to talk to Jonathan.'

Ray smiles. 'Ask him how his misconduct investigation is going.'

His smirk fades as he picks up his laptop and strides out, glancing back and muttering something under his breath. Ray turns back to find Aidan and Sydney staring at him, Sydney open-mouthed. Aidan shrugs. He's seen it before.

Ray exhales. 'Okay, let's debrief.'

They take their seats. Sydney gathers the loose paper spread over the table – network diagrams and server configuration baselines. 'The attack originated from the inside – laptops infected by trojan malware, lying dormant until today. It executed as soon as users logged in.'

Aidan takes over. 'It uses PowerShell to connect to servers each user has access to and deploys its payload. A second-phase attack kicked in. Looks like another trojan, installed on the out-of-support Windows servers. That locked up our production apps and database servers.'

Ray absorbs it all silently, like a general surveying the aftermath of a battle, with casualties and smoke still rising, anticipating a follow-on attack. He glances down and realises he is still wearing his holiday clothes of checked shirt and jeans. It's the first time he has been in the office without a suit and tie.

He looks up. 'Is there any good news?'

Aidan and Sydney exchange a look.

'If we hadn't activated the kill switch, it would have taken out everything,' says Sydney.

'The R&D network is okay. The firewall did its job,' says Aidan.

'And our backups are safe. They're immutable, so we can do a restore,' says Sydney.

Ray feels relief as he thinks about what might have happened. From the outside, it might look like a disaster, but they have contained the attack: malware isolated, R&D network untouched, backups intact. All things considered, this is a good position to be in.

To Ray, it now feels oddly exhilarating. The company is in crisis and he's the one who has to steer them out of it. He needs to update the board first thing tomorrow. He's never been in the boardroom before and the thought makes his pulse quicken in a different way.

He turns to Aidan and Sydney, jabs a finger towards the whiteboard. 'We need a recovery plan.'

For the next two hours, the three of them thrash through their steps: isolate infected devices, prioritise systems for recovery, map dependencies. They are working from out-of-date paper documentation, which means they are dealing with a web of assumptions and unknowns. But a plan is forming: update the intrusion detection system, staged recovery of systems and full-scale laptop restore. But all the while they are conscious of a second-stage attack and the fact that someone on the inside – a staff member – must have been involved. How else would they find their way around the network and known host names? They need to investigate. They would have left a trail somewhere in the network event logs.

'Anything else we need to consider?' asks Ray.

'Some people who came in this morning were angry,' says Sydney. 'They're going to come back and have words with you.'

Ray smiles. 'Good.' He enjoys confrontation, and if they want to get him started, they've picked just the right moment.

Ray fields calls during the afternoon: Winstanley, demanding timelines; HR fretting over staff communications; random people inflating their own sense of importance. He gave them the same response: *We'll be working through the night. I'll have an update for the board tomorrow morning.* Then, when necessary, *piss off and let us do our job.*

It's after eleven o'clock when Ray arrives home. The house is quiet and Kirsty's already in bed. He goes to his home office, spreads the paperwork across the desk and the floor and translates their sketches and rough notes into slides for the board meeting tomorrow: diagrams, timelines and who did what and when. He told Aidan and Sydney to go home and get some sleep. They all need clear heads tomorrow.

This has been a day like no other for Ray. One minute he was pacing the room like an excited tiger; next, he was shaking with fear that the company would blame him for a preventable cyber-attack. People like Winstanley always look for scapegoats and Ray is in his sights. He'll likely send in the auditors who will find gaps – unpatched servers, expired certificates. Nothing related to the attack, but enough to get him fired. Juliette –

his friend in HR – has often told him he should invest time in building relationships rather than pissing people off all the time. He knows she's right. No one will have his back on this one.

It's past one in the morning when he climbs into bed. Kirsty breathes softly beside him. He thinks of the holiday she had organised and how much she had been looking forward to it. She had prepared a detailed itinerary, right down to the pubs they would visit. Traditional real ale pubs she knew he would enjoy. He hasn't given it a second thought all day. Flowers and presents won't fix it this time.

15

Dear Catherine and Team

We are Ninja Magpie, an organisation that specialise in cyber insecurity. We have infiltrated your network to show you the many weaknesses in your cyber defences. Although highly disruptive, our actions typically help organisations improve their security in the long run. Your systems are now encrypted and unusable. Only we can decrypt those servers and restore your network to normal.

*The fee for this service is **90 Bitcoin**. Once you have made payment, we will immediately send the decryption keys and the scripts to perform the decryption. If your security team gets organised, this recovery process should take about one day. As a show of good faith, we will also provide you with a report outlining the security weaknesses across your tech-*

nology footprint. A support service is also available to help you with any difficulties you may encounter during recovery. Payment is to be made to the Bitcoin wallet address provided. The deadline for payment is **Friday, 8.00 a.m.** *After then, the cost will double.*

Best regards,

Ninja Magpie

Mike Chester is first to break the silence. 'Who the fuck are Ninja Magpie?'

'And how much is ninety Bitcoin in real money?' Winstanley adds.

Catherine Davenport, perched at the head of the table, nods towards the visitor sitting beside her. 'Jude?'

'At today's price, just short of eight million pounds,' he replies, not missing a beat.

'Is it even true? Are our servers encrypted?' asks Catherine.

Ray nods. 'All the important servers are –– production databases and application servers. They knew which ones were most important and targeted them first.'.

The room falls into stunned silence.

'And Ninja Magpie?' says Catherine, her tone sharper now.

Jude Wiseman rises from his chair, a touch theatrically, Ray thinks. He's in his twenties and looks like someone who's just stepped out of a Paul Smith fashion parade. Too young to be credible, and he's probably never even worked in a security operations centre. But Catherine brought him in from the National Cyber Security Centre. So, he has her ear.

Ray watches from the far end of the oval-shaped board table, his laptop closed, hands clasped while listening to Jude describe Ninja Magpie: a prolific, organised, financially motivated threat actor, who use tactics such as social engineering and technical exploits to gain access to company networks. They've earned tens of millions through ransomware and data-theft extortion and have even resorted to physical violence. They do business through the dark web, buying and selling services with other criminal groups. Despite being tracked by multiple law enforcement agencies, they evade capture and remain anonymous.

Ray feels heat rising in his chest. He could have told them all of this. He's well-connected with the NCSC, attends their weekly threat intelligence briefings and knows all about Ninja Magpie. And the others: Scattered Spider, Cozy Bear, Lazarus, Envoy Panda. He feels undermined. He's worked in cyber security for twenty years, yet the board would rather put their trust in someone they've known for ten minutes.

Winstanley leans forward. 'Should we pay?'

'Our advice is you should not,' replies Jude.

Mike Chester clears his throat. 'Jude, I'm in charge of manufacturing and distribution in this company. Our systems are down and production lines have stopped at both of our manufacturing sites. I can't tell you how many trucks we have parked up in loading bays, when they should be on the road delivering medicines. I estimate we're losing two million a day.'

You should have planned for this. Ray holds back his interjection, re-membering he was told to remain silent until asked to contribute. His jaw tightens. He gazes towards Catherine, gesturing to his laptop.

She catches the cue. 'I want to hear from Ray. And please, in language we all understand.'

Ray stands. Pauses for a few seconds, heart pounding. This is his moment, and he needs to get it right. He toggles his slides and walks through his rehearsed presentation, describing the sequence of events, and how he activated the kill switch to contain the attack. He talks through his plan to restore systems from secure backups and how every laptop will have to be scanned, upgraded and hardened. There are complexities and dependencies to consider but they will prioritise the most important systems and users. He finishes by stating that Ninja Magpie may be the architects of the attack, but they had help from someone on the inside. Someone with detailed knowledge of their network.

'How long for full recovery?' Winstanley cuts in.

Ray hesitates. 'Four to six weeks.'

There are sharp intakes of breath around the table and Chester lets out a low whistle.

Ray continues, explaining the complexities of legacy tech, undocu-mented integrations and the need to verify each restore is malware-free.

Chester turns to Jude. 'Can we trust them if we pay?'

Jude's pause is telling. 'Yes. To them, this is business. They will hand over the decryption keys.'

Chester glances at Ray. 'I don't mean to piss on your plan, Ray, but we can't afford to wait six weeks for your team to get their act together.'

Ray struggles to hold back his frustrations. He feels like a boxer, accept-ing punches with his hands tied. But he can't have an outburst here.

Winstanley jumps in, smiling. 'No disrespect to Ray and his team. They're working hard, but this is a multi-faceted crisis. It needs more strategic leadership.'

And you're a multi-faceted idiot. Ray clenches his fists. 'This could have been so much worse. Thanks to our quick response, we're now able to recover without paying a ransom.'

Catherine turns to Sean Bristol, head of Research and Development. 'Sean, you've not said much. What do you think?' asks Catherine.

Bristol leans back and clasps his hands. 'I think Ray's done a good job under challenging circumstances. The firewall held up and kept the research vault secure. If our scientific research data got breached, well...' He shakes his head. 'The company may not have survived. I say, we back Ray's plan.'

Chester and Winstanley shoot him a look. Bristol's vote of confidence is a surprise given that Bristol, Winstanley and Chester are close friends. Ray exhales with relief.

Catherine whispers something to Jude. He nods. She looks back to Ray. 'Okay. We're relying on you, Ray. This board will meet every day until we recover. We'll expect a daily progress report from you. You will work in partnership with Jude. He will advise and guide.'

Ray feels the tension release from his body. He was on the ropes for a minute, his recovery plan almost trashed by a couple of morons. He'll take this victory. Having pretty-boy Jude shadow him will be painful, but a price worth paying for being back in control. He picks up his laptop and makes to leave along with Jude. The board members remain in the room to continue their meeting, which makes Ray curious. What else is so important they need to discuss?

Back in the cyber operations room, Ray introduces Jude, choosing his words carefully. 'This is Jude Wiseman, from the NCSC. He's here to help us.' In Ray's mind, Jude hasn't yet earned the status of expert or specialist. And he's certainly not going to be in charge.

Jude raises his hand in a wave. 'Hi, guys. Think of me as your knight in shining armour.'

Aidan and Sydney exchange a glance.

Ray disguises his laughter with a cough. 'Can you two bring Jude up to speed?'

They all take a seat at the round centre table. Ray opens his notebook and pulls out his pen, ready to take notes. Aidan and Sydney run through the last twenty-four hours with Jude: attack vector, malware behaviour, propagation.

'Sounds like it started as a drive-by download from a malicious website,' says Jude.

'We think it originated internally,' says Sydney.

Jude shakes his head. 'Probably polymorphic malware, designed to by-pass your end-point security.'

Aidan laughs. 'It's a PowerShell script, hard-coded with host names. There's nothing polymorphic about it.'

Jude glances at Ray, looking for support. Ray shrugs.

Jude changes the subject. 'What's your recovery strategy?'

Ray folds his arms, watching the developing dynamic between the three of them. Jude offers half-baked theories, Aidan counters with specifics. He finds it mildly entertaining: Aidan – towering over everyone, defiantly unshaven and wearing a shirt that's never felt a warm iron – contrasts with well-groomed Jude, whose vocabulary seems borrowed from LinkedIn. Ray had already pigeonholed Jude as a bit of a fake. He's interviewed people like him. But senior leadership doesn't see that and until they do, he'll play nice and keep him onside.

The door swings open. Mike Chester strides in, suited, polished brogues, smiling with an air of self-importance. He gazes at the video wall, then wanders towards the meeting table. 'How's it going?'

Ray straightens. 'Can I help you, Mike?'

'Don't mind me, just observing,' he says, standing over the table with a poise of entitlement.

But Ray minds. This is his space.

Chester strolls towards a workstation, takes a seat, leans back and laces his fingers behind his head. 'Don't stop on my account.'

The atmosphere has changed, but Sydney restarts the conversation, explaining that all the laptops will have to have a rebuild because they don't know how many were infected and some may still have dormant malware, ready to activate.

Ray's focus has shifted. He wants to know why Chester is here.

'Two million a day,' Chester announces as he reclines in the chair. 'That's how much this is costing us.'

Ray drops his pen and swivels to face him. 'Would have been more if we hadn't pulled the plug when we did.'

Chester rises from his seat and wanders over towards the table. 'Ah, yes, the famous kill switch. More like a self-inflicted outage that's left the entire workforce standing idle.'

Ray stands, walks towards him until they are face-to-face. 'I'd ask for your help, but I think these pot plants might have more to offer. So, with all respect, get out.' Ray thumbs towards the door.

Chester points at Ray. 'Don't get above your station, Dunlop.' He jabs his finger into Ray's chest. It was only the slightest touch, but enough.

Ray has a surge of rage and thrusts his open hand against Chester's throat, driving him backwards, pinning him against the standing cupboards.

Ray's grip is tight against Chester's throat. 'Don't throw your weight around in here, Chester.' He leans in closer until their faces are inches apart. 'Now, I suggest you go back to counting your trucks and let these smart people get on with their jobs.' He shoves Chester towards the door. Chester stumbles, barely stopping himself from falling.

From a safe distance, Chester points with a shaking hand. 'Big mistake, Dunlop.'

Ray shrugs and returns to the table. Sydney and Jude look on in stunned silence, mouths hanging open. Aidan keeps his head bowed. He's seen Ray's anger flare up like this before and knows the type of person who can fire him up in an instant.

The three of them ease cautiously back into their discussion, outlining the recovery plan: the service desk will work round the clock on laptop rebuilds, the hosting team will recover servers from backup and the security analysts will scan and re-harden systems before bringing them back online.

Ray's burning rage subsides as quickly as it flared, and he's now enjoying a feeling of triumph after seeing off Chester. It brings back memories of growing up in Glasgow, when that would have been an everyday conversation. Chester probably had a more sheltered upbringing.

Sydney hesitantly raises her hand to speak. 'Whoever wrote the malware knew a lot about our network and systems, even our host names. We could have a bad actor on the workforce. Someone technical.'

Ray nods. 'Agreed.'

'We should mine the system logs and reassess all the alerts,' says Sydney.

'Can you tackle that?' asks Ray.

'With the right software, yes.'

'Then you have my approval to license whatever software you need.'

If there *is* a rogue insider, Ray wants to discover who. But a pang of unease hits him. Maybe they've missed something obvious. The one alert out of thousands that could have helped them prevent the attack. This could come back to him. People like Winstanley and Chester would love to make him the scapegoat. He pushes the thought to the back of his mind. That's something to deal with when and if it happens.

'What more can we find out about this Ninja Magpie crowd?' asks Ray.

Jude leans in. 'I'll focus on attribution. I have a sock-puppet account on the dark web so I can listen in to chatter amongst hacker groups.'

Ray smiles. 'Thanks, Jude. That would be a good use of your time.'

Jude nods in acknowledgement. 'Think of me as your intelligence agent, working in the shadows, behind enemy lines.'

Ray holds back a smirk. 'I'm really happy you're here to help us, Jude. We couldn't manage this without you.'

16

An atmosphere of tension and irritation has replaced the happy chill vibe that is normal for a Friday. The open-plan work zone resembles a boarding queue for an overbooked budget airline flight. Hundreds of staff, laptops in hand, snake through makeshift lines around hot desks all the way back to the staircase. Greasy pizza boxes, half-eaten croissants, takeaway coffee cups and empty Red Bull cans lie strewn across the desk space. Computer manuals litter the floor, and the smell of stale food and sweaty bodies drifts through the air-conditioned office space.

Rachel's job is to calm the chaos. She's already had to break up one fight when a heated argument between two men escalated to fisticuffs because they couldn't agree whose job was more important. The next fists that fly might be hers, if she doesn't get out of here by tonight because this is her family weekend. She didn't go home last night and is still in yesterday's clothes, running on caffeine and adrenaline. Her team have pulled an all-nighter, grabbing catnaps whenever they can, showing loyalty to a company who, one week ago, were ready to outsource their jobs. If she's honest with herself, it's guilt rather than loyalty that's driving her.

A small woman with thinning grey hair materialises beside her, cradling a dead laptop like it's an injured child. 'Sorry to barge in, Rachel, love. I need this restored asap.'

Scottish, well-spoken. To her knowledge, they have never met. From her ID badge, Rachel learns her name is Maureen McMillan.

'What department do you work in?' says Rachel.

She thrusts her laptop towards her. 'Regulatory Liaison Office. We've got a submission deadline. Do you need my password?'

'Sorry, you're not on the priority list,' says Rachel, too tired to be diplomatic.

Maureen's friendly demeanour drops. 'That's not acceptable. Who do I escalate this to?'

Someone who gives a shit. 'You'll just have to wait.' Rachel sighs.

Maureen stamps her foot and walks away in a huff.

Rachel feels like an abandoned foot soldier. She has twice asked for management cover to deal with interruptions like this. Her patience for politeness is wearing thin, and the lack of sleep doesn't help.

She retreats to an office, shuts the door and slumps into a chair. Tiredness is draining her energy levels and her head throbs. She pops two ibuprofen and glances at her phone. Two messages from Richard, the first at 7.05 a.m. asking if there's anything he can do to help. Fresh clothes would have been useful. The second was to say he's heading off to the airport and will be back Monday. She's not used to this sudden consideration and thoughtfulness. Not that she's reconsidering anything. Lost love can never return. Still, she wishes him no ill-will and is relieved he's gone to Germany for his pickleball tournament because having him, Tony and Florence under the same room for the weekend would have taken her stress levels off the scale. She thinks of Adam, again. He's never far from front-of-mind. She couldn't see him this week as she was dealing with this crisis, but they manage to FaceTime nightly.

A ping from her computer interrupts her thoughts: a Teams message from Jonathan Winstanley.

Jonathan: Have you read my last email?

Rachel: No! I've been upgrading laptops and dealing with obnoxious staff. Did you read my last message?

Jonathan: Yes. The board just discussed it. You need to speed up the laptop upgrade process. One hour per laptop is too slow. You need to get it down to 45 minutes. 30 would be better.

She slaps the desk.

Rachel: Why don't you come down and help?

She stopped herself from appending, *you useless shit-face*. It's probably best he doesn't come down. She'd only slap him.

She glances out of the office window into what is a chaos zone. She doubts her team will get much in the way of recognition for their efforts. People like Winstanley are all about cutting costs or money making. He'll likely still go ahead with the outsourcing.

She turns to her monitor and stares blankly at a random document she'd opened earlier, still unable to focus on its contents. She feels emotionally exhausted and angry. Angry at herself. She's not stupid, but she's acted like she is. She plays back the sequence of bad decisions she's made over the last three weeks and it's like watching herself in slow motion, unable to stop the inevitable crash she is now trapped in.

It was as if her own delusions drowned out any rational thinking: Tony and Florence, a disintegrating marriage and an unmanageable debt pile consumed her. Aleks and his Bitcoin payments were the solution, but she failed to consider what she was committing to. Instead, she became consumed by her dream of a future life, one where she might be a mother. That's what led to her recklessness. Now, once again, she feels like a puppet. But this time, the strings are being pulled by Aleks and Izabela. No more. She wants out. Now.

One anonymous message to the cyber-security office would do it. Ray Dunlop would pick it up and this nefarious campaign will end. Izabela would plead innocence but forensics on her laptop will reveal the truth – every system she logged into, every malicious program she built. But then the trail leads to Rachel. Fast-track recruitment, missing background checks. How can she defend that? Then there are the research files. Another stupid mistake. But the company know nothing about that, and that's how it must remain.

She presses her palms together, trying to steady the tremor in her fingers. Izabela is one big liability. She picks up her phone, taps open Telegram, and creates a new message to Izabela:

Rachel: I think you'd best make your excuses and leave. Security could track you down any minute. Give me your laptop. I'll wipe it and cover for you.

She watches her pick up her phone and finger tap a reply.

Izabela: If the company cooperates, I'll be out of here tonight, otherwise I'm staying. Keep your head down and await further instructions. Remember whose side you're on.

Rachel's fear continues to build. She stands up and kicks the office wall. She feels her heart thumping. Her phone pings.

Izabela: I've just checked with Aleks. We need you to do one more thing.

Rachel: No. I'm out.

Izabela: We need you to send through the remaining research files.

Rachel shudders, as if she's sitting on an electric chair that just discharged its current.

Izabela: That will be enough to finish this job.

Aleks appears in the group chat. Another ping.

Aleks: Rachel, stay with us. The job's almost done.

Rachel returns to her computer, opening File Explorer and her *shopping* folder. A list of over 200 files appears: spreadsheets, documents and PDFs. It could be any collection of files. But it's not. They all come from the R&D digital vault. She wonders how much they have sold the first batch for. She only gave them twelve. Obviously not enough. She right-clicks on the folder, selects *Set Password*, pauses for a moment to think of a memorable but impossible-to-crack password. She smiles and types in a unique fourteen-character password.

Her phone pings again:

Aleks: We are going to cut you in. If we succeed, you'll receive one million.

For a second, she forgets to breathe. The number blazes on the screen. It's hypnotic. *One million.* Her heart lurches as the thoughts unfurl: financial freedom, new home, no more debt, no more fear. For a heartbeat, she lets herself imagine it. A new start in life.

Then the cold reality returns. She's entangled in a world she doesn't belong to. One she's ashamed to be part of. This is not the person she is.

Her fingers tremble as she types out a reply.

Rachel: I have no more files.

Thirty seconds later, the office door swings open and Izabela marches in. She plants both hands on the desk and leans in until Rachel can feel her breath.

'We know you have more files. All you have to do is transfer them,' she says softly, dangerously. 'Then you walk out of here clean – just like me.'

Rachel steadies herself, draws in a breath. 'No can do.'

Izabela's eyes narrow, her tone dropping. 'We paid you for a job. It's time to deliver.'

Rachel rises to her feet, holding her gaze. 'I think I'm done being used.'

For a heartbeat, neither woman moves. Then Izabela smiles. 'Big mistake. You'll regret this.' She turns and storms out.

Rachel stays frozen. She's proud of standing her ground, even with adrenaline surging through her veins. But the game has just escalated. They're determined to get their pay-out and have probably found some dodgy company willing to pay big money for these research files. She could have taken the money and disappeared. But it's time to salvage what's left of her conscience and get out.

8.30 p.m. Rachel steps out into the cold night air. It hits her like a slap after thirty-six-hours in the office. She's done. Until Monday, at least. She had a debrief with Lionel before leaving. Despite doing an all-nighter, he's as happy as a kid in a sweet shop to be left in charge over the weekend.

Her legs ache, and her head is throbbing. She just wants to get into her own bed, fall asleep and not wake up for a long time. She could take the Tube but the thought of screeching rails and body-heat-packed carriages turns her stomach. A walk to Kings Cross will clear her head as she thinks about the weekend ahead: Tony and Florence will arrive mid-morning and will stay until Sunday. She's ordered some storybooks from Amazon which should have been delivered by now.

The streets are bustling as late-to-go-home office workers mingle with early-night partygoers. Both cohorts spill out of crammed pubs onto pavements and patios. Beer and wine flow freely, conversation volumes are loud, and it's reached that time of night when macho-rowdiness comes into play. On the opposite side of the road, three motorcycle scooters with rear-fitted food delivery boxes are lined-up outside a pizza restaurant, impatiently awaiting their orders. Pigeons are picking at scraps of food strewn on the pavement, and a black cab performs a perfectly judged U-turn to pick up a suited man with his hand in the air.

Rachel walks towards a group of pavement drinkers. One man, cradling a half-empty beer glass, elbows his mate and smirks towards her. She crosses the road without breaking her stride, then cuts diagonally through Russell Square gardens. It's a darker, more secluded route, but preferable to weaving through emboldened drunk men. She's not in the mood for cheap chat-up lines, and if just one stray hand were to grab her bum, she would throw punches, and it would not end well.

As she nears Kings Cross station, she zig-zags through quieter side streets and her thoughts turn to shopping – breakfast cereal, milkshake... What else do five-year-olds like to eat? She's startled by the sudden buzz of an engine behind her and turns to see a moped heading towards her with a pillion rider. It's close. Too close. She steps into a shop doorway; the bike mounts the pavement, slows and the second man leaps off and lunges for her bag. She grips the handles with both hands, pulling back with all her weight. He's too strong and wrenches it out of her hands. He dashes back to the getaway bike. Fuelled by rage, she launches herself towards his lower body and takes him to the ground with a rugby tackle. They both slam into the concrete. Her hands go to the front of his neck, and she clasps his windpipe, digging her nails in. He releases the bag, and she grabs it. She scrambles to her feet, ready to run faster than she's ever done in her life when a hand grabs her hair and yanks her head backwards. She cries out as she falls to the ground.

The second man's on top of her. His breath stinks of sweat and weed. She thrusts her knee upwards between his legs, but doesn't make the connection she was hoping for. He tries to yank the bag free. She sees the gap in the open visor crash helmet and stabs her two fingers into his eyes. He screams and falls back.

She has the bag. A short sprint and she'll be back on the main road. Safe. A leather-gloved punch slams into the side of her face. She collapses to the ground and her grip on the bag loosens. Then a second one comes, harder this time, followed by a large boot stamping on her wrist. She curls into herself, shielding her head. She's done. No more.

Then she hears the faint whirr of the moped, disappearing into the distance. They have her laptop. Nothing else. The empty bag and mobile phone lie on the pavement. She peels her hands away from her bleeding face. Her vision blurs and the world seems to spin. She tries to stand, but her limbs don't respond, and she collapses back into the darkened shop doorway. Then silence.

One minute later – or it may have been five – she hears footsteps running in her direction.

A hand rests on her shoulder. 'Are you alright?' says the woman.

Rachel removes her hands and looks up.

The woman flinches. 'Oh my God.' She crouches. 'My name's Tasha. I'm a nurse.'

Rachel grips her wrist as if it were a lifeline. She tries to speak, but her voice catches as blood trickles from her mouth. She shivers. Tasha takes her wrist in her hand and takes her pulse, then looks into her eyes. 'Can you tell me your name?'

'Rachel,' she mutters.

Tasha pulls a phone from her back pocket and makes a call. She's a few years younger than her, tall, slim with long red hair in a plaited ponytail. Steady hands.

'Yes, the patient is breathing... I'm a registered nurse... Head injury and bleeding... Found at the side of the road... Conscious but low GCS score.'

Rachel looks at her. *Please stay with me.*

Tasha finishes the call and puts her hand on Rachel's shoulder. 'The ambulance is going to be at least thirty minutes.' She removes her puffa jacket and puts it over Rachel's body. 'I'll stay with you,' says nurse Tasha.

Rachel's body is shuddering, tears streaming into the cuts in her head. *Why did I try and fight them? It wasn't worth it.*

'Is there anyone I can call for you?' asks Tasha.

Yes. She's shaking and terrified and needs someone to look after her. She thinks for a moment. 'Can you call my mum and dad?'

Tasha picks up Rachel's phone from the pavement and makes the call. Rachel grips her trusting hand. She tries to stand, just about makes it. Then collapses again.

17

Subject: Unpaid Fees

Dear Catherine and team,

*We are disappointed not to have heard from you, especially as we made a perfectly reasonable offer. The initial deadline for payment has expired, which means we have had to escalate our campaign. The attached link will take you to a private website where you will find a sample of confidential files extracted from your digital research vault. We have many more. We understand how crucial these are to the future success of your drug development programme – and your company's valuation. We have now set a revised fee of **200 Bitcoin**. Once we receive payment, these and every other file in our possession will be destroyed. The new deadline is*

Monday, 9.00 a.m. Your failure to comply will result in public release of all files.

Respectfully,

Ninja Magpie.

Jude rises. 'This is a tactic known as double extortion. They steal sensitive data, in addition to locking you out of your systems—'

'We've worked that one out for ourselves, thank you,' Sean Bristol cuts in.

Jude returns to his seated position, next to Catherine Davenport, as always.

'And they're now demanding eighteen million pounds,' says Winstanley, stating the obvious.

Davenport leans forward. 'Sean, as head of R&D, can you verify if these files are authentic?'

Sean stands. 'Yes, they are. Some of them are from an ongoing phase two clinical trial. Others relate to pre-clinical research. They provide valuable insights into our experimental drugs and *are* competitor-sensitive. They are of limited value to competitors on their own. But if they leak more like this...' He pauses and clenches his fists. 'We're ruined.'

The room is still. The weight of his words hangs in the air. The board members appear stunned, except for Harriet Barker, head of HR, sitting at the far end of the table, tapping away at her phone. Ray doesn't even know why she's here. It's Saturday morning and there's not much she can contribute.

Catherine turns to Ray. 'You've had twenty-four hours to investigate this. What can you tell us?'

Ray straightens in his chair. This was supposed to be his moment. He had prepared his presentation: a neat update on status of the recovery operation, showing they were ahead of schedule. But that's irrelevant now. The trumpet he was ready to blow lies dented on the floor. This new ransom demand hit him like a truck. He's read it multiple times. *Unpaid fees.* That subject line still grates. They make it sound like a service agreement rather than criminal extortion. They also mentioned *company valuation.* Do they know something he doesn't?

He stands, pausing long enough to gauge the room, thinking of his opening gambit. 'We've investigated as thoroughly as we could in the short timeframe. Jude and I found no evidence of an external breach.'

Mike Chester snorts. 'Can't wait for the punchline.'

Ray ignores him. He explains that to access those files, an attacker would have to breach two layers of security. First, the firewall protecting the R&D network, then the role-based access safeguarding the digital vault. A multi-stage exploit would have generated security alerts, and they would have been on it immediately. But they've seen nothing. He's overstating the strength of their security and simplifying the threat scenario. But he's more convinced than ever that it's someone on the inside and he intends to find out who. Maybe then, he'll get a permanent seat on the board – no more than he deserves. This crisis proves how much they need him. But he still needs to win their confidence.

'So, how did they get hold of these files?' asks Sean.

'Two possibilities. Either they hacked through multiple security defences without detection, or, more likely, an insider passed them on.'

Sean frowns. 'Are you suggesting one of our researchers has gone rogue?'

'Or someone else with that level of access, such as an IT support engineer,' says Ray.

'Which narrows it down to, what... a thousand people?' says Chester, leaning back with his arms folded.

Ray's frustration continues to build. He's being provoked. It's hard not to retort, but he keeps himself in check.

At that moment, Harriet gets to her feet and walks towards Catherine and crouches to whisper something. This riles Ray even more than Chester's arrogance. She's been glued to her mobile all morning, has contributed nothing and now disrupts him in mid-flow.

Ray clears his throat. 'If I may continue.'

'Hold on.' Catherine raises her hand. 'Harriet has something important to tell us.'

Harriet stands at the front. 'Fellow board members, there's been a serious incident.' She stands like a headteacher addressing a misbehaving class. 'Last night, a female staff member was attacked and robbed after leaving the office.'

Gasps fill the room and heads turn to face each other. Ray takes his seat.

'Who?' says Winstanley.

'Rachel Carter. She manages the tech service desk. She was walking to the train station after working late on this *disorganised* recovery effort. Two men assaulted her and stole her bag.'

Ray sits back, stunned. *Rachel?* He remembers her from their interview. Confident, articulate. He nearly recruited her.

'She took multiple blows to the head and body,' Harriet continues. 'A passer-by found her and stayed with her until the ambulance came – nearly two hours later.'

People look at each other, murmuring. Shock. Sympathy. Guilt.

Winstanley raises his hands to his head. 'I'm her mentor. Is she... alright?'

'I don't know,' replies Harriet, 'but no one – *no one* – should walk home alone after a shift like that.'

Ray thinks of Sydney. She too works late and leaves alone. Then his thoughts flash to Kirsty, his wife.

'Was it an opportunistic robbery or do we think it's connected to what we're dealing with?' asks Catherine.

'They stole her laptop. That's all I know,' says Harriet.

'It could be related,' says Jude. He turns to Ray. 'Are all company laptops encrypted?'

Harriet slams her palm on the table. 'We don't care about the fucking *laptop.*'

The room falls silent.

Catherine drops her head into her hands. 'This is terrible, and it reflects badly on the company. Harriet, prepare some comms. *No one* should be expected to walk home alone after hours.'

'We should fund taxis for staff who work late,' says Winstanley.

'Small comfort for Rachel,' says Harriet.

'Jonathan, as you're her mentor, I'd like you to visit her in the hospital,' says Catherine.

He hesitates, then nods. 'Of course.'

'This is a shock. We'll take a fifteen-minute break,' says Catherine.

As the room breaks into murmured conversations, Ray notices Winstanley, Chester and Bristol huddle together in some sort of confab. Always the same trio, having their side conversations, talking a little too quietly about something that seems important.

Ray feels a sense of unease as he turns Jude's question over in his mind again. Could there be a connection? If this had happened a week or two ago, he'd say yes. Stealing a company laptop might help an attacker gain access, especially if they coerced the password from her. But Ninja Magpie don't need another device. They're already inside.

Was Rachel just in the wrong place at the wrong time?

Catherine Davenport re-enters the boardroom and resumes her seat. The side conversations break off, and she instantly has everyone's undivided attention.

'When we received the initial ransom demand, we made the right decision not to pay because we were in a good position to recover. Good job, Ray.' She offers him a thin smile. Polite. Not quite warm. 'But I feel we are now back to square one.'

'And the stakes are higher, in my opinion,' says Bristol.

Catherine turns to him. 'What's the worst-case scenario?'

He shrugs. 'With those twelve documents, it's mostly reputational damage. Normally, we could manage that. But this is bad timing.'

'It could wipe millions off our valuation,' mutters Chester.

Catherine shoots him a glance. The room falls silent.

She turns to Ray. 'There is something you need to be aware of, Ray, which must stay within these four walls.'

Ray's already pieced it together. He nods. 'Understood.'

Catherine folds her arms and discloses that they are in late-stage discussions with a large pharma firm, who want to make an acquisition. Their primary motivation is our experimental Alzheimer's drug. They have seen the early-stage clinical trial results and see the potential for a new class of treatment, significantly better than current therapies. Only a large pharma firm has the resources and economies of scale to take this to a large-scale trial and, if successful, move it forward for regulatory approval.

Ray nods, unsurprised about a takeover bid. He's seen this before. GSK bought IDRx, Novartis bought Anthos, Gilead bought CymaBay. She didn't mention who's interested, but that doesn't really matter. He knows the game. The small fish do the early-stage innovation, and when it looks promising, the whales come to feed. It might fail late-stage trials, but big pharma can afford to take that risk. Synaptonica cannot. Normally, it's the directors with equity stakes in the small company who benefit most. He casts a slow glance around the table. Winstanley, Bristol, Chester and Davenport. They're all carrying large stock options. No wonder they're worried about this breach. If Ninja Magpie have found a leak in their research vault, then the deal is dead, and they miss their golden payday.

Ray noticed something else. Catherine spoke only to him, not Jude, who sits beside her, expressionless. Like someone who's already been briefed.

Sean rises from his seat. 'Same question as before, do we pay?'

No. Ray stands. 'I would like to present my plan first.'

Heads glance at each other; he senses impatience around the table.

Sean folds his arms. 'Cut to the chase, Ray. Can you identify the leak before Monday? And recover our data? All of it?'

Ray hesitates. 'We've no evidence they have more than those twelve files. If they do, why don't they show us?'

Ray outlines his plan. It's all about digital fingerprints. They've designed a process to comb through the DLP logs. If the files were exfiltrated from the vault, the logs will show it. They will then correlate that with event logs on the user device to confirm what was accessed, when and *by whom*. Once they identify the culprit, this extortion ends.

'You're assuming the insider is still here and hasn't already done a runner,' says Chester.

Catherine looks to Jude. 'What's your view?'

Jude nods. 'I helped build the plan. It's doable.'

Ray resists the urge to clarify that his team built the plan, while Jude sat at the table dropping technical terms, not adding anything meaningful.

'Jude, what is Ninja Magpie's record? Can we trust them?' Sean asks.

Jude shuffles in his seat. 'In every case I know of, they've kept their promise and destroyed the data after receiving their payment.'

Sean nods. 'Good to know.'

Ray feels something twitch inside him. He glances again at the faces round the table, knowing they are on the verge of paying. He hasn't yet won their confidence.

'Ray, you have until tomorrow night,' says Catherine.

He exhales with relief, but his heart is still racing because he knows there is no guarantee they will find the culprit. There are billions of records to analyse, and the logs get deleted after four weeks. If the exfiltration happened before then, he'll come up empty. Then they'll pay, and he'll probably get sacked, because that's what normally happens after a crisis. Find a fall guy, and who better than the chief information security officer? He feels like he's standing at the roulette table and just gambled with his job.

'One last thing,' says Catherine. 'No one outside this room – except for Ray's team – must know about these files being leaked.'

18

Rachel is sitting up in bed, thankful for the privacy of the cubicle curtains that cocoon her from the rest of the ward. Her right arm, bandaged and resting in a sling, is throbbing with a dull, persistent ache. Her head feels swollen and heavy. She hasn't looked in the mirror this morning. She's scared of what she'll see.

She had arrived in the ward just after dawn, after spending most of the night on a trolly, in a corridor next to accident & emergency. The intermittent beeping of medical equipment, the clatter of trolleys being adjusted and other patients' conversations kept her awake. Two drunks had been shouting, one bloodied from a knife, the other just shouting obscenities.

Compared to that, the ward feels calm. But whenever she closes her eyes, she's back there, in the darkened street, facing her two attackers, the gloved fist hitting her. It feels like she's trapped in a waking nightmare.

'What time is it?' she asks.

Her mum places a trembling hand on hers. 'Just after two o'clock, dear.' Her eyes are puffy, her voice shaky. She looks scared.

Rachel feels safe with her parents at her bedside. They'd driven through the night and have been with her ever since. They've had to abandon their usual weekend routine: Saturday tennis, coffee shop, bell-ringing. Sunday walks on the Dales. They do everything together, just like in any good marriage.

She thinks of the friendly nurse who came to aid her last night, kneeling beside her, looking after her and keeping her safe for what seemed like hours. Other passers-by stopped, asking if they could help. One came back with a takeaway hot chocolate she wasn't able to drink. Good people, who cared.

The important people now know. Adam, Richard, Tony and work. Word has spread and there's been an outpouring of love. Richard's flying back and will be here soon. Her phone has been pinging with messages all morning; she's read all of them but hasn't replied. Adam wanted to come in, but that would have been awkward. She won't tell her parents of her new domestic arrangements. It's too soon, and they don't need that worry added to their burden.

This was supposed to be her weekend with Tony and Florence. They had such a fun day planned. Tony wanted to come and see her until he heard their parents were here. They used to be such a close-knit family, always enjoying spontaneous day trips. Four of them in the car. Blackpool was their favourite. It may have been wet and windy, but they always had something to laugh about. She still blames herself for this estrangement. She was the big sister who refused to take him in when he asked for help. It all went downhill from there.

The curtain pulls open and her dad steps in. 'Rachel, love, I've just been talking to the police officers. Are you okay if they ask you some questions?'

She nods. 'Yes, that's fine.'

She reaches out to her mum's hand. She's not sure what to tell them. Her skin prickles as another flash of memory causes sickness to rise inside her.

Two uniformed officers step through the curtain: a young man who looks as though he's trying to grow a beard and a woman with a calm, watchful face. He remains standing; she takes a seat by her bedside and removes a notebook from her pocket, flipping it open.

'Rachel, I'm Sergeant Wells and this is Constable Clarke. You can call me Jenny. This is awful and we're really sorry this happened to you. We'll do everything we can to find who's responsible.' She pauses. 'Would you be okay to answer some questions?'

Rachel adjusts herself against the pillows; the IV line pulls slightly at her wrist.

She tells them about the incident. Two men. Young. Dressed in leathers. Open visor crash helmets, one with a spider-web tattoo on his neck. Both about her height and medium build. As she talks, she realises how little she's giving them. Except for the tattoo, perhaps.

The sergeant leans in slightly, watching Rachel closely. 'And all they wanted was your laptop?'

Rachel nods.

'We have phone-snatch robberies by bikers every five minutes in London. These thieves are difficult to catch,' says the constable.

Her dad stiffens. 'Does this look like a drive-and-snatch robbery to you?' He towers above the young police officer.

The young constable recoils. 'I'm sorry, sir, that wasn't what I meant.'

Jenny holds her pen over her notepad, 'Rachel, I have to ask – was there anything of value stored on your laptop?'

Rachel hesitates; she knows this was not a random robbery. She shakes her head. 'It was just work stuff.'

Jenny's eyes narrow slightly, pen poised over her notebook, waiting for Rachel to fill the silence.

Her heart pounds as it occurs to her that the answer to their questions, and more, is on her phone, which is sitting beside her atop the bedside cabinet. The message exchanges with Aleks and Izabela. If they ask to see it, they'll discover the significance of the laptop and how desperate those two were to get their hands on those files. She needs to delete every incriminating message as soon as they've gone.

The constable exhales and closes his notebook. He and Jenny exchange a glance as if communicating the same thought: *just the laptop. Why not her phone and purse?*

Jenny stands and wishes Rachel a speedy recovery. She hands over a card with her phone number. 'Just call if you remember anything else.'

They slip through the curtain and leave.

Rachel grabs her phone. More messages have come in. She taps on the Telegram app:

Aleks: *This didn't have to happen. You need to give us your password to the encrypted folder. Now!*

She takes a deep breath. Was it worth it? She could have given them the files yesterday and she would be at home now with her brother and niece instead of lying here recovering from a beating. No, she will never hand over the password. What more can they do to harm her?

She glances at her mum and dad, sitting by her bedside. She feels protected.

She holds the business card between her thumb and forefinger: Police Sergeant Jennifer Wells. She seemed to sense there was more to this story. Rachel could call her and tell her everything: Aleks, Izabela, and how they're desperate to get the research files so they can sell them to some unscrupulous agent on the dark web marketplace. But how would that play out? To her knowledge, the company knows nothing about the theft of those files. No one does, except Izabela and Aleks. As for her laptop – well, probably best if it's never recovered. Who knows what incriminating evidence it stores?

A nurse appears, carrying an iPad.

'Just need to do your obs, Rachel, love,' she says.

Rachel's had neuro-obs done every four hours: light in the eye, touch your head, flex your arms. The nurse is a black lady of solid build, about the same age of Rachel. She straps a blood-pressure cuff to her arm and inserts a thermometer in her mouth. Rachel notices her large hands. She would have given the attackers a fight.

'A couple of visitors came in asking for you,' says the nurse. 'They said they were friends from work but didn't want to disturb you while the police were here.' She presses a button on a device and the blood pressure cuff starts to inflate and tighten round her arm.

'That was nice,' says her mum.

Her dad stands with his arms folded. 'Your company should have organised a taxi to take you home last night.'

She thinks about her team at work, who are working through the weekend. It was probably Lionel who came in. He's a caring person. Maybe one of the ladies as well.

'They said they will see you soon. Didn't give their names. A tall, slim lady. The man had round-rim glasses. I think they were from one of those Eastern European countries. They were very polite.'

The nurse administers the painkillers and leaves. Rachel feels a shudder pass through her body, and she can feel herself trembling. It can only be Aleks and Izabela. They're desperate. How far will they go?

Outside, it is getting dark. Inside the ward, background chatter of other patients' visitors blends with the sounds of medical instruments and footsteps. Rachel has been drifting in and out of sleep, scared that she might be alone, but a quick glance confirms her mum and dad are still by her bedside, having a whispered conversation. She sits up and browses through social media and WhatsApp. Messages of love are coming through from friends and colleagues, such as Cathy and Lionel. Someone has launched a Facebook appeal to hunt down the attackers. There was even a long message from Deirdre, the night cleaner she's made friends with. She'll call her sometime to see how she's coping with her domestic problems. Then a message from Jonathan Winstanley, saying he would like to visit. He probably got his admin to write it.

A familiar voice drifts from the corridor, asking for her by name. It's Richard.

He appears at the doorway. 'Oh my God.' He rushes over to her bedside. 'I got here as soon as I could.'

He looks across at her mum and dad. 'Arthur, Annie. I'm so glad you're here.' He reaches out his arm to shake hands.

Her dad shakes his head. 'Don't bother,' he says, his voice tight with anger.

'What?'

'Where the hell have you been?'

Richard holds his arms out, as if in defence. 'I was out of the country. The flight just landed. What did you expect me to do?'

'You should have been looking after your wife!' he shouts.

Her dad's face and balding head have turned red. He doesn't get angry often, but when he does, it's very visible. He's never truly taken to Richard due to his cosy upbringing and reluctance to get what he would consider a proper job.

Her mum stands. 'Arthur, let's get something to eat and give these two some time together.' She taps him on the elbow. 'We'll pop back later, love.'

'Thanks, Mum. By the way, one of the senior managers from work is coming in later.'

Her dad scoffs. 'Well, don't expect me to keep my mouth shut.'

She watches them head off down the corridor, holding hands. They probably haven't spent a night apart in twenty years.

She turns to Richard. Her voice is weak. 'Thanks for coming back.'

She means it. After everything that's passed between them this last week, she wouldn't have blamed him for staying in Germany.

His face is pale, eyes rimmed red as though through lack of sleep. 'I wish I'd never gone,' he says, voice cracking.

'It's not your fault,' she whispers.

He leans in closer, fingers twitching as if unsure whether to reach out and hold her hand. 'Is there anything I can do?'

Rachel studies him. Her husband. The man she told she didn't love anymore. The man she's been resenting for months. They are supposed to be moving on with their lives, separately. But something loosens inside her and having him at her bedside fills her with a warmth she didn't expect. She wants him to stay so they can talk. About anything.

She looks into his eyes and recognises that look – concern and fear. Her throat tightens and the tears flow. She reaches for his hand and clasps it tight.

She wants to tell him everything. The full story.

19

Ray, Aidan and Sydney huddle around the same debrief table they've occupied every day for the past week. The office – their command post – feels like their home. They've shared long nights and made some big wins, like restoring almost 2,000 servers from backup. They're fatigued and the finish line keeps shifting.

'Jude not joining us today?' asks Sydney, twisting the cap off her water bottle.

Aidan smirks. 'Maybe superheroes don't work Sundays.'

'Or maybe this is his day for a manicure,' offers Ray.

The building is silent except for them and the twenty-four-hour security downstairs. They arrived at eight, had their first coffees at eight-thirty and are about to finish the croissants and muffins.

Ray paces with agitation. He stares at a data-flow diagram scribbled on the whiteboard, disappears into his office then re-emerges a minute later. He's searching for answers without knowing what questions to ask.

At their adjacent workstations, Aidan and Sydney are drowning in data. Their triple-monitor set-ups are glowing with spreadsheets, log files and code. Ray gazes over their shoulders. Aidan is browsing a spreadsheet, which is dense with data: time stamps, IP addresses, event IDs, severity ratings.

'What are we looking at?' asks Ray.

'Just the alert logs,' Aidan replies, scrolling rows of data. 'Thousands of them, but nothing useful.'

'That's because we configure the rule set for bulk data theft,' Sydney adds. 'Zip files, multi-attachment emails and batch uploads to unauthorised domains.'

'We need the source data logs,' says Aidan.

'I'm downloading that now.' Sydney points to her monitor. 'A hundred gigabytes of telemetry. I'm dumping it into a new table in the data lake.'

'How long?' says Ray.

Sydney shrugs. 'Download's the easy bit. Running queries against ten million rows is what's going to take time.'

Ray nods. He misses this. Twenty years ago, he would have been sitting beside them, hands on the keyboard, writing queries and co-joining tables. He loved his days as a programmer. He still dabbles. He's tempted to jump in, but knows he'll likely be counterproductive.

'More coffee?' he offers.

'Mango smoothie, please,' says Sydney.

Aidan gives him the thumbs up. 'Triple shot soy latte.'

Ray steps outside. The shock of the cold breeze hitting his face cuts through the fog in his head. Kirsty was still asleep when he slipped out this morning. He hadn't wanted to wake her just to see the disappointment in her eyes again. They've seen little of each other this week. Every night, when he's got home she's been in bed. Then he leaves in the morning, before breakfast.

Fortunately, he hasn't had to explain why he has to go in. The television news has done that for him, with film crews pitched outside head office, generating headlines about a *sophisticated cyber-attack, bringing the company to its knees*. She knows this crisis is on his shoulders.

The coffee shop is empty. The two baristas are deep in conversation about boyfriends. He stands at the counter, feeling invisible. After ten seconds, he shouts his order.

As he stands in line waiting on his drinks being prepared, he questions why he is here, when everyone who seems to think they are important is at home. The board members, sitting comfortably in their cosy homes. Golden boy Jude hasn't shown his face once this weekend. That leaves him and his team, fighting alone on the frontline. When this is over and the finger pointing starts – and it will – he'll be the one in the firing line: the security officer who failed to prevent the biggest breach in the company's history.

He thinks about Kirsty. Sundays are *their* day. Always have been. Woodland walks, pub lunches, visiting family. Simple things that are precious. His first marriage failed, in part, because he spent so much time at work, obsessing over matters no one else cared about. He once spent an entire weekend rewriting a program to improve system response times by a second or so. No one asked him to do it. He just couldn't leave it alone. He and Kirsty have been together for eight years, and it's perfect. They don't argue; they talk. When he feels himself getting angry about something unimportant, she's there to give him a nudge. He can't imagine not having her in his life.

Maybe he should have just let them pay the ransom. Maybe his loyalty to the company is a symptom of some misguided obsession. He thinks of Aidan and Sydney. He didn't need to ask. They just show up, ready to fight. Are they becoming as misguided as him? What would happen if the three of them just went home, right now? He would salvage what's left of the Sunday.

But he's not going to do that.

His phone vibrates with a WhatsApp message:

Jude: *Hey guys, kudos for going in on a Sunday. You're doing a great job. Just call if you need anything from me.*

Ray shakes his head. He collects his drinks order from the counter, mutters a thank you to an indifferent server and strolls back to the office. He checks his watch. Davenport and Bristol want a progress update. He'll try to time that to interrupt their Sunday lunch.

By 5.30 p.m., Ray has had enough. This is pointless. They need a machine-learning system that can churn through the logs and pick up those meaningful signals. They could build one, but that would take at least a week. Right now, he's relying on team heroics. He may as well have asked them to row a boat across the Atlantic to save on the airfare. He wanders out, leans on the desk between Sydney and Aidan.

'Let's call it a day,' he says.

Their heads shoot up.

'No,' says Aidan.

'We're exhausted. It's time to go home,' says Ray.

Sydney flashes a grin. 'We've found something.'

Ray's heartbeat stutters as he circles behind them.

Sydney points at her monitor. 'Look.'

Ray stares at the spreadsheet on screen, with coloured mark-ups.

Sydney points. 'Twelve log records, representing twelve emails. Each one has a single file attached, and all going to the same destination – an unknown Dropbox account.'

Ray's mouth drops open as he reads the familiar file names.

Sydney highlights each of the data elements: time stamp, threat level, user ID, hash value. 'I've compared the file hash values. They match. These are the emails that leaked the research files,' she says.

Ray leans in. 'Can we see who sent the emails?'

Aidan brings up a list of names on his monitor. 'Here they are. Four different people, all of them from R&D: a placement student, a senior clinical scientist and two lab scientists.'

Ray examines the names. One person – James Craig, senior clinical scientist – sent six. The others sent two emails each. They look at each other.

'Collusion?' asks Aidan.

Ray shakes his head. 'That's hard to believe.'

'Password hack?' suggests Sydney.

Ray nods. 'Most likely. Someone compromised their credentials and logged in as them.'

Sydney points to the spreadsheet again. 'They came from our internal network. Definitely an insider.'

Of course it is. Ray's pulse quickens. This is a breakthrough. 'Can you tell me if anything else went to that Dropbox account?'

Sydney types a SQL statement and hits run. 'We'll soon find out.'

Ray drags a chair beside her and watches the status icon spin. Ten million records to search through. The minutes that pass feel like hours, then the results fill the screen. Twelve records only.

They look at each other.

'Nothing else went to that Dropbox account,' says Sydney.

Ray exhales. Exactly the answer he was hoping for. Ninja Magpie are bluffing. They have no more than the twelve files.

He glances between the two of them. 'Thank you.'

'Good job you didn't shut down the DLP tool,' says Aidan with a dry smirk.

Ray laughs. 'But we must rethink the alerting rules.'

Ray heads back to his office and makes the phone calls. First to Bristol, then Davenport, confirming that only twelve files were leaked and not the two hundred they claim. They thank him. He's just saved the company millions of pounds in an unnecessary ransom payment. Maybe he'll get to keep his job, after all.

His new focus now is to identify the rogue insider. Someone smart enough to breach multiple security defences and steal users' passwords. *How did they do it?*

He checks the time. It's 6.17 p.m. 'Let's go home. Tomorrow's a big day.'

They both log off.

'Should we trigger a global password reset?' says Sydney as she fastens her duffle coat.

'Absolutely,' says Ray, 'and tighten the complexity rules – twelve characters, minimum.'

Aidan raises an eyebrow. 'You mean, do what we should have done years ago.'

Back home, in his study, Ray gazes into his monitor. Soft lamplight warms the desk as he clicks between three browser tabs: a multi-city rail tour of Italy, a walking holiday through the Dordogne or a wellness retreat in the hills of central Portugal. He'll choose one, just him and Kirsty – no work. Something he knows she'll enjoy.

His door creaks open and he minimises his browser just as Kirsty steps in. She thrusts his phone towards him. 'It's Catherine Davenport.'

His stomach tightens. He stands and takes the phone. 'Hi, Catherine. Everything okay?'

'No,' she snaps. 'Board meeting on Teams in five minutes.' She hangs up.

Ray stares at the screen, heart rate rising. *What now?* Disaster scenarios run through his head. He dashes to the wardrobe, pulls on a shirt, brushes his hair, then drops into his chair and joins the familiar faces on the video call: Winstanley, Chester, Bristol, Davenport and Jude.

No friendly pre-amble. Catherine launches right in. 'There's been an escalation, which will need some swift decision-making.'

Ray takes a deep breath. Something's gone wrong, and he wonders what could have happened in the few hours since he left the office.

'Ninja Magpie have sent me this file,' says Catherine. A spreadsheet appears on screen. 'Sean, do you recognise these filenames?'

Sean leans forward, squinting at the list. 'I recognise the format: three-character project code followed by a unique ID. It looks like a list of files from our research vault.'

'They claim to have copies of every single one of these. I've counted 200.'

The number hits Ray like a body blow. His hands tremble.

'Ray, you told us they only have twelve files. How do you explain this?' says Catherine, sneering into the camera.

They're bluffing. 'Somehow, they've got hold of a file index. But they haven't got the files.'

'How certain are you?' asks Catherine.

Ray lets the question sink in. Did he miss something? Is there another Dropbox account? Did they miss it? Can he rely on the log records? He wants to say he's certain, but he isn't. His head drops.

'Oh yes, and the ransom payment has gone up,' says Catherine, slamming her hand on the table. 'Fifty million pounds,' she yells.

Ray checks the time. 10.30 p.m. A return to the office with Aidan and Sydney is feeling inevitable. But then what? If they find no evidence – no log records to show a transfer – could he still conclude they definitely do not have the files? It would just be a throw of the dice at the casino table, setting himself up to be the fall guy. No, there's nothing to gain from going back to the office for another all-nighter.

'Everyone in the boardroom for 7.00 a.m. tomorrow,' says Catherine.

Nods of agreement and thumbs-up icons appear.

'Jude, can you stay on the call?' she asks.

Ray exhales slowly, and he sinks his head into his hands. His holiday tabs sit in the background, nothing actioned.

20

'They've just parked the car, so should be here any minute now,' says Rachel, pulling herself upright in the hospital bed and sinking into her pillows. Her dad stands, awkwardly rearranging the hard plastic chairs to make space. Her mum fumbles with the magazine which she hasn't been reading.

Rachel's heart beats faster, nerves and anticipation winding together. Then she hears them, heels clicking on the hard floor and the unmistakable sound of a child skipping down the corridor.

Sarah and Florence appear at the doorway to the side-ward, Florence clinging to her mum's hand and holding what looks like a homemade get-well card in the other. Sarah stops short, pauses, and her mouth drops open as she catches sight of Rachel. She's had a similar reaction from most of her visitors.

Rachel smiles. 'It's not as bad as it looks.'

They walk tentatively towards the bed, glancing at her mum and dad, who are setting their eyes on their granddaughter for the first time.

'Mum, Dad. This is Sarah and Florence,' says Rachel.

Her dad holds out his hand. 'Very nice to meet you, Sarah.' Her mum repeats the gesture. There's an awkwardness, everyone navigating unfamiliar ground. Florence walks towards the bedside and hands Rachel her card. On the front is a crayoned drawing of a tabby cat and on the inside, in coloured writing, *Get well soon, Aunt Rachel*. Rachel has a lump in her throat. This means so much to her.

'Did you make this, Florence?' she asks.

She gives a shy nod, then climbs onto the chairs next to her grandmother.

The awkwardness soon melts as they get to know each other. Sarah tells them about her job as an assistant manager in a pub restaurant and explains how she relies on her mum for childcare when she's on split-shifts. Florence pulls books from her backpack and Rachel's mum offers to read to her. Soon, the ward has a new energy. Florence tells her grandmother that she's five-and-a-half years old and shows her a picture of her school from her mum's phone.

There are tears in her mum's eyes, and her father's face twitches, as if he's holding something in. Rachel's heart warms as she watches her parents get to know their granddaughter, five years late. Her dad and Sarah are still chatting. Rachel gazes at Florence. Her parents must see the likeness to Tony. He should be here. He said he's working, but she knows that's an avoidance excuse.

She remembers how it all started. She was eighteen, Tony fifteen. She had passed her driving test and had the freedom to visit her boyfriend in Skipton. Their parents thought she was out with her best friend, staying the night at her house. Tony knew the truth. She'd slip him a fiver to keep quiet. Enough to buy his silence and give him a good weekend.

Some older lads – street drinkers – befriended him. He was young, impressionable and eager to be accepted. That was the beginning of his downfall. At first, he hid it well, then he started hitting the vodka. One night, he stumbled through the front door, reeking of it, barely able to stand. Their dad went ballistic, demanding to know where he got the money from and where he bought it. To his credit, he never snitched. They grounded him for a month while Rachel's misdemeanours went undetected and unpunished.

It hadn't been worth it. She dumped the boyfriend after two months. His shared student house was a smelly, rodent-infested shit-tip. He talked about himself constantly and the sex had been forgettable. But by then, the real damage had been done. Tony's drinking habit had taken hold, and his new friends had accepted him into their fold.

By the age of nineteen, their parents had had enough. Complaints from neighbours, warnings from the police. They told him to leave. He did and vowed never to come back.

She still remembers the night he phoned her, when she was staying in her student house in Liverpool. If she hadn't been so wrapped up in her own life, she may have sensed the desperation in his voice and taken him in, just to help break his cycle of self-destruction. She wasn't there for him when he most needed help.

Richard would tell her not to blame herself for Tony's life choices. Even when he was with Sarah – the girl he loved and had a child with – he couldn't keep it together. Rachel puts it down to circumstances and toxic influence rather than personality. Having seen the way he's rebuilding his life, she's sure she's right. Regardless, he's her only sibling and she'll do anything to help him get back on the straight-and-narrow. Most of all, she would love to see her family reunited and today feels like a step in that direction. Little Florence might be that magic wand that makes it happen.

Sarah and Florence stayed for over an hour. Sarah and Rachel chatted while Florence sipped a hot chocolate her granddad bought from Costa. The two of them agreed they will try to get Tony reunited with his mum and dad. Sarah said she would talk to him.

They say their goodbyes. Florence stands on a chair to give her aunt a hug and Rachel tries not to wince with pain. Rachel glances at her mum and dad. The smiles on their faces tell her that today has been as special to them as it has been for her.

It's dark outside. Rachel has enjoyed a lot of love and attention these last two days. Her friend Cathy dropped in. She had a long chat with Adam after her mum and dad left, then a shorter call with Richard. Many more messages through Facebook and WhatsApp.

She closes her eyes, attempting sleep, but every sound unnerves her: the distant sound of a television, the soft squeak of trolley wheels, footsteps from the corridor. Izabela's last words repeat in her mind: *You'll regret this.*

She felt safe while she had visitors. But now she's alone, the haunting threat of Aleks and Izabela plotting revenge consumes her once again. They still have her laptop and can see everything on there, except the encrypted file-folder. The folder containing the company's secret research files, which they are so desperate to get their hands on. The files that someone is prepared to pay a lot of money for – millions, it seems.

A nurse comes in to tell her that as her neuro obs are normal now, they will probably discharge her in the morning, and she should arrange to be collected.

She feels ready to go home now. She reaches for her phone, thinks for a moment, then sends one more message.

She tries to relax by gazing through the window at the full moon and the flickering stars on what is an unusually clear night. She closes her eyes but can't fall into a proper sleep. It's more a state of nervous calm. She senses a presence by her bedside.

'Are you awake?' comes a familiar voice.

She opens her eyes and glances sideways to see nurse Tasha. 'Oh, hello.'

Rachel was so hoping to see her, just to say thank you for phoning the ambulance and looking after her. The jacket Tasha had put over her must be blood-stained.

'I've just finished my shift, so thought I'd pop by and see how you are.'

'Thank you. Why don't you have a seat?' says Rachel.

She sits. 'How are you feeling?'

Rachel thinks for a moment. 'Physically, fine. Mentally, all over the place.'

Within five minutes, they're chatting like best friends on a confess-all night out. Rachel tells her about how she's trying to get out of her marriage to Richard and start a proper relationship with Adam; Tasha tells her about her controlling boyfriend, who's installed tracking software on her phone to follow her whereabouts. But she's going to move out of his flat as she has an offer of a room in a shared house with two male doctors, one of whom she fancies, and this will be a way of getting noticed. Rachel goes one better, telling her how much she wants children of her own and she's hoping Adam will have a vasectomy reversal, but they're still getting to know each other so she'll have to wait a bit before broaching what may be a delicate subject. They continue, as if raising each other at a card table. If it were a contest, Rachel would clear up, with her winning hand of living in fear of being discovered as the person responsible for a crime that brought her company to its knees. But that's not something to boast about. She's still ashamed of everything she did. It may not be over yet. The threats of Izabela and Aleks come back into her consciousness. She shudders. *How far are they prepared to go?*

Nurse Tasha stands ready to leave, reaches out and clasps Rachel's hand. 'You take care now,' she says.

They connect with each other on social media, say good night and promise to keep in touch.

21

R ay gets his feet and takes a breath. 'We know how the original twelve files were leaked. It was by email to—'

'Do we know by whom?' Catherine cuts in.

He hesitates. 'It was a password hack.'

Winstanley lets out a scoff. 'We'll take that as a no.'

Ray clenches his fists. *Stick to the facts and don't get emotional,* Kirsty had told him that morning. But it's easier said than done when his nemeses are circling.

'It's a work-in-progress investigation,' he says through gritted teeth. 'So far, we've found no evidence that any additional research files have been exfiltrated.'

Sean Bristol is on his feet, pacing, gesturing with his hands, agitation radiating from him. 'Then can you explain how they obtained a very accurate listing of our research files?'

Ray takes a breath. 'All the evidence points to an insider, someone with access to the research vault, who took some screenshots and passed them on.'

Chester snorts and rolls his eyes. 'Genius. I would never have worked that one out.'

Catherine shoots him a look.

She turns to Sean. 'Please explain to us the value of these files, and the impact of their loss,' she says in a sombre tone.

Sean walks to the front of the room. He scans the table, like a teacher, checking he has everyone's undivided attention. He takes a breath. 'Most of the files contain raw data from studies - lab experiments and clinical trial results for our new Alzheimer's drug. This data will tell us if our new treatment is safe and efficacious, which helps us determine if it's worth progressing to a large-scale, phase 3, trial.'

He pauses, glancing round the table, as if gauging reactions. 'As I've reported before, early results show it reduces amyloid plaque buildup in the brain and improves cognitive function, which means slower disease progression. It seems to be more effective and with a better safety profile than current therapies, which could make it game-changing for patients with early-stage Alzheimer's. And their loved ones. That's why the big pharma companies want to buy our company. They want our Science.'

'And can you tell us what they can realistically achieve with these files?' asks Catherine.

He leans forward, resting both palms on the table. 'A single file is meaningless, but those spreadsheets and lab reports together provide insights into the protein structure, the mechanism of action and the formulation of the biologic. They also show the dosing regimens and how the medicine gets absorbed, distributed, metabolised and extracted from the body. This is the cumulation of six years of tireless research. *Our* intellectual property.' His head drops as he sighs. 'Losing this to some competitor would be catastrophic. They could compromise out patent or produce a similar molecule and beat us to market.'

Silence. Heads drop around the table. Ray sinks lower into his chair. *It's over.* Even if he had another week, he's not confident that he could prove conclusively that those files have not left the company. He may get to ninety-nine per cent certainty, but the stakes are too high. He's played his hand and has nothing more to offer.

Catherine breaks the silence. 'Jude, can you give us an update?'

Jude rises, as if stepping up to perform. 'I've been talking to Ninja Magpie overnight, using secure messaging on Tor,' he pauses for effect, but stern faces return his gaze. 'They will accept forty million, so long as it's paid this morning.'

Catherine lets out a heavy sigh. 'Do we have everything ready?'

Jude nods. 'Payment infrastructure's in place.'

Catherine scans the room. 'I've authorised payment. Forty million.' Her voice tightens. 'Does anyone have anything to add?'

Ray feels sick. This is one of the biggest cyber extortions in corporate history and it's happened under his watch.

Catherine nods at Jude, who packs up his laptop and exits the room. 'It will take about ten minutes,' he says.

Ray watches him leave with a skip in his step.

Catherine browses something on her phone. Bristol, Winstanley and Chester break into one of their whispered, suspicious-looking side-chats. Ray wonders what can be so secret. They must be worried that the buyer will find out about the leak and will walk away, which means they lose out of their big payday. They seem relieved now.

Catherine turns back to face the room, visibly shaking with fury. 'This does not end here.' She points at Ray. 'I'm expecting you to come back with answers. If it's an inside job, I want to know who. Whatever it takes, find them.'

'Better late than never, I suppose,' says Winstanley with a smirk.

Ray feels a surge of rage. 'What's that supposed to mean?'

Winstanley shrugs. 'Just saying. It's disappointing you couldn't have prevented this.'

Catherine slams her palm on the table. 'And what the hell have you done to help, Jonathan?'

Winstanley recoils slightly, but she's not done.

'Call yourself a leader.' She points at him. 'You've contributed *nothing* this past week – nothing but smart-arse remarks and excuses.'

Ray can barely conceal the grim sense of satisfaction rising in his chest. *I couldn't have put it better myself.*

She continues, points at Chester. 'Mike – you've said little this entire meeting.' She folds her arms. 'What do you have to say about paying forty million to criminals just to keep this company alive?'

Chester flinches, fumbles for words, but nothing coherent comes out.

She slams the table again. 'This is the worst day in my professional life,' she says, voice rising with rage. 'Does anyone have anything to say?'

Heads drop and silence reigns. The door opens. Jude re-enters, takes one look at the room, sinks into his seat and fiddles with his laptop. 'The transfer's gone through,' he murmurs.

No one speaks. No one moves.

Ray feels defeated. This is the worst day of his professional career too. He just wants to go to the pub and get drunk. He thinks of Aidan and Sydney. The three of them have given everything this past week, fighting an invisible enemy. And it isn't over. They still need to find the rogue insider. It's personal now.

'So, we've just bankrolled a ransomware gang,' Aidan snaps, arms folded in disgust.

'They'll come back for more,' says Sydney.

Ray nods. 'I know. But there was too much at stake. The company would sink if those files went public.'

Ray glances at the two of them. They look dishevelled and demoralised. Exactly how he feels. He'll take them to the pub tonight. They all need to let off steam.

He glances at the whiteboard. A new multi-coloured diagram has appeared. He points. 'What's that?'

'Misuse cases,' says Sydney, 'showing all the possible paths for transferring data out.'

Ray smiles. 'Catherine's determined we find out who's responsible.'

'Are we convinced it's an insider?' asks Aidan.

'Whoever it was knew our technologies, our network architecture and worked out how to evade our monitoring systems. They knew too much,' says Sydney.

Ray nods. 'Agreed.'

They sit around the briefing table, brainstorming next steps in the hunt for the rogue insider: scanning all laptops, reanalysing system logs, going through all indicators of compromise. And they still need to put in place enhanced monitoring to prevent any copycat attacks. They agree the actions, aware that they are taking on more work than they can humanly manage. But somewhere in the data are the clues that will identify the perpetrator.

'We should also go through all the user-reported security incidents,' says Ray.

'Most of those are trivia and noise,' says Aidan. 'Requests for dodgy websites to be unblocked or hard discs running out of space. Hardly any are security related. We haven't had the time to look through them in months.'

'Okay, you focus on network telemetry and any newly developed code,' says Ray, 'I'll plough through the incident log. No stone unturned. This is too important.'

Ray steps back into his office, slumps into his chair, shakes the mouse on his desk and watches his monitor flicker into life. Something new is nagging at him. He replays the board meetings of the last week, each one a theatre of power. He was always the outsider, brought in for answers. They goaded him, while bestowing Jude with unearned superhero status. It was the body language that bothered him. Winstanley, Chester and Bristol with their side glances, knowing nods. Communicating in their own code. It was like trying to read ciphertext. They were all friends before joining the company and he senses there's something rotten going on between them. They were relieved when Catherine approved the ransom payment. That's money off the bottom-line. Less profit means reduced bonus for them. Are those files really worth so much? He can't see the full picture. Not yet. But he will.

Rachel sits in the hospital's corridor ward, holding a box of prescription painkillers. She plans to take one week off work, hoping by the time she returns, the recovery of systems and laptops will be complete. She dreams of getting back to the tedium and frustrations of managing the service desk, dealing with the daily dramas then going to the pub on Friday after work. But it won't be normal because the threat from Aleks and Izabela is omnipresent, like a whispering voice, continually reminding her they will get their revenge.

The double doors to the ward swing open and she smiles as Adam walks through. She links her arm with his and they walk out together.

22

Ray stands in the lift, watching the floor numbers light up one by one as it climbs to the top floor. He's either going to get sacked or promoted. Why else would Catherine Davenport ask to see him?

Despite attending the board meetings these last two weeks, he has never had the privilege of meeting one-to-one with Davenport, unlike Jude. But he's not one for kowtowing to superiors or spinning bad news into something politically correct. Perhaps that's why he doesn't fit in at the executive level. He prepares himself for one of her tirades, when he tells her they are no further forward in identifying the rogue insider.

He steps out of the lift, walks along the hushed corridor. Modern art adorns the walls. Her admin appears from nowhere, taps the door, opens it and ushers him inside. Her office has more space than a six-person meeting room and the floor-to-ceiling windows frame a striking view of the city, but he barely registers it. Instead, his focus locks on to the two women seated across from him.

Catherine's expression is unreadable, her iPhone face down on the desk. Next to her sits Claire O'Donnell, the head of communications and external affairs, with hair tightly pinned and a posture so upright it looks painful. He recognises her from the all-staff broadcasts and the monthly newsletters with their subliminal messaging, reminding everyone what a great company they work for. He can guess why she's here: to spin some good-news story.

She jumps to her feet and offers her hand. 'Ray, lovely to meet you at last. I'm Claire.'

Ray shakes her hand. 'It's a pleasure.'

Ray sits, laptop ready in case they need details.

Catherine forces a smile. 'Ray, I would first like to say a massive thank you. This crisis could have been so much worse, and I think you've done an excellent job.'

Ray hesitates. Not what he was expecting. 'Thank you. I owe it to my team, who have been heroic, working through the night and at weekends.'

'Pass on my heartfelt thanks. We'll ensure they're rewarded. And you too, for excellent leadership.'

Maybe it is a promotion, after all. 'I appreciate that, Catherine.'

'As you probably know, we must prepare and submit a regulatory disclosure statement, stating what happened, the impact and action we are taking.'

Ray nods. 'I'm familiar with the disclosure requirements.'

'And we also want to issue a media statement. There's already too much fake news circulating,' Claire adds.

Catherine nods to Claire, who slides a document across the desk.

'At this stage, we need to rebuild stakeholder confidence. We just need your signature,' says Catherine.

Company Disclosure Statement

Subject: Cyber-Attack Investigation Update

Incident Overview: On 13th October 2025, Synaptonica experienced a cyber-attack that resulted in disruptions to our production operations and head office functions. This incident involved the deployment of malicious software to the computer network.

This was a sophisticated and fast-moving attack. Our cyber defence team took pre-emptive actions, and forced an emergency shutdown of all systems, which included closing all internet connections. This prompt action allowed our internal team to contain the threat and activate recovery procedures.

This incident resulted in an outage of key operational systems for three days. Over ten days, we restored them using secure backups.

Current Status

After ten days of intensive investigation and crisis management, we can confirm that:

- All critical and essential systems are operating securely.

- Recovery of non-critical systems is ongoing; we estimate full restoration within one week.

- Additional security measures are in place to safeguard our systems and prevent future incidents, including copycat attacks.

- Customer orders are being fulfilled once again and all operations, across research and manufacturing, are returning to normal.

The exact cost is unknown at this stage, but we do not expect it to be material.

Identification of the Perpetrator

The cyber-attack originated from a cybercrime gang commonly known as Ninja Magpie. We are working with specialists from the National Cyber Security Centre to identify the specific threat actors who have infiltrated our network. We are also conducting a thorough internal investigation and taking measures to prevent recurrence; this includes disciplinary action on internal staff who may have violated our Secure Computer Use Policy.

Ray reads it twice. No mention of research files being leaked, no mention of ransom payment. He wants to rewrite it for them. This has too many gaps, which makes it misleading. He retrieves his pen from his inside jacket pocket, smiles back at them. 'I would like to suggest some alterations.'

Catherine smirks. 'I appreciate it's probably light on technical detail for you. But it's just a confidence-building statement for investors. Bottom line, we had a crisis and now it's resolved.'

Ray clears his throat. 'With respect, disclosure statements must follow the principle of transparency and accuracy. This omits relevant facts required by regulators, which makes it misleading.'

Claire chuckles. 'It's fine, Ray. Our stakeholders trust us to do our jobs.'

Ray shakes his head. 'I'm sorry, but as it is an official submission to the regulators, it has to follow the principles of truthfulness and transparency. It doesn't do that, in my professional opinion.'

Claire looks towards Catherine.

Catherine leans forward on her desk. 'Ray, you don't normally get involved with board matters. But maybe you will, soon.' She smiles. 'Think of this as... practice.'

'Proactive reputation management,' Claire chimes in, with a condescending smile.

Ray pauses. The hint is clear enough: a seat in the boardroom. A position he has always strived for. One where he could make a difference. He glances back at the document. It is factually accurate, and he knows of other companies who have failed to disclose ransom payments. But this is about doing the right thing. He glances back at the two ladies.

'Can you tell me a bit more about the last sentence?' He points to it in the document: *This includes disciplinary action on internal staff who may have violated our Secure Computer Use Policy.*

Catherine's smile returns. 'You gave us names; we investigated further.'

'I gave you the names of people whose accounts were compromised. They're victims.'

She nods. 'One of them was already on a disciplinary. A bit of a loose cannon and having a weak password was the last straw. We parted company, amicably... Sort of.'

Ray nods. He knows her priority is the acquisition, and she's trying to clean up the house after a flood so they can get the best price for the company, and the board can cash out. He thinks of the other board members. Winstanley and Chester are lying rogues. He doesn't know Sean Bristol that well, but he's in their inner circle. A circle Ray would never be part of. He studies Catherine, someone he's always admired from a distance. But now, close up, he sees a different person. There's insincerity in her face and desperation in her body language.

He slides the document back across the desk. 'I'm not signing.'

Silence. Catherine's smile fades. She points at him. 'These past two weeks have been the worst and most stressful of my life. I've sacrificed more for this company than you can imagine. I'm really not in the mood for your petty stubbornness.'

Ray holds her gaze. 'Truthfulness and transparency are not petty.'

Catherine leans back in her chair. 'Ray, you've made a lot of enemies in this company. In fact, I don't know anyone who has a good word to say about you. That's what's held you back.'

Ray stands, gathers his laptop. 'Thanks for the feedback. But I care more about professional integrity than my bank balance.'

As he leaves, her fist lands hard on the desk.

Ray walks back into the cyber operations room, still shaking after his disagreement with Davenport. That was a career limiting exchange if ever there was one. But he has principles, and he is proud of his stance.

He repositions the waste bin, adjusts the room temperature and manoeuvres the two office plants an inch or two so they are in line and equal distance from the door. Then he slumps into a chair at the briefing table.

'I'm back,' he announces.

No response.

Aidan and Sydney are sitting side by side, fingers tapping at their keyboards, eyes flicking between display monitors. They're deep in conversation about an infinite loop they found buried in a source code file.

Sydney laughs. 'No wonder this application kept crashing.'

'We should cross-charge the DevOps team for finding and fixing their bugs,' says Aidan.

Ray stretches out his legs and folds his arms. 'In your own time,' he calls over.

His gaze falls on a brown padded package sitting on the table, addressed to him. He rips it open and finds a laptop inside. Just the device – no note, no instructions. He's guessing someone wants a forensic job done on it. The last time he had one of these, he found a sex video. He smiles at the memory. But there's no paperwork. No chain-of-custody documentation. There isn't even a return address on the envelope.

Aidan and Sydney saunter over and take their seats at the briefing table.

'How did your meeting with the big boss go?' Sydney asks.

'Not very well.'

Ray's still holding the laptop, flipping it over to check for distinctive markings other than silly stickers. 'By the way, she sends her heartfelt thanks to both of you for your hard work. You might even get a bonus in next month's salary.'

Aidan and Sydney exchange a smile and give each other a high five.

'Nice to be appreciated,' says Aidan.

'So what was so bad about the meeting?' asks Sydney.

Ray leans back. 'She told me that no one in this company has a good word to say about me.'

Aidan smirked. 'I could've told you that.'

Ray shoots him a look. 'I don't come here to make friends.'

Ray considers how much to reveal. They deserve to know the truth. That the board is planning to sell the company, and the people-friendly culture they believe in is a lie. The disclosure statement they're about to release is a steaming pile of corporate spin, designed to soothe investors rather than tell the truth. The board want to cash in on a takeover deal which will probably mean most of the loyal workforce losing their jobs. He'll sit on that thought for a bit.

He gestures to the laptop in front of him. 'Any idea where this came from?'

Aidan and Sydney both shake their heads.

Ray frowns. 'It looks like one of ours.' He slides it across the desk. 'Perhaps you can repurpose it as a honeypot.'

Aidan reaches for it.

'Stop.' Sydney slams her hand on top of it. 'It could be a trap. Pre-installed with malware for a second-stage attack. I've seen this before. They may have created BIOS-level malware, which will launch before the anti-virus even starts up.'

Aidan nods. 'Good point. If they're planning another attack, they've likely installed command-and-control software.'

Ray nods. He thinks that's unlikely, but he likes the way they're thinking.

The entrance door swings open and they look up to see Jude enter.

'Morning, team,' he says, slipping off his coat and hanging it in the cupboard.

He strolls over and takes his seat at the briefing table, placing his coffee on the coaster in front of him, grinning.

'We've not seen much of you these last few days, Jude,' says Ray.

He shrugs. 'Everyone wants a chunk of my time.'

'And I thought you'd left without saying goodbye,' says Ray.

He laughs. 'I had to brief the National Crime Agency this morning. But don't worry, you've got me back now.'

Ray turns towards Aidan and Sydney and asks them to give an update on their investigation. They talk through the machine-learning algorithm they've built to identify suspicious patterns of activity from the network logs. They enthusiastically describe how they are using open-source

Python libraries to do multi-dimensional array processing and data visualisation. It does exactly what they need, but they have another problem: data gaps. Some servers, such as the jump server connecting into the R&D network, had event logging turned off months ago for performance reasons.

Ray shakes his head. Yet another example of the server operations team ignoring his security policies. He needs to dispense another bollocking. He turns to Jude. 'Why don't you give us an update on your dark web investigations?'

Jude clears his throat, explains that he can't go into specifics about his covert work, but he has picked up some interesting crypto transactions taking place. Big Bitcoin payments to known threat actors. He opens his iPad and displays what he refers to as a crypto transaction graph, showing crypto-transfer activity between wallets on the blockchain. He spends ten minutes describing blockchain architecture, then finishes by saying he hasn't yet linked those wallets to people in the real world.

Ray feels he's just wasted ten minutes of his life listening to crypto gibberish. He's tempted to berate him, but decides he's done enough pot stirring for one day and instead thanks him for his insights.

He calls the meeting to a close. 'Keep digging, team. The evidence is out there; we just need to find it.'

As the team disperse, Sydney points to the laptop. 'Don't anyone power that up. Not until we've examined it properly.'

'Understood,' says Ray, smiling. He picks it up. 'I'll safeguard it in my office.'

Ray sits in his office, staring at his monitor, pensive. His morning meeting with Catherine replays in his head. He's still troubled by them sacking someone. He looks up the four names he passed to Catherine. Three are still active on email. One – James Craig – is missing. He is the one they sacked, Ray concludes. He doesn't know the man or anything about his background, but scapegoating someone for getting their password hacked is unjust and he'll have a good case for unfair dismissal. There's something more behind this. He's sure of it.

He switches to his browser, and does a Google image search, smiling as he finds what he's looking for: a bold red triangle with a skull and crossbones, and *DANGER* written in bold white lettering. He prints it off on A4 paper and tapes it to the mystery laptop, smiling to himself. It's likely nothing more sinister than a standard laptop needing a rebuild, redirected here because the service desk is still busy doing recovery work. Aidan and Sydney are being over-paranoid. He'll humour them.

As he reclines in his chair, his mind drifts towards thoughts of alternative employment. He may have pushed things too far with Catherine, which could mean their next meeting will see him get shown the exit. Maybe he should have made life easier for himself and just signed. Despite his disdain for the upper echelons of this company, he doesn't want to leave. This job gives him routine: the daily commute, the team huddle, the rhythm of the shared mission. He would miss Aidan and Sydney and the weekly threat intelligence briefings with the NCSC. And despite what Catherine says, he has friends here. Juliette from HR, for one.

23

Rachel sits on the sofa of the high-ceilinged, wood-panelled waiting room, glancing at the parenting magazines neatly arranged on the pinewood coffee table. Soft background music plays through speakers she can't see. The couple sitting opposite her are having a whispered conversation. She guesses they are in their early forties, perhaps here for IVF treatment. Maybe they left starting a family too late or maybe this is a second marriage, and they want to have a child together. She thinks about striking up a conversation with them, just out of curiosity, but notices their furtive glances in her direction. They must be equally curious about her – a single woman who looks as though she's stepped out of a cage fight.

It's been almost a week. The memory of the attack, like the cuts and bruises, is still fresh. She still has that same recurring nightmare: walking to the station, in the dark. Alone. Then the whistling sound of the moped. She knows what's coming and jolts herself awake in sheer panic. Richard asleep in the spare room is oblivious. She keeps her bedside lamp on and tries to read, but the fear of Ninja Magpie's next move still haunts her.

If she had co-operated and given them all the files, she wouldn't have been attacked. If she had disclosed the password, she wouldn't be spending every waking hour looking over her shoulder in fear of the next attack. But she didn't like the person she had become. It was as if she had fooled herself into thinking it wasn't really a crime because the company didn't know about it and would probably never find out. The perfect victimless crime. Delusional thinking. Then there was the chaos caused by Izabela. The very visible cyber-attack. Everything stopped and no one could work. The company must have lost millions, all because of her naivety – or is it selfishness? And yet, here she is, about to spend her illicit gains on something she wants more than anything else in the world.

She unlocks her phone, glances at Telegram Messenger. Nothing since that last message on Sunday: *Big mistake, Rachel*. She wants to focus on her future, the one where she lives a normal life and becomes a mother, but the threat of retribution-to-come dominates her thoughts. She needs protecting. The trouble is there's no one she can talk to.

She closes her eyes for a moment and exhales, taking deep breaths, trying to calm her anxiety and focus on the procedure she's about to go through. She flips open a fact sheet she picked up at reception and skims over a diagram illustrating the eight-stage process of egg freezing. Images of ovaries, injection needles and test tubes submerged in liquid nitrogen stare back at her. She wonders about her ovary reserves and how many eggs she might produce. She'll soon find out. She checks her watch. Her appointment time has arrived.

From the open door, she hears the receptionist rescheduling another patient's visit. Then a tall, slim woman appears, glasses perched on her head, thick greying hair swept back.

'Rachel Carter?' she calls softly.

Rachel stands. The woman extends a hand. 'Dr Lamb.'

They shake hands, exchanging brief pleasantries about travel times and the traumas of trying to park a car anywhere in London.

Dr Lamb settles behind her desk in her consultation room. Rachel sits opposite. The doctor's gaze lingers on Rachel's face, showing concern. 'Looks like you've had quite a knock,' she observes gently.

Rachel hesitates. 'It was an opportunistic mugging. My fault for taking a shortcut home and trying to fight back. It's not as bad as it looks and I'm going back to work soon.' She keeps her voice light.

'If you wanted to do this another time…'

'Oh no, I'm fine. Thank you,' says Rachel.

The doctor gives a small nod, and turns to her screen, typing as she speaks. 'I have your blood test results here. Your Anti-Müllerian Hormone level is 1.5, which means your ovarian reserve is about average for a woman your age.'

Relief washes over Rachel. 'So this would be a good time to freeze my eggs?'

Dr Lamb nods. 'The sooner the better.'

Rachel smiles. 'I'm ready.'

'That said, success rates vary depending on the number of good eggs we can collect and your age at the time of use. If we retrieve around fifteen eggs, you'll have a solid chance of a successful pregnancy. If not, we can repeat the procedure.'

Rachel exhales, some of the tension in her shoulders loosening. She still has time to conceive naturally, with the right partner, and she has someone in mind. But she cannot outrun biology, so this will be her safety net.

Dr Lamb continues. 'We'll begin on day two or three of your cycle. You'll need daily hormone injections to stimulate your ovaries. These are self-administered. After about two weeks, a trigger injection will mature the eggs, and we'll schedule a minor procedure, under sedation, to retrieve them for immediate freezing.'

Rachel nods. She's read about this already.

'If you are ready to start, we can post the syringes to your home,' Dr Lamb offers, 'or you can collect them here, and the nurse can show you how to administer the injections. They're quite painless.'

Rachel smirks. *Post them to my home?* No. The last thing she needs is for Richard to see them. 'I'll collect them.'

Dr Lamb makes a note. 'That's fine. Just call when you're ready and the nurse will show you how to administer them.'

Rachel steps out of the clinic, walking back to her car with a sense of fulfilment. One step closer to the one thing she wants more than anything in this world. She does a mental calculation. Her illegal earnings have cleared her debt and paid for this treatment, but there isn't enough left for a second round, so she'll need to produce as many eggs as possible the first time. She may not even have to use them, but who knows what the future holds. As she imagines herself being pregnant, holding her enlarged belly then going through labour, she thinks of Florence. Wouldn't she love to have a little cousin? Then the dark thoughts creep in. *Do I deserve that happiness?*

She takes a breath, checks her watch and jumps in her car with a sudden sense of excitement for her lunch date with Adam.

Rachel and Adam sit upstairs in the Coffee Shop, tucked into a quiet corner surrounded by dusty potted palms. The air is rich with the scent of roasted coffee and toasted teacakes. It's quiet except for acoustic background music coming from ceiling speakers. An eclectic collection of artwork lines the walls, some vibrant, some abstract. All local artists. Opposite them, a lone customer hunches over his laptop with headphones clamped to his ears. A young barista walks nervously towards them holding a tray with two lattes and a pair of paninis. Rachel takes the one oozing with mozzarella, not quite remembering what she'd asked for as her mind is still buzzing with thoughts of her ovarian reserve.

Adam drops a sugar cube into his coffee cup, stirring it and destroying the delicate tulip pattern on the foam.

'I was thinking about you this morning,' he says, glancing at her with a smile.

Rachel raises an eyebrow. 'Pleasant thoughts, I hope.'

He glances from side to side. 'How much detail do you want?'

She grins. 'I don't mind being inappropriate.' She nods towards the other customer. 'He won't hear anything with those headphones on.'

She places a hand gently over his, allowing herself to enjoy the moment. A warmth passes between them, but a question is burning inside her chest. Would he want more children – a second family? Would he consider reversing the vasectomy he so casually mentioned after their first night sleeping together? But they're still at the lovey can't-keep-our-hands-off-each-other stage in their relationship. She can't just blurt out such a desperate-sounding question. She reminds herself to enjoy the present and see where they go. They need to clear a few more relationship hurdles first. After she's met his children and they've become more entwined, if it is true love, then he will say yes, won't he?

They finish eating and step outside into the brisk daylight. She won't see him this weekend because he has his children again.

'Perhaps I could pop over during the day,' she says hopefully, 'just to say hello.'

Adam shifts his feet and glances away. 'Trouble is, they'll report back to their mum, and she'll start poking her nose in, and that's a can of worms I'd rather not open right now.'

Rachel nods. 'I understand.' *Don't be too pushy.*

They kiss, properly. It gives her warmth and a feeling of security. *Small steps.*

She drives home and parks a few doors down from her house, having multiple attempts at aligning the car with the kerb. Her phone buzzes with another message.

Lionel: *Hope you are feeling better. Everyone in the office is asking after you. If you'd like an update before your return, check out this story – just published on the BBC News website.*

Yes, thank you Lionel, she's desperate for an update. She taps the link, her heart thudding a bit more than normal.

Synaptonica Issues Update Following Cyber-Attack

Synaptonica confirms no research data leaked following swift containment efforts

Ten days after a cyber-attack caused a significant outage across its IT infrastructure, Synaptonica has issued a public statement confirming that most systems are back online and there is no evidence of research data being compromised or leaked because of the incident.

They have attributed the attack to Ninja Magpie, a sophisticated e-crime group known for targeting organisations with ransomware – a form of malicious software that encrypts computer systems and demands payment to restore access. They are known for using social engineering tactics, where employees are duped into providing access or disclosing credentials, often through impersonation tactics.

According to the company press release, the breach began when trojan malware – malicious code disguised as legitimate software – infected several employee devices, then later activated.

However, Synaptonica said they promptly invoked their incident response protocols, including a critical containment referred to internally as the 'kill switch.' This action immediately severed infected systems from the wider network, helping limit the spread and isolate the threat.

'We took swift action to contain the incident and protect our systems,' the company stated. 'Our priority was safeguarding our intellectual property, and we are pleased to confirm that, based on digital forensic investigations to date, we have found no evidence of research data being leaked.'

The outage caused major disruptions to internal operations, including research laboratories and supply chain functions. System restoration has been successful, they claim. The company has not commented on whether this required a ransom payment.

Cyber security experts have noted a rise in ransomware attacks targeting life science and pharmaceutical firms because of the high value of their intellectual property. Ninja Magpie is one of several e-crime syndicates operating in this space, often employing multiple tactics to evade traditional security systems.

Synaptonica say they continue to work with cyber security specialists from the National Cyber Security Centre and are co-operating with the National Crime Agency to fully investigate the incident.

Rachel exhales with a sense of relief: *no evidence of research data being leaked*. Maybe she's got away with it. But her gaze lingers on the final paragraph: working with the *National Crime Agency*. They are still investigating, of course they are. The company probably lost millions. If there's a trail that leads to Izabela, that brings Rachel into the frame. She needs to prepare for this. *Why did you recruit her without following the standard recruitment procedures?* She was desperately short-staffed and Izabela seemed the perfect fit. Others will support her on that – she fitted in well and learned quickly. That's the truth, although not quite the whole truth.

She is living on a knife edge. Every noise makes her jump; she flinches when her phone rings. The panic is never far away, ready to ambush her. She's fragile, and needs to talk to someone, but she can't open up without revealing her crime which leaves her alone with her guilt and the constant fear of being uncovered as the linchpin to what has become a newsworthy crime.

She then imagines the investigation digging deeper, and they discover she downloaded those research files. There's no plausible deniability on that one. But they would first need to recover her laptop, and even then, the folder is password protected. She presses a trembling hand to her chest and feels her heart pounding. If they catch her, it wouldn't just be an ignominious exit. It's a crime that could see her end up in court, maybe even prison. Worst-case.

She closes her eyes and breathes, trying to clear her mind. In for four. Hold. Out for four.

Five minutes later, she steps out of the car, feeling calmer, and walks to her front door. Richard's standing at the bottom of the stairs, waiting to greet her like an excited dog who's been left on his own too long. 'You're back. How are you? Did you have a good morning? Cup of tea?'

Too many questions. She's only been out half a day. She prefers the old Richard who barely noticed if she was in or out and would never offer to make her anything.

As he heads to the kitchen, she tries to relax, but something is unsettling her – Adam's reaction when she suggested popping round during the day at the weekend. He seemed to recoil at the suggestion she meet his children. She only meant a casual hello. They're teenagers, so probably indifferent to meeting his dad's girlfriend. Unless there's more to it. Perhaps there's still something between him and his ex-wife. Maybe they're only on a trial separation and the children expect them to get back together.

She shakes the doom thoughts from her mind as she's probably over-thinking again. Adam's a genuine person and they were friends before they got together properly. In his mind, it's probably too soon for her to meet his children.

24

Rachel takes her familiar route to work, the tall boundary railings of the British Museum, once a spectacular landmark, now a regretful reminder of the night she crossed a line she can not uncross. She shivers at the memory of that meeting with Aleks. She was selfishly thinking only of herself, ignoring her moral compass and suspending any sense of right and wrong. Disturbingly, she had found it easy.

And yet, she got what she wanted. She's going back to the clinic tomorrow for the first injection and to pick up the supply of twelve syringes. She's even booked in for the egg collection procedure two weeks later and paid in full for three years' storage. Everything is in motion. Now she has to live with the knowledge of how she got there and the fear of it catching up with her.

She hasn't heard from Aleks or Izabela this past week. No more threats. But that doesn't stop her looking over her shoulder, scanning for danger at every corner. She now knows what they are capable of. Never again, she promises herself.

She's glad to be going back to work. Being stuck at home with Richard had become suffocating. He would ghost in and out of rooms, being overly polite. It seemed a lot easier when they were shouting and arguing. It felt more genuine.

The October air is sharp and the breeze bites, but her brisk pace and layers keep her warm. The pavement smoothie cart is now selling hot chocolate. She blends into a throng of commuters spilling out of the underground station and is grateful for the anonymity. She's tired of people staring at her, taking a second glance, probably thinking she's been in a drunken brawl. It will be another week before the bruises fade.

A loud slam makes her jump. Her heart races before she realises it's only a food delivery – frozen boxes dropping onto the tailgate of a delivery vehicle. She takes a breath and slows her pace. In a shop window, she notices cobwebs, cardboard skeletons and grinning pumpkins. Halloween is coming up. An idea forms. Florence is visiting on Saturday. She pictures her niece dressed as a witch, with a pointed hat, broomstick and plastic bucket, and the two of them going trick-or-treating. The thought warms her. The joy children bring is uncomplicated.

She reaches Charing Cross Road, passes through the revolving door of her office, scans her pass at the barrier and walks into a waiting lift with three strangers who look at her, then take a second glance. No conversation. Her reflection in the mirrored wall stares back. Her makeup and concealer are doing their best, but faint shadows remain.

Her heart kicks as the doors slide open on the sixth floor. She tells herself the crisis is over, and she just needs to ease back into her routine. It's 8.50 a.m. Too late to get a window desk. She walks the short corridor, pushes through the double doors and creeps into the open-plan zone. Heads turn, one person stands, headsets are removed, calls abruptly end. Someone claps, then applause fills the room. People drift towards her. She freezes, her throat tightens and her eyes well up with tears. Lionel reaches her first, wrapping her in a tight wordless hug. She barely has time to react before Priya – a long-time colleague takes both her hands in hers.

'I prayed for you, Rachel,' says Priya, her eyes full of emotion.

Lionel places a guiding hand on her elbow. 'We have a desk for you.'

He leads her to her favourite spot by the window. Waiting on the desk is the most beautiful bouquet of lilies and carnations, carefully arranged in a box tied with a pink ribbon. Deep reds, soft pinks, warm peaches. The scent reaches her immediately, fresh and sweet. A new laptop sits beside it together with a box of handmade chocolates from a Covent Garden chocolatier, and a large brightly coloured card: *Welcome Back, Rachel*. Every inch is filled with loving messages.

For the next half an hour, she's wrapped in hugs and kindness. She has never felt so welcomed. So cared for. The guilt she has been living with these last two weeks has escalated to a new level. They think she's an innocent victim. She's not, and she wishes they hadn't gone to this trouble because she doesn't deserve any of it.

Ray strides into the cyber operations room, carrying the morning coffees. It's his day to buy and fetch. He places them down on the circular team table, each cup landing neatly on its designated coaster.

Sydney makes a show of checking her watch. 'Let me guess – they had to remake them for you again?'

Ray shakes his head as he drops into his chair. 'New barista. Still being trained. It took a while to explain the order, but he got there in the end.'

The three of them pop the lids, the familiar scent of fresh roasted coffee fills the room as they take their first sips.

Ray leans back. 'What's new?'

Aidan rubs his temples. 'We've gone as far as we can with the server telemetry. It's throwing up some new indicators of compromise, which we dug into.' He shrugs. 'Nothing useful.'

'We've started scanning source code in the GitHub repos, looking for back-doors or anything suspicious. We're finding plenty of bugs – null pointers, stack overflows – but nothing out of the ordinary,' she says.

Ray sips his latte. 'We probably need to think a bit more out of the box on this one.'

'What about the crypto analysis Jude was doing?' says Sydney.

Ray rolls his eyes. 'I haven't seen him for a while.'

'Did you say something to upset him?' says Aidan.

'Not that I know of.'

Ray notices the sense of urgency that had been driving them forward these last two weeks has dropped. The adrenalin's gone and the thrill of the chase evaporated after the ransom payment. Ray feels the same. Disillusioned by the lack of recognition and undermined by that press release. They didn't even give Ray the courtesy of a preview. No more board meeting invites, either. It feels like they are drifting back into their routine security monitoring. A thankless job, working on a shoestring budget. But unanswered questions still nag him. Namely, who is the rogue insider? And what happened with that scientist they sacked? He knows he won't settle until he's got answers.

Sydney breaks the silence. 'How about I do the forensics on that mystery laptop?'

Ray smiles. 'The booby-trap device, you mean?'

Sydney drains her coffee. 'I'll take it outside to power-up, and once I've checked the BIOS, I'll bring it back in.'

Ray smiles. 'Always best to play safe.'

Rachel closes the front door behind her and exhales. It's only 4.30 p.m. and she's grateful for the short workday. It's been emotional. She places the boxed flowers on the kitchen table and takes a moment to admire them. They're beautiful but she can't display them at home. It's just a reminder of what she's done, and this guilt is gnawing at her.

She hears Richard moving around upstairs. He's probably getting ready for pickleball coaching, which means she'll have a chance to FaceTime with Adam later. She crosses to the sink, fills her miniature watering can and drizzles her window garden. The salad leaves are perfect for cutting. She smiles, thinking of her own growing follicles.

'Nice flowers.'

She jumps and spins around. Richard stands in the doorway.

'From work. Everyone was so lovely.'

He picks up the kettle. 'Tea?'

'No thanks.'

He fills the kettle and flips the switch. She takes a seat at the table. The two of them remain silent for an uncomfortable moment.

'My parents called today, asking after you.'

'That's kind of them.'

'They want to come up on Saturday and take us out for lunch.'

Rachel sighs. 'I'm assuming they don't know yet?'

He shakes his head. 'Didn't seem like the right time to mention it.'

That fair. She hasn't told her parents either. They are at that awkward limbo stage of separation. Not yet public, still living under one roof. But this gives her another problem.

'I've got Tony and Florence coming over Saturday afternoon. I thought you would be at a tournament.'

'I cancelled. For my parents,' he says flatly.

She watches his face as he pours boiling water into his mug. There's a sadness in him she's not used to seeing. Eyes dull and emotionally drained. For a second, she wants to hug him, as a friend, even though she's the one who's hurt him.

She sighs. 'Okay, let's make an effort. They haven't been here in a while.'

He leans against the worktop, mug in hand. 'What about Tony and Florence?' he says with a hint of resentment.

'I'm not cancelling.'

He nods, then wanders back upstairs.

It's 5.15 p.m. Ray blinks at the screen. For the last two hours, he's been trawling through the incident backlog, looking for clues. Perhaps a report of suspicious activity, like someone logging into another person's account. But nothing has come up. Most of the reported incidents are trivial: someone accidentally emailing the wrong people, a request to unblock YouTube, another user wants Netflix blocked. One in ten might justify investigation, but rarely is anything serious reported. The more interesting stuff – fraud, whistleblowing – go to the integrity line and only land on his desk if they need digital forensics. His incident backlog stretches four months. It will take at least a couple of weeks to go through it.

He checks the time. Fifteen minutes until he leaves. He opens LinkedIn and scans a few job postings. Some CISO roles have caught his eye. Tempting. It would be difficult to adjust to a new company, but he's been so disillusioned of late, that it may be his best option. If he could find something similar to what he has now, and take Aidan and Sydney with him, he'd seriously consider jumping ship.

He shuts down his laptop and starts his end-of-day routine when he hears movement outside his office. He looks up to see Aidan and Sydney standing in his doorway, looking serious.

He raises his eyebrows. 'Spit it out, then. And be quick, I'm about to leave.'

They exchange a glance. No jokes. Even Sydney seems to have lost that infectious *I've got a theory* sparkle.

'We need you to look at this,' says Sydney.

He follows them over to the operations table. Aidan grabs a spare chair and the three of them sit side by side facing the monitor.

Ray nods to the laptop in front of him. Smiles. 'Is it safe?'

'This is a gift,' says Aidan.

Ray folds his arms. He has a train to catch but something in Aidan's voice tells him he might have to miss it.

'Multiple user accounts have logged into this device,' Sydney begins.

Ray shrugs. 'A loaner laptop.'

They both shake their heads.

'What are the chances of the same laptop being used by multiple people, in the same day, after hours?' says Aidan.

'Every night for a week,' adds Sydney.

She hands Ray a printout. 'These are the names of the accounts that have logged on.'

Ray scans the list of forty accounts and names. Amongst them are the four accounts they identified last week as compromised.

'Someone had the credentials of all these people, logged in to the research vault and downloaded the files here.' Aidan moves the mouse pointer. 'It's an encrypted folder and password protected. We can't see its contents. But the event logs tell us everything. Over 200 file downloads from the research vault. The same filenames Ninja Magpie gave us.'

Ray's mouth drops open; his pulse quickens. After all those dead ends, all those late nights, have they just discovered a lead?

'How did they get all those passwords?' asks Ray.

'We don't know,' says Sydney.

Ray runs his hands through his hair. 'Can we tell who this machine belongs to?'

Sydney and Aidan glance at each other again.

'There is one user profile that always remains on the computer. After every session with a compromised login, this account logs back in,' says Sydney.

She nudges the mouse. The screen flickers, the pointer hovers. Then a double click and the name appears:

» Rachel Carter

Ray stares. The room falls silent. He opens his mouth, but no words come out.

'That was our reaction too,' says Aidan.

Ray continues to stare at the name in disbelief. The woman she interviewed. The one who got attacked. The one person no one would ever suspect.

He looks at them, shaking his head, trying to think of a rational explanation. There is none. 'Make sure we clone this hard disc,' says Ray.

25

Rachel's hands shake with nervous excitement. She's watched the videos, spoken to the doctor, and now here she is, back in the clinic, sealed syringe packet in her hand.

She rolls up her blouse, tears open an antiseptic wipe and swipes a spot on the right side of her stomach. Peeling open the wrapper, she pulls out the syringe, removes the plastic cap from the fine needle and, as instructed, pricks her skin and injects herself. It's over in seconds.

'That's all there is to it,' says the nurse, with a reassuring smile.

Rachel laughs. 'Quicker than sex.'

The nurse laughs. 'And you'll be doing this every day for the next twelve days.'

Rachel nods. 'I'll build it into my morning routine, right after brushing my teeth.'

'All being well, we'll be ready for the egg retrieval in two weeks.'

She thanks the nurse, collects her box of syringes, and leaves the clinic, singing to herself.

She arrives at the office just before ten, still on a high. The usual cacophony of noise surrounds her – colleagues chatting, keyboards clicking, the occasional burst of laughter. Everything feels normal. Familiar. She notices her favourite window seat is free. She wonders how much longer she'll get this privilege. She has a quick good morning chat with a few people, takes her seat, starts up her laptop and opens up her email.

One message jumps out, marked urgent. From Ray Dunlop. Her heart pounds, she glances from side to side. He's all about work and security. It's a short message asking her to come to the cyber operations centre as soon as she gets in. No further details. Many senior managers have checked in on her since her return, offering sympathy and support. Not Ray. He's not really that type of person.

She can only think of one reason he wants to see her.

She takes a deep breath, rises from her chair and makes her way to the Cyber Operations Room. *You can do this.* She runs through her pre-prepared story. Yes, she recruited Izabela and fast-tracked her into the organisation, skipping the usual pre-employment screening procedures. She was so short-staffed and desperate for a new team member quickly. She came highly recommended, with good references from previous employers. She slotted into the team quickly, getting along well with everyone. Her team will vouch for that. *Oh my God. I did not know she was hacking our systems. Are you sure? What did she do?* She can act, and she'll have to be convincing on this one. *No, she hasn't returned to work this week. I've been off, so I haven't caught up with all the staff admin.*

She walks into the relative calm of the cyber security office. Two people sit at the far end of the room, throwing her a lingering glance before turning back to their screens. That's the woman who got the job she interviewed for.

'Rachel.'

She turns. Ray stands in the doorway, expression unreadable. He gestures for her to enter.

She steps inside. Nothing's changed since the interview. Sparse and spotlessly clean. He sits opposite, elbows on the desk, fingers interlocked. He says nothing, just studies her. She feels uncomfortable and shuffles in her seat.

'Sorry I wasn't in earlier,' she says, filling the silence. 'I had a medical appointment.'

He nods. 'You've been through a lot. How are you?'

She forces a smile. 'I wish I'd got a few punches in,' she jokes, 'otherwise, I'm recovering well.' Her hands won't stop trembling.

Ray leans down, picks a laptop up from the floor and places it on the desk. The first thing she notices is the three smiling emoji stickers on the lid.

'Yours?' he asks.

Blood drains from her head, and she suddenly feels faint. 'I'm not sure. Did the police find it?' The question trips out; she feels stupid.

Ray shakes his head. 'Delivered to us. Anonymously.'

She jolts, as if taking a punch to the gut. The memory of Izabela's last words – *You'll regret this* – comes back to her. This is their payback. She drops her face into her hands. She hadn't prepared for this and doesn't know what to say next.

She trembles, visibly. 'Sorry. I've just had a sudden flashback to the attack.'

'Take a moment,' says Ray with no hint of malice.

She takes a deep breath, then sits up again. 'I'm okay,' she says holding back her tears.

Ray leans forward on his desk, tapping the laptop. 'We've run a full forensic analysis on it. Event logs tell us who logged in and when. It's like digital DNA. We can't access the encrypted folder but we know what's in there and how it got there.'

Her palms go to her face as tears stream from her eyes. She can't deny any of this. 'I'm so sorry.'

'Do you understand the consequences of what you have done?'

She shakes her head. No, she doesn't. But actually, yes. She knew it was wrong, and she should have known the consequences.

'Would you like to tell me your side of the story?' says Ray.

She nods and starts talking. The password hack, the downloads, passing them on to someone she only knows as Aleks, who would pass them off as competitor intelligence. Only twelve files, though. When she saw the impact of the cyberattack, she stopped cooperating, which led to her being attacked because they wanted all the files and she wouldn't hand them over.

Ray listens without interrupting. His mouth dropped open when she explained how easy it was to get the password hashes and crack them.

'And the cyber-attack which took out all the systems?'

Rachel continues, starting with recruiting Izabela. She had no idea what they were planning. She didn't want to know. They launched the attack; that was when she realised she had made a stupid mistake.

Ray sits impassively, as if contemplating all those security weaknesses she's just described.

'Does anyone else know about the research files?' asks Rachel.

Ray nods. 'Ninja Magpie threatened to release them. I was in the board-room, saw panic and desperation. That's what led them to pay the ransom. Forty million.'

Forty million. Rachel closes her eyes. Her pulse is loud in her ears. 'I've screwed up,' she says as if asking for pardon.

'How much did you get?' asks Ray.

She sighs. 'Thirty-five thousand.' She drops her head. 'Mostly to cover my debts.'

'Small change compared to the extortion payment.'

She wipes at her eyes, but tears keep coming. The room seems to tilt, and nausea rises within her. 'What happens now?'

Ray studies her for a long moment. She senses a change in his face. Something like compassion.

He exhales. 'I want you to self-report this.'

Rachel's head jerks up. 'What?'

'If I report you – as I should – you'll face the worst possible consequences,' he says, voice measured but firm. 'If you self-disclose and show remorse you'll have some mitigation. It's the best I can offer.'

She opens her mouth, but no words come.

Ray leans forward. 'Find a quiet room. Call the integrity hotline. Tell them everything, just as you've told me.'

Rachel sits at her desk, staring at her email inbox, which has now become meaningless. She's surrounded by the usual hubbub of chatter and keyboards tapping. She had meetings this afternoon, which she's cancelled. There's no point. She's finished in this job and this company.

Forty million pounds. The figure reverberates inside her head. They offered her a million for the rest of those files. She refused because she didn't trust them.

The man on the integrity hotline started off calm and professional. Maybe he thought it was a prank call. But she repeated the story and went into details few others knew. She could hear his breathing rate increase. He couldn't tell her what would happen next but he said he would escalate the matter immediately. So now she waits. She also wonders why Ray Dunlop did what he did. Was it out of sympathy or her open confession? But will it make any difference?

She is now expecting to be called in by HR. This could be a police matter. Hopefully, they will be discreet. She glances across the open-plan zone at her colleagues and friends she is going to miss. Will she find another job? How does she explain the absence of a reference from her employer of seven years?

Her mind keeps looping back to how well today had started. The injection. The first step towards the future she wanted. And now, everything is falling apart.

There's a commotion at the other side of the office. Raised voices. People shifting towards the windows, peering down at the street below. Something's going on outside. Maybe a demonstration or a protest. At least she hopes that's what it is.

Then she sees it. The double doors swing open and the first people she sees are the two uniformed building security men whom she knows by sight but not by name. Then a man and woman, smartly dressed. Behind them, two uniformed police officers. All of them stride towards her.

So much for the discreet exit. Everyone else is on their feet, looking around, perplexed. Only Rachel knows why they're here. She could run but doesn't stand a chance. Her chest tightens. Panic takes over. Her arms and legs tremble.

The man steps forward. 'Rachel Carter?'

She forces herself to stand, head bowed, voice barely a whisper. 'Yes.'

'Rachel Carter, we are arresting you on suspicion of offences under the Computer Misuse Act, specifically unauthorised access with intent to commit further offences and obtaining company secrets through illegal means. You do not have to say anything, but it may harm your defence if you do not mention, when questioned, something you later rely on in court. Anything you do say may be given in evidence. Do you understand?'

People stand, aghast. Lionel comes over, tries to intervene, but the uniformed female officer holds him back.

Rachel nods. There is nothing she can say. For the second time this week, she has caused the office to fall into sudden silence.

The other uniformed officer steps forward and grips her arm. There's a metallic click as handcuffs lock around her wrists. Tears flow down her face as they walk her through the office. Colleagues she's worked alongside for years look on, their eyes wide with shock; others have their hands pressed to their mouths in disbelief.

She keeps her head down as they march her into the lift. No one speaks. When they step out onto the ground floor, the first thing she sees is a marked police van with flashing blue lights, encircled by onlookers. She hears her name being called, but she ignores it.

The van door slams behind her with a thud that echoes through her chest. The sound feels final, like the end of everything. Through the narrow mesh window, she glimpses faces, her colleagues and others. Professional people in business attire, just like her.

As the van moves off, she feels her life collapsing inwards. How is she going to explain her actions to her mum and dad? Her friends, like Cathy. Then there's Adam. The steel of the cuffs bites into her skin. She thinks of her husband, Richard. He was at her side in the hospital, despite what she'd said to him the week before. She wishes he were here now.

Never in his long professional career has Ray felt so dumbfounded. He had imagined this investigation leading him to some shadowy hacker from Russia or North Korea, stealthily orchestrating a ruthless cyber-extortion campaign. Instead, it led him to Rachel. Out of her depth, unwittingly getting herself embroiled in corporate extortion. But she was just a pawn in a bigger game. The serious players have escaped. That's probably why she opened up so quickly, telling him everything, as if it were a relief to unload her burden. It felt more like a debrief with an ethical hacker who had just tested the company's cyber defences. He thinks back to when he first met her. When he interviewed her. He underestimated her technical talents. She was methodical, insightful and organised. She would have been great in his team. He shakes his head at the thought of his security systems being breached so easily.

Ray knows what's coming. Earlier, he received a call from the head of Integrity and Compliance, asking him to confirm Rachel confession. He was then asked to provide details on how he discovered Rachel was the one responsible. He provided a full and accurate account of receiving the laptop and their forensic analysis – one week after he received it. It felt like he was suddenly under investigation. Thirty minutes later, he watched Rachel being taken away. The whole office stopped to observe. People from other neighbouring companies looked on.

The lift doors slide open, and he strides towards the CEO's office. He raps his knuckles on the door and walks in without waiting for a response.

Catherine Davenport sits behind her desk, poised but visibly seething. Beside her is John Lucas – chief legal counsel, who seems to regard Ray with the weary detachment of a man who's done this a hundred times before.

'You sent for me,' says Ray. He remains standing.

Catherine fixes her gaze on him, like a sniper preparing to fire. She places both palms on the table. 'Words cannot express my *anger* strongly enough.'

Ray crosses his arms. 'Now you know how I've been feeling.'

Her shoulders tighten. 'You really don't know how to help yourself, Dunlop.'

Lucas leans forward and taps a printed document on the desk. *A prepared script*. Catherine exhales sharply before continuing.

'As chief information security officer,' she begins, 'your job is to ensure adequate controls are in place to protect this company. That includes reporting any material findings to me and the board *promptly*. You failed to do that. You sat on that laptop for a week, discovered last night who the insider was, then waited until today and calmly told her to self-report. She could've run. You've fucked up, Dunlop.'

He suspects the last bit was unscripted. *Now, here it comes.*

'I have no choice but to terminate your employment.'

He was ready for this. He draws breath. 'I've found you and your board members to be lacking in integrity. That includes issuing misleading statements to external regulators.' His tone is level, every word deliberate. 'Under these conditions, it has been impossible for me to fulfil my duties. And I'll make that argument to the employment tribunal.'

Catherine slams her palm against the desk. 'We took appropriate action based on the best information available.' Her eyes flick to the lawyer.

Ray stands tall. Defiant.

The lawyer clears his throat. 'Mr Dunlop, we recognise the breakdown in professional relationships. So, all things considered, we'd like to part company *amicably*. Therefore, we've prepared a settlement.' He slides a document across the desk. 'In return, we expect you to sign a non-disclosure agreement covering all board-level discussions related to this incident.'

Ray glances at the document, scanning quickly. Nine-months' salary. They want him gone – quietly. But he's not ready to give them that satisfaction. His instinct is to tell them to go to hell. He could walk into a top city law firm tomorrow, put his evidence on the table and they'd take his case on a no-win-no-fee deal. Davenport and her shady board would have their reputations shredded. Exhilaration rises the more he thinks of it.

'I'm not signing.'

Catherine leans back in her chair, arms crossed. 'We can terminate for cause. Negligence.'

Lucas interjects, 'You'll need a strong legal team if you intend to make any accusations against the company.'

'And you'll never work in this field again,' adds Catherine.

Ray's jaw tightens. He reminds himself that he's just about to become a man out-of-work. Before stepping off the edge, he wants to talk to Kirsty. She's always been his best council. What would she say? As he pauses, he hears her soft, sensible voice in his head.

He slides the paper back. 'Nine months isn't much time to find another job.'

Catherine and Lucas exchange a quick glance. She murmurs something, he nods, scribbles on the document and pushes it across again.

'Twelve months' severance,' says Lucas.

'This is beyond generous,' Catherine adds, her tone barely concealing her resentment.

Ray holds her gaze. 'Okay. I'll take it.'

Lucas hands him a pen. Ray signs the non-disclosure, then the second copy. His hand trembles slightly as he dates it. He folds his copy and slips it into his jacket pocket, then slides the second copy back across the desk.

'Can I say goodbye to my team?'

'We'd prefer if you didn't return to your office,' says Lucas. 'We'll handle your belongings.'

'We wish you well, Ray,' Catherine adds with obvious insincerity.

Neither of them offers a handshake. Not that he would have accepted it. He turns and walks out.

As the lift descends to the ground floor, emotions overwhelm him. It was so sudden. Ten years here and it ends like this. He steps out onto the ground floor, drops his employee pass in the bin and exits the building for the last time. He'll miss Aidan and Sydney. And his long-time friend Juliette from HR. He shoves his hands into his pockets, and his fingers close around a small, familiar shape. A USB drive. A full clone of Rachel's laptop hard drive. Everything's on there. He doesn't know what he's going to do with it, but something tells him it will come in useful sometime.

Part 2

26

Rachel lies on the surgical bed, legs in stirrups and trembling with anxiety. She's lucky to be here. The room hums with the quiet buzz of computers and the medical equipment that surrounds her. The air smells of antiseptic and scented hand gel. A loose-fitting gown and thin cotton blanket provide minimal warmth.

'Big day, Rachel. Are you ready?' says the anaesthetist, smiling warmly.

She laughs nervously. 'I've got everything crossed – except my legs, of course.'

The woman laughs, taps the back of Rachel's hand to find the vein. 'Just a small scratch,' she says.

The needle slides in. The anaesthetist tapes the plastic cannula down and loops the tubing gently over her wrist. Rachel hears her heartbeat and her stomach flutters. She's nervous. But she's here, on the launchpad. It's really happening.

Dr Lamb wheels a machine to her bedside and starts tapping icons on the touchscreen. The thin probe looks harmless. She scrolls something on the chart. Pre-flight checklist, Rachel imagines. The blood pressure cuff strapped to her arm inflates, compresses then slowly deflates, and the doctor notes the reading.

The anaesthetist returns. 'Okay, Rachel, just lie back and relax.'

Rachel starts the countdown: ten, nine... Her eyelids close, and she's gone.

She wakes to the same ceiling, the same clinical smell and tries to work out if she's still dreaming. She squints at the wall clock. She was only out for thirty minutes, but that was the most relaxing nap she's had in weeks. Her hand reaches for her belly, and the dull ache and inner tenderness tells her the procedure is complete – or something has been done. *How many?* That's all that matters to her right now.

The curtains swish open. Dr Lamb steps in, carrying an iPad.

'How are you feeling, Rachel?'

'I feel fine. What's the result?'

The doctor's smile falters. 'Everything went as planned,' she says. 'We successfully retrieved five eggs.'

Rachel stares. Her chest tightens and her heart sinks. *Five*. She had hoped for fifteen. Even ten would've been a win. But five? She feels like she's scratched a lottery card and come up empty. The tears build, but don't fall. Not yet.

The doctor softens her tone. 'It's a lower yield than we were hoping for, so I'd recommend a second round. Maybe after three months – give your ovaries chance to recover.'

Rachel doesn't answer. She's furious and wants to shout and swear and let everyone in the clinic know how angry she is. She clenches her fists and holds back, for now.

'There's tea and coffee in the recovery room. Your friends are waiting. If you're okay in an hour, you can head home,' says Dr Lamb.

Head home? *If only she could.* 'Thank you. I'll join them now.'

She gets dressed quickly, then emerges from behind the curtain. She takes the printout the doctor hands her – numbers and outcomes, dates and instructions. She folds it into four and stuffs it in the pocket of her jeans.

'If you decide to book a second round, we'll give you a discount,' the doctor adds as she holds the door open for her to leave. They shake hands. 'Hope to see you again, Rachel.'

She walks towards the recovery area. The two officers – a man and a woman in civilian clothes – are waiting for her. She takes the seat between them.

'Cup of tea?' Officer Woods asks, his voice softer than usual.

She nods. 'Thank you.'

They sip tea and watch the clock. At the hour mark, they make their way to the exit, stopping at the front desk as Officer Evans informs the receptionist they are ready to go. The receptionist glances at Rachel. Her eyes dart between the two officers and her brow creases faintly.

'Would you like to make a follow-up appointment?'

Rachel lowers her eyes. 'Not today.'

The receptionist hesitates before asking, 'Are you heading home now?'

'Yes,' Officer Evans replies, 'we're taking her home.'

The receptionist's smile is polite; confusion flickers across her face but she asks no further questions. She was much more conversational when Rachel was last here – talking about her diet and her personal trainer. There's no such chit-chat today. They've probably never had a prisoner in here before.

The three of them walk outside. The sky is overcast, the air damp and a light breeze chills her face and hands as they cross the short path to the car park.

Officer Evans slides into the back seat with Rachel, reaches into her coat pocket and pulls out the handcuffs. She nods and Rachel presents her wrist.

The cuff clicks shut. The other end fastens to the officer's wrist. Officer Woods sets the destination on the satnav, which calculates that it will take fifty-four minutes to return to the prison.

The electric car glides through suburban streets, then joins a slip road onto the motorway. Rachel breaks the silence.

'Thank you for your discretion back there,' says Rachel.

'You needed privacy,' Officer Evans says, 'and you behaved yourself.'

Rachel suspects they broke a few procedures by pretending to be her friends and not handcuffing her as they walked to and from the clinic.

'How long can the eggs remain frozen?' asks Officer Woods.

'I've pre-paid for three years.'

No response. They all know this could be pointless. She wonders if the two officers have children. They both wear wedding rings and are about her age.

She stares out the car window and thinks of her new 'home.' She's dreading visitors and doesn't think she can face her mum and dad. Tony will come, but will she even she Florence again? Adam will probably abandon her. Then there's Richard. He's the sort of person who would gloat with satisfaction that her life is a lot worse without him. It's true. Her life is a mess, and it's her own fault. And what has she done to her family? Her mum and dad were ashamed when Tony was in prison. What must they be going through now? But the most painful thought of all is the fact that she may never have children of her own. Her body shudders, her vision blurs, her free hand reaches her face, and the tears come in a flood. The two officers remain impassive.

The car pulls off the motorway and joins a town bypass. After a short drive, it curves into the prison entrance road. Rachel sits rigid, still hand-cuffed to Officer Evans. The car going over the speed bumps makes her nauseous. The jail is new, and if it weren't for the mesh panel fencing, topped with coils of barbed wire, it could be mistaken for a business park. Landscaped grass, paths and a few trees surround modern brick buildings. But nothing about this place is welcoming.

They follow the winding road and stop in front of a large impenetrable gate. Officer Woods announces his arrival on the intercom, and the gate slowly creaks open. He crawls forward into the holding spot, in front of a second gate. An officer does a security check of the car, then the second gate creaks open. He parks the car and the three of them walk through an entrance door, and into a reception area. The air smells stale. In the background, someone is speaking into a walkie-talkie. A male prison officer sits at the desk, separated by security glass. A bank of monitors behind him provides visuals of each of the halls, the images switching every ten seconds. She tries to pick out her area, but they all look the same and she can't recognise anyone in the video.

'Well, well, the privileged princess has returned,' says the seated officer.

'Checking in prisoner Carter,' says Officer Woods.

'Did you have a good jolly?' He makes a show of checking his watch. 'Four and a half hours, you've been gone. Stop off at the pub on the way back, did you?'

'Have you moved your arse of the chair today?' retorts Woods.

'Watching 200 prisoners.' He thumbs to the monitors behind him, then stares back at Rachel. 'If it were up to me, you wouldn't have stepped outside that door.'

Officer Evans leans into the glass partition and points. 'Listen, Denton, you're not the one who decides. So stop wasting time, and check the prisoner in.'

Denton smirks, turns to his computer and punches at the keyboard, using just one finger. It's painful to watch. Rachel can write faster than he types. He passes a logbook beneath the glass partition. Woods signs and dates it and shoves it back.

Denton points to a side door. 'Take her through there.'

Rachel looks at him. He smiles back malevolently.

'Body scan is all that's required,' says Evans as she points to the air-port-style X-ray scanner.

'Can you confirm you were with the prisoner for the entire time you were out?' Denton asks.

'She was having a medical procedure,' she shouts back at him.

He shakes his head. 'Level two search.'

They face off each other, but he won't budge. Evans leads Rachel into the side room. 'Spiteful prick,' she mutters. She removes the handcuffs and Rachel sits and waits. A box of single-use gloves sits on the table. She knows what's coming next.

A second female officer enters, and it begins. She stands, undresses, closes her eyes and follows each instruction as the officer completes the procedure with mechanical efficiency. Her thoughts are a haze of frustration and fatigue. *Just get on with it.*

When the search is done, she puts her prison clothes back on – cheap underwear, grey trousers and a navy sweatshirt. She stuffs her civilian clothes into a bag for storage. The next time she'll see them will be for her journey to court.

Evans returns, and leads her down the corridor, through two more locked doors and into the remand hall – her home, for however long it will be until her sentencing hearing. Three to six months. Maximum term, fourteen years, her solicitor had said. It's still sinking in and the more she thinks about it the angrier she becomes. She made a stupid mistake. The real criminals are Aleks and Izabela. Why aren't they in prison?

The wing echoes with women calling to one another across the hall. A radio plays somewhere – young-person's music screeching from behind a half-open door. The sharp odour of bleach hangs in the air from the freshly mopped floor. At one table, three women are playing Monopoly. They pause their game and glare at Rachel as she passes. Other prisoners emerge from their cells, watching silently. Two women, playing pool, stop their game. One of them stands, facing her, legs astride, holding her cue, staring at her. Taunting her. Looking for a fight.

'The posh bitch is back,' someone shouts.

Never in her life has she been called 'posh' or 'privileged'. It's a reminder that she's stepped into an unfamiliar sub-culture. One she doesn't belong in. But she has no choice and must adapt. She keeps her eyes forward and wonders how long they will hold their grudge against her. It started after she'd reported her hormone syringes stolen, leaving her with seven injections rather than the full course of twelve. That led to a full-scale search of every cell. Nothing turned up, but they found a batch of hooch in someone's locker, which was confiscated. And now she's become their object of hate.

Amanda – her cellmate meets her just outside their cell, arms wide.

'Darling,' she shouts, folding Rachel into a warm hug. 'How did it go?'

Rachel nods towards their cell, and they slip inside. Amanda turns and gives the pool-playing women the finger. Rachel's thankful to have one friend, at least. Amanda's of a similar age, tall, broad-shouldered – a gym regular – with shoulder length hair curled up at the ends. And she's loyal.

Before arriving at prison, she envisioned her cell to be cramped, with a concrete floor, graffitied brick walls and iron window bars. Instead, it's more like a room in her university hall of residence: magnolia-painted walls, bookshelves, a desk and chair, curtains and even a mirror. The pine effect furniture looks like it came straight from IKEA. She has to share, but they have their own toilet, shower and even a television. At university, she shared a bathroom with six people and couldn't afford a television licence.

Some people call their cells 'rooms'. Rachel can't. It's a cell. The door locks at 6 p.m. every night. The prison's comforts and facilities don't soften the punishing lock-up regime. University creates opportunities; prison removes them. She wonders if she will ever be employable again and if so, what type of job?

Her canteen delivery lies on the top bunk: sachets of cappuccino and Horlicks, cherry tomatoes, a carton of plums, Dove shampoo, Colgate mouthwash, Highland Spring sparkling water, writing paper, pen, stamps.

'I hope you don't mind, love, I had one of your cappuccinos. They're delish,' says Amanda.

Yes, Rachel minds. That box of eight are to last the week – her little luxury. She's all for sharing, but Amanda seems to have spent her earnings on skincare, makeup and mascara. Her only food contribution is a packet of Oreos, and they're already half gone. She lets it go.

Amanda settles onto her bed. 'Tell me all about it, darling.'

Rachel walks her through the day – the clinic, the relaxing nap, the news of only five eggs. And now she is in a panic because she might not get out in time to use the eggs or have children. Amanda listens, interrupting occasionally her with usual affirmations: 'Everything happens for a reason, love – even if you can't see it.' Amanda is intelligent – an accountant. She's facing embezzlement charges she insists weren't her fault. Superstitions, mantras and signs from the universe guide her life path. She believes in fate the way others devoutly follow their religion.

'Would you like a reading?' Amanda asks, her tone enthusiastic but oddly serious.

Rachel imagines her for a moment in long velvet robes, like a well-meaning vicar, about to deliver some cosmic sermon. Amanda reaches for the drawer and pulls out an oversized tarot deck.

Rachel shakes her head and smiles. 'No thanks. I just need to try and make peace with my predicament.'

But Amanda's already clearing the desk, sweeping aside her clutter of lipstick, half-used mascara tubes and glossy magazine scraps. She places a small blue crystal in the centre, like it's sacred, then shuffles the deck.

'Sit,' she says, gesturing to the chair.

Rachel sighs. It will fill the gap until dinner.

Amanda fans the cards out across the desk. 'What would you like to ask of the cards?' Her voice has shifted – lower now, deliberate.

There is only one question that claws at her thoughts, night after night.

'How long will I be in prison?'

Amanda closes her eyes, recites a mantra Rachel doesn't understand, and glides her hands over the cards. She taps them.

'Pick three.'

Rachel chooses. Amanda slides out the three cards, explaining that these represent her past, present and future. She turns over the first and second cards and makes exaggerated facial expressions as she explains the meaning of each. *The Tower* – lightning strike, flames and two figures falling represents upheaval and the breaking down of the old foundations of life. The second card is of *The Hanged Man*, gracefully suspended upside down from a tree representing powerlessness and gaining new insights.

Amanda doesn't turn over the third card. Instead, she selects three more and adds a second row below the first, flipping them in turn. Her brow furrows with focus and her mouth moves silently as she considers their meanings. It's an elaborate ritual and Rachel's attention drifts. She's thinking about the upcoming visit from her solicitor and how she is going to string together a convincing defence – mitigating circumstances, cooperation with the police. The story she'll have to tell about Aleks and Izabela being the masterminds and how she was just used by them. That is what she should focus on, not this mystical twaddle.

Amanda flips the final card – a woman, sitting on a throne, sword in one hand and scales in the other. *The Justice* card.

Amanda's mouth opens, then closes without an utterance.

Rachel stifles a laugh. 'And this means?'

Amanda meets her gaze. 'The truth will come out.' She taps the card gently. 'And there will be consequences.' Her tone quietens. 'This is your karma, Rachel.'

Rachel breathes in. 'Something more uplifting would have been nice.'

Amanda reaches for her hand and squeezes it. 'The cards don't lie. But they're not final either.' She leans in towards Rachel. 'They tap into your energy and show you what's beneath the surface.'

Her tone is serious enough to cause Rachel to wonder what justice would look like.

Amanda gathers up her cards, carefully shuffles them and puts them back in their box with the crystal. They make their way to the dining hall and insert themselves amongst four women in their twenties who sneer. Rachel wonders if it was one of them who stole her injections. If not, they probably know who.

The tension eases when Amanda shares gossip about a male officer, who has recently separated from his wife. 'He's probably desperate for sex,' she says. The women smile. They'll probably work out a ploy to entrap and corrupt him before they even get back to their cells for the night. Amanda always seems well-informed on the goings-on in the prison. She chats to everyone and anyone and probably pieces together enough nuggets of information to concoct a rumour juicy enough to share. Rachel imagines her to be a social media conspiracy theorist on the outside.

A jug of over-diluted squash sits in the middle of the table. They pour some into their plastic cups. The younger women down theirs then refill. Kitchen workers hand out mess trays loaded with cottage pie, overcooked broccoli and a dollop of rice pudding. Rachel makes this at home, always using fresh ingredients, and she can stretch it out for three or four days. What she has in front of her is a sad excuse for a simple dinner – over-creamed potatoes and too much gravy, forming an unappetising mush. It may not be the worst food she's ever tasted, but it's not far off.

In the ten days she has been here, Rachel has learned much about prison life. Accumulating debt is easy as drugs and alcohol are often available, for a price. Prison work pays little, but today is canteen day and the conversations revolve around who owes what to whom, resulting in trading and repayment. The girls mention that Tanya – one of their gang – got into an argument, which escalated into a fistfight and she is now in the segregation wing for the next four days. Rachel's spoken to her before. She's distraught over being separated from her six-month-old baby. She seemed friendly when they chatted. Then again, she's inside for assault.

Back in the cell, Rachel lies on the top bunk staring at the ceiling. Amanda watches *Married at First Sight – Australia* while swinging her legs off the side of the bed and laughing like a defiant teenager staying up late on a school night. The locked door will confine them to their cell until morning. Then, someone will start kicking at their door, someone else will thump with their fists, then the shouting will start: 'When are we getting out?' It's like an alarm clock without a snooze button.

She closes her eyes, attempting sleep, but that damn tarot card comes back into her mind. *The Justice* card. She can't unsee it. Then Amanda's warning: *and there will be consequences*. But that should apply for everyone. Yes, she did wrong – cracked passwords, stole sensitive documents. But she didn't extort forty million from the company. She tried to stop it, and they attacked her. She owned up to everything, is cooperating with the police and hasn't put a foot wrong inside. That must count for something. Her solicitor said the maximum sentence for her crime is fourteen years. That's not justice. Not in the tarot world and not in the real world. But Amanda's words still haunt her:

The truth will come out.

She buries her head in her pillow. The tears are unstoppable as the thought of multiple years in here weigh down on her.

27

This is not Ray's usual choice of pub. The laughter's too loud. Gaming machines flash and jingle in the corner. A group of students in costume, sprawled across the bar, line up shots for some drinking game. He hates it. But a deal's a deal. The last Thursday of every month, he, Aidan and Sydney will meet for drinks, taking turns choosing the pub. Tonight is Aidan's pick – Wetherspoons, another unsympathetic conversion of a historic building, once a bank.

At the bar, the barman sets down three pints. Aidan flashes his watch at the payment machine, and they make their way up the grand staircase to the balcony.

'Cheers,' they say in unison, clinking glasses.

Aidan nods towards Ray's pint of hazy golden ale. 'Verdict?'

Ray sips, nods his head. 'Better than expected.'

'How low were your expectations?' says Sydney with a grin.

Ray laughs, but there's a lump in his throat. He's more emotional than he expected to be. It's been a month since his unceremonious exit from the company and he's finding it difficult to adjust. His job gave him routine, responsibility and intellectual challenge. Even the confrontations were energising. That's gone. He feels he's lost his sense of purpose and struggles to get out of bed in the morning. Kirsty's days are always full: teaching

Pilates, coffee mornings, book group or taking the neighbour's dog for a walk. But he feels like a dog without a ball to fetch – restless and bored. Tonight is a welcome reprieve. Something to look forward to in a week that was otherwise shapeless.

Aidan and Sydney bring Ray up to speed with company goings-on. The big news is the announcement of a proposed takeover by one of the big pharma companies, a multi-national, ten times the size of Synaptonica. News of the acquisition has doubled the share price, and the internal communications machine has gone into overdrive with staff briefings and newsletters, explaining the exciting transition the company is about to go through. But there's an undercurrent of trepidation amongst the staff. Rumours of office closures, staff being relocated to Cambridge or Manchester. They sound more disillusioned than ever, not helped by the fact the reward Catherine Davenport promised them for working round-the-clock during the crisis never materialised.

Ray could have warned them a takeover was coming, but he stayed silent, bound by the non-disclosure agreement. When the news broke, he felt a surge of anger as he pictured the board members celebrating their success and congratulating each other. All of them calculating the value of their share-options and bonuses.

A takeover was always inevitable. Companies like Synaptonica need the resources of a big pharma backer to push their drug into phase three trials. What stings is the way it had been done. Winstanley, Chester and Bristol – opportunists, all of them. Carpet-baggers who treated the company as a means for personal enrichment. They'll move on, leaving behind a toxic legacy.

He tells himself it shouldn't matter now. He's out and needs to move on. But somehow, they still get under his skin. Deeply held resentments he can't let go.

He thinks about the people left behind. Loyal staff who've worked there for years, now facing redundancy. Aidan and Sydney will be okay. They're smart and have in-demand skills. But it will be more of a wrench for others, and he makes a mental note to call his friend, Juliette.

The conversation drifts, as it always does, to cyber talk and they are back recounting the events of the double-extortion cyber-attack. It's a war story that puts them in the cyber defender's hall of fame. Then, the twist they never saw coming: Rachel.

'Looks like she's taking the rap, all on her own,' says Aidan, finishing his pint.

Ray nods. 'She gained the least and lost the most.'

'But why?' Sydney frowns. 'If it was just greed, then she could have leaked all the documents, taken the money and vanished.'

Ray pictures Rachel again, sitting in his office. Shaking. Bruised. The way her composure cracked when he mentioned the forty-million-pound ransom. He shrugs. 'I still can't fathom it out. She was clever, but something broke inside her and it all came pouring out.'

They order more drinks at the bar and settle back into their seats. A silence settles between them. Not awkward, just reflective. Ray senses they have something they want to say. He sips his beer and lets it linger.

'How's your new boss?' he says, eventually.

Aidan shrugs. 'Chris. External hire. He's a nice guy.'

'But we miss the morning huddle with you,' says Sydney with a laugh.

Ray smiles. That means more than he lets on. The sparring, the banter, the rituals. Everything he misses from the life he used to have.

Sydney leans forward, eyes gleaming. 'We've discovered something interesting.'

Ah, here it comes.

'Remember the backlog of incident reports?' she says.

Ray nods. 'I was working through those before I was... you know.'

'Chris asked us to review all of them and close them off. He said it would improve our key performance indicators. Most are non-events, but there's one we'd like your thoughts on,' says Aidan.

Sydney pulls out a folded A4 sheet from her jacket pocket and hands it to him. 'This one dates back to before the cyber-attack. Buried amongst the trivia.'

Subject: Suspected Research Misconduct

Dear Cyber Security Team,

I would like to report a suspected case of malpractice in the clinical research department. Specifically, falsification of clinical trial results, resulting in a flawed statistical analysis.

Inconsistencies and anomalies have emerged in a recent trial that suggests tampering of test result data. I do not have access to the source files because of data protection protocols, so I cannot provide direct evidence. However, as a clinical scientist with almost thirty years' experience, I recognise anomalous results when I see them.

I initially reported this through the official integrity channel, but the case was closed as unsubstantiated. It is my belief that the investigation failed to apply due diligence in examining data lineage. I am therefore contacting you directly as I believe it needs a technically qualified team to investigate.

Yours sincerely,

James Craig, Ph.D. Senior Clinical Scientist.

Ray's eyes lock on the name. 'He's one of the staff whose password got hacked... and the only one who ended up getting sacked.'

They both nod.

'Correct. Even now, with the truth out in the open, he's not been reinstated,' says Aidan.

Ray's pulse ticks up. 'Are you investigating?'

'We started, but were told to stop,' says Sydney.

Ray's gaze sharpens. 'Told by whom?'

'Winstanley,' says Aidan. 'He told Chris not to waste any time on it.'

Ray takes a slow sip of his beer. A clinical trial is a critical milestone for a new drug. A positive outcome will see it progress to the next stage, increasing the chances of an eventual market launch, which would be a licence to print money. If it fails on clinical trials, then that's several years' research wasted. That's just the nature of their industry. Some you win, some you lose. Tampering of trial results is a serious accusation, but what's needling him is the mention of Winstanley's name. His old nemesis. Always meddling in matters he doesn't understand. Suppressing an allegation of research fraud takes deceit to a new level, but he has nothing to do with clinical research. Why would he be interested? Then he thinks back to the boardroom and the side-chats between Winstanley, Bristol and Chester. Huddled together. Close. Too close.

'I would never have dropped this without a proper investigation,' says Ray.

'We tried,' says Sydney, 'we even followed up with someone on the integrity team, but they said the investigation found no violation of protocols.'

'The integrity team don't have access to clinical data. They need to come to us for that. Which means they didn't really investigate,' says Aidan.

They glance at each other, unsettled, probably because they know they have crossed a line by sharing this. Ray knows he should just hand back the sheet of paper and forget about this conversation. But he is suddenly back in his old job, sitting at the briefing table in the cyber ops room: the three of them, theorising and challenging each other. The adrenalin is flowing again. He smelt a rat when he learned they had sacked James Craig. *Leave no stone unturned*, was what he used to say. He feels proud to have been their manager and had this influence. He wishes he was back.

Aidan folds his arms. 'The whole thing just doesn't sit right with us, and Chris is new, so he doesn't question his boss.'

Sydney finishes her drink and gives him a look. 'We've probably shared more than we ought to have done.'

Ray smirks. He considers telling them about the USB drive he has back home – the clone of Rachel's hard drive – but decides against it. He'll take it from here. He folds the sheet of paper and slips it into his inside jacket pocket. He drains his pint and sets it down. 'Sometimes, after a few drinks, I wake up the next day with a few memory gaps and can't remember a damned thing about the previous night.'

They order one more round and continue reminiscing. When it's time to say goodnight, they hug, fist bump and promise to meet again next month. Ray nods and says 'thank you' to the barman on the way out. It's not actually that bad in here.

Ray slumps into a window seat in a half-empty first-class carriage. He closes his eyes, but his mind is wide awake. Is it conceivable that some large-scale fraud is going on? Protocols and controls are in place.

He pulls out his phone and makes a call.

'Hello, Ray,' says Juliette. 'Long time no speak. What's the occasion?'

'Nothing special, just thought I'd call for a chinwag.'

She laughs. 'Are you pissed?'

'Just returning from a night out with the old team.'

The two of them slip into easy conversation, as close friends do. She asks about his job hunting and mentions the mood inside the company is low as people fear they may lose their jobs.

The train slows and Ray glances out the window.

'Listen, my station is coming up. Could I ask a favour?'

She laughs. 'I knew you weren't calling just for a chinwag.'

'Guilty as charged. It's about James Craig, the sacked scientist. He raised an integrity case, which was closed down. Could you check that out for me and give me some background on why it was closed?'

She sighs. 'Of course I can't. You don't work here anymore.'

Exactly what he expected. 'I know, but if you can just tell me it was a full and proper investigation, then I'll drop it.'

'Why do you want to know?'

'Like me, he got forced out and something smells off.'

The train glides into the station. Ray stands, balancing with one hand on the overhead rail.

Another pause. 'Okay,' Juliette answers. 'I'll have a look. But if there's anything untoward, then I'll deal with it. Not you.'

They say goodnight and promise to meet up soon, with their respective spouses.

28

Ray sits in his home office staring at his laptop screen. He skims through his inbox. No interview requests or job leads today – just the usual subscription special offers and spam. He glances at the paper copy of James Craig's email that Sydney handed to him last night. This interests him more than anything else. He opens up a spreadsheet, then picks up his phone and makes a call, which is answered promptly.

'Jim Craig speaking.' A soft Scottish accent. Good start.

'Jim, my name is Ray Dunlop. I was the chief information security officer at Synaptonica. How are you?'

There's a slight pause. 'I know who you are,' he says coldly.

'I'll get straight to the point, Jim. I know they forced you out, unfairly. The same thing happened to me. We all know you didn't leak those files because we found out who did. I think we can help each other.'

'Why are you interested if you don't work there anymore?'

Ray sighs. 'Unfinished business. If there's fraud, I want the satisfaction of discovering it.'

He snorts. 'Why should I help you?'

Ray grimaces. This is tougher than he expected. He needs to build rapport, which doesn't come naturally to him. He describes the details of the breach, the password hack, the download, the look of fear on the faces of the board members, the misleading communications and his own dismissal. Then how his old team were told to drop it when they tried to investigate.

'Listen, Dunlop. I've been a clinical scientist for thirty years. Longer than Sean Bristol and almost everyone else working there. I was on my way out because I was asking awkward questions. Do you know what it's like to work for someone who doesn't understand the job you do and has no sense of professional integrity?'

Yes, I know exactly what that feels like.

'Jim, I have a list of the files that the cyber criminals claimed to have. I saw panic on the faces of the board. Over 200 research files were on that list. Is it possible they contain evidence of data tampering?' asks Ray.

'Tell me what the files are, and I'll let you know.'

Ray reads from the spreadsheet he has on screen, the one they generated from the event logs. They include daily test results from the clinical investigator, data preparation files for statistical analysis and statistical summaries. Jim is silent. Ray pauses.

'Do you have copies of those files?' asks Jim.

Ray grips his phone tighter. 'Could these files contain evidence of fraud – data tampering?'

'Some of those are from the latest phase two study, so potentially, yes. Now, answer my question. Do you have them?' says Jim.

Ray pauses. 'I think I can get them.'

Another pause. 'Well, if you get them, call me back. Otherwise, I don't want to hear from you again.'

They say their curt goodbyes. Ray reclines in his chair, pleased he's taken this first step. Jim Craig is obstinate and would be difficult to work with, but his tone shifted when Ray listed those files. But he hasn't got them. That has to be his next step.

Ray reaches into his desk drawer and retrieves his backup laptop, the one he has on standby in case his primary one dies. He powers it up and changes the BIOS settings so when it next starts up, it will boot-up directly from the USB drive rather than the internal hard drive. From his top drawer, he withdraws an unmarked and sealed brown envelope. He opens it and retrieves a USB stick. He looks at it and smiles for a moment. He knew this would come in useful.

He restarts the laptop; it boots from the USB drive and the restore process begins. This will take time.

One hour passes, and the restore is complete. He has just recreated Rachel Carter's laptop and can see her email, browser history, favourites. Everything. Nothing unusual stands out. He remembers the encrypted folder and browses file explorer until he finds it – the folder named *Shopping*, with its distinctive padlock icon and Zip file extension.

This is where the files are. The folder the company paid forty million pounds to protect. But he's staring at a locked safe. It's impenetrable and only one person knows the password.

Ray and Kirsty sit opposite each other in the living room, each with their legs stretched out in their own sofa. A bottle of red wine sits on the side, which they will finish between them tonight, as they do every Friday evening. Some comedy panel show, which they're only half watching, plays quietly on television. Their early chat had been light. Kirsty taught two Pilates classes, caught up with friends for a late lunch, then did a bit of shopping. Ray mentioned a job he applied for and vaguely alluded to a personal project he was working on. They have fallen into their laid-back Friday-night rhythm. Relaxed contentment.

Ray's phone rings. Unusual for a Friday evening. He frowns at the screen as he sees who's calling.

He hesitates and answers. 'Hi, Juliette. How are you?'

Kirsty shoots him a look.

Juliette launches right in. 'I looked into that case you mentioned, the one submitted by James Craig.'

Ray glances across the room as Kirsty picks up the television remote and turns down the volume. She's alert to his conversation.

'And what did you discover?'

'This is a specialist area, and the original investigator didn't have the right expertise, so it got passed up the chain to Sean Bristol. He looked into it and reported back that all protocols were being followed and there was no sign of any data tampering. So the case was closed. Jim Craig had a reputation for confrontation and stirring up trouble.'

Ray exhales. 'Okay. Are there any specifics on how Bristol investigated the claims?'

'Ray, he's the head of R&D. Are you seriously suggesting he would be complicit in fraud?'

Ray's voice softens. 'No. That would be a stretch. But thanks for checking.'

He tries to say goodbye, but Juliette sighs, then launches into a conversation about her day: one person off sick and another just left; she's juggling the work of three people and will likely have to work over the weekend. Ray nods along, making appropriate noises. He enjoys chatting to Juliette, but it's uncomfortable with Kirsty watching and listening.

After ten minutes, he finds a lull, wishes Juliette a good weekend and ends the call.

Kirsty looks at him, raising her eyebrows.

'That was Juliette, from work,' he says.

'I worked that one out. And I think you mean your *old* work.'

Ray gets to his feet, picks up the wine bottle and tops up both of their glasses. 'I asked her to check something out for me. A historic incident I'm looking into. Potential fraud, which could be big.'

'And why is that your problem?'

Ray exhales and tells Kirsty about the conversation with Aidan and Sydney last night, and the conversation with Jim Craig this morning and how he has an urge to scratch beneath the surface, because if the allegations are true, it would be a major scandal. It's the right thing to do.

'Then hand it off to someone else.'

Ray takes a sip of wine and nods. 'I just need to dig a bit more.'

Kirsty places her wine glass on the side table and leans towards him. 'And why do you need to talk to Juliette about that?'

Ray quickly shakes his head. 'I don't anymore. I've got everything I need now.'

'Good.'

Kirsty turns the volume back up on the television and the sound of comical laughter fills the room again, but Ray's focus is elsewhere. Jim Craig could just be an obsessive, disgruntled employee looking to stir up trouble for his old company. His accusation seems far-fetched. Even if it were true, the truth would come out eventually, wouldn't it? Wouldn't the company who are planning to buy Synaptonica verify the trial results as part of their due diligence? And what about Sean Bristol? He doesn't know him well enough, not in the way he knows Winstanley and how he operates. His mind ticks through possibilities. He needs to get to the bottom of this.

He glances towards Kirsty, browsing her phone. She wants him to focus on job hunting.

29

Rachel sits on a hard plastic seat, hands splayed across the laminate table in what looks like a converted storeroom – four blank walls, grey laminate flooring and a faint buzz of strip lighting overhead. She has a cup of watery vending-machine tea by her side. It's barely drinkable, but it's warm, and she clings to that. Officer Denton is loitering outside, sneering through a small door window, like a visitor to the zoo.

Her heart sank when she first saw the man sitting opposite – Matthew McLeod, her new lawyer. He's young. She thinks of the graduates she used to hire for the service desk – ambitious and over-confident. They would learn on the job then move on to something more interesting within a year. Is he remotely interested in her or is she just a fleeting case to help his learning curve? How much can he practically do to help her? She thinks about asking for a different lawyer – someone more experienced? A woman. The trouble is, she's no money to pay.

Matthew positions his iPad carefully at an angle beside a leather notebook. The suit he's wearing looks new and he's styled his blond hair and splashed on aftershave. He flips open a blank page.

'Okay, Rachel,' he says brightly. 'What I want to do today is start building your defence.'

Rachel nods. 'Do you think there's a chance of avoiding a prison sentence?'

He smiles sympathetically. 'You are facing some big accusations, but we can create a narrative based on mitigating factors and cooperation. Let's start with that.'

She lets out an exasperated sigh. 'Mitigation and cooperation. I've got lots of that.'

He leans his hand across the table. 'Trust me, I'm on your side.'

He reminds her of an old boyfriend, back at uni. He too had a cocksure way about him. That didn't end well.

Matthew smiles. 'First, I need to outline the charges that are being brought against you.'

He scrolls his iPad screen and reads in a calm and precise tone, using long sentences and legalistic speech, explaining that the charge falls under sections 1 and 2 of the Computer Misuse Act: unauthorised access to computer material and access with intent to commit further offences. Also, the theft of confidential research material from a pharmaceutical company.

'The *maximum* sentence would be fourteen years.' He stabs his index finger onto his open notepad. 'My job is to reduce that. And, if our mitigation is strong enough, argue against a custodial sentence.'

A shudder passes through her, sharp and fast. Fourteen years. The words pound in her skull like the drumbeat of doom. In fourteen years, she'll be fifty-two. Too late for everything she's ever wanted. She drops her head. She can't imagine surviving that long in here. She just wants to curl up in the corner and cry and hope someone – anyone – can get her out of this mess.

Matthew runs his hands through his hair and continues. 'The sentence can vary depending on circumstances and magnitude of harm.' He leans in, his tone shifting. 'You made an early guilty plea. That *could* reduce your sentence by up to one third.'

She takes a deep breath. 'Nine years is still a long stretch.'

He picks up his pen and smiles. 'Let's build on what we have,' he says.

He lays it out: she did not know of the planned cyber-attack. She stopped cooperating with the criminals and refused to send them any further documents, even though they offered her a seven-figure bribe. The assault, which landed her in hospital, was her punishment. The circumstances clearly show her to be outside the inner circle of the cyber gang. In fact, no more than a pawn in their sophisticated crime. A victim, even.

Rachel nods. Yes, that is all true. She'd made a mistake and tried to make amends. But she imagines the prosecution argument: she only confessed in the face of irrefutable evidence, and she still spent the money she received from the gang. Not exactly remorseful.

'They're claiming material loss – several years of research compromised.' He scrolls his iPad again. 'Since then, a multi-national pharma company has made a takeover bid, with an offer at a premium to their market capitalisation,' he says, smiling at his insightful discovery.

Rachel tilts her head. 'So, they're lying about material loss?'

'That's what we will argue. If we can undermine their damage claim, their credibility wobbles.'

She nods. 'What about the ransom payment? Ray Dunlop told me forty million.'

'They've said nothing about that,' says Matthew. He pauses. Thinking. 'That can work two ways: you only received thirty-five thousand – a fraction of the supposed ransom, which also proves you weren't really part of the big plan. But if the ransom payment were to be raised, it would add weight to their claim of material loss.'

Rachel nods. 'We should keep quiet then?'

He raises his eyebrows, furrowing his brow as he considers her question. She suspects the crypto currency angle is confusing him. 'Let's not decide just yet.' He scribbles in his notebook.

Despite his inexperience, Rachel's warming to Matthew. He has at least read the files and done the groundwork, unlike her first solicitor who'd barely skimmed the summary. But she needs realistic expectations. She leans forward, staring into his eyes. 'Can you tell me realistically, how strong is my defence against the prosecution's case?'

He pauses. The smile fades. He puts his pen down, holds out his palms and moves them like balancing scales. 'Two to five years.'

She closes her eyes. In five years, she'll be forty-three. Late in life to get pregnant, even if she skips the finding a partner part and goes it alone as a singleton. Two years would be a painful penance, but that's more doable.

Matthew continues, as if running through a pre-prepared monologue. 'There is a lot being done to track the masterminds of this attack – the people you know as Aleks and Izabela.' He glances at his iPad. 'The National Crime Agency and cyber experts from a company called... CrowdStrike. This seems to be Ninja Magpie's biggest hit yet. If you can provide intelligence that leads to their arrest – even one of them – we can broker a deal, possibly avoiding a custodial sentence altogether.'

She presses the heel of her hand to her forehead, hard, willing something else would surface. She recalls every single meeting: Victoria Park Plaza, the British Museum, the Telegram chat history. She spent four weeks working with Izabela. Yet still no names, no traceable data. It's as if they are hallucinations. She thinks hard. The night of the attack – the man with the spider-web tattoo on his neck. Can that help? If she can join some dots, evoke a memory, it could save her from this godforsaken place. But she has nothing else. A chill ripples through her body as she pictures herself being guided into the prison van, in handcuffs. Tears form in her eyes. She raises her hands to her face but can't stop herself from crying.

Matthew looks towards the door, his mouth hanging open. Officer Denton is still watching, still smiling. Rachel waves her hand at Matthew. 'I'm okay,' she mumbles. The last thing she wants is Denton's gormless face gloating at her distress. She wipes her eyes with her sleeve, and her breathing steadies.

Matthew goes back to scribbling notes and talks her through the next steps: she should hear soon about the date for her court hearing. No trial, as she has pleaded guilty. Just a sentencing hearing. He'll continue reviewing the prosecution's case and will gather material to support mitigation. He promises to return within the next two weeks. He closes his notebook and folds his iPad. He stands, offering his hand.

Rachel hesitates as she thinks about something Amanda suggested. 'If I change my plea to not guilty, how would that change things?'

Matthew's expression falters. He sinks back into his chair.

'Could you build a defence for that?' Rachel asks.

He crosses his arms and tilts his head towards the ceiling. He clearly wasn't expecting that one.

'That would be a fundamental change in strategy. We'd need to prepare a full trial defence. That means identifying and disclosing all relevant evidence. If the case was based on coercion or duress, we would have to establish that you were under genuine threat. It would also delay proceedings. That's a big decision.'

She studies him, then nods. 'You will still defend me, won't you?'

'Of course, I'd...' He hesitates. 'I'd need to discuss it with my senior, and we'd have to apply to the court to vacate your guilty plea. But I'll stay with you, whatever your decision.'

They shake hands and Rachel watches him go, a flicker of something stirring in her chest. Not hope exactly, but something.

Officer Denton, smiling, steps inside and instructs her to accompany him back to the wing.

Rachel strolls back to her cell, with anger rising within her as she thinks about smooth-talking Aleks and conniving Izabela. They should be in prison too. For this, and every one of their premeditated cybercrimes. They take their reward; she takes the jail time. The dreaded words of a judge saying, 'take her down' reverberate inside her head as the possibility of a multi-year imprisonment nightmare becomes more real every day.

She arrives back at her cell and lets the door clank shut behind her. The air is thick with lavender oil, which probably means Amanda's been performing some ritual. On the desk is a dog-eared paperback book, its curled corners and cracked spine evidence of near-religious use. A loose piece of paper lies beneath it, scribbled with symbols and numbers.

'How was your solicitor?' Amanda asks brightly, not moving from her lying-down position.

Rachel doesn't answer. She just climbs straight onto the top bunk, her jaw tight, throat full. Rage is simmering beneath the surface. She wants to scream at her cellmate for taking her notepaper, drinking her coffee, crowding the table with her makeup and perfume bottles, staying up late to watch trash TV, and talking about dumb stuff all the time. But she holds back, throws herself down and buries her face in the pillow instead.

'I'm here for you, babe,' says Amanda, softer now.

Rachel keeps her eyes shut. 'He said... with mitigation, it should be a reduced sentence.' Her voice cracks. 'But that could still mean five years, maybe more.'

Amanda gasps. 'Bloody hell, babe, anyone would think you'd hacked the Bank of England.'

'He said my best chance of avoiding prison is if I can help track down the cyber gang members. But I've given them everything. I don't know what to do next.'

Amanda swings her legs out of the bed and stands. 'What's your solicitor like?'

'His name's Matthew McLeod. He's young. I bet this is his first proper case. But I like him. He actually gives a shit.'

Amanda's eyes gleam. 'Fit and good-looking?'

Rachel lets out a short, tired laugh. 'He's fresh-faced and not long out of uni.'

Amanda grins. 'Would you still shag him?'

Rachel shoots her a look. 'I want him to get me out of prison.'

'Just asking.'

Rachel lies side on to face her cell mate. 'I haven't thought about sex since the day I arrived.'

'You will,' Amanda says, 'eventually.'

Rachel closes her eyes. Amanda's world seems built on distraction, superstition and flirtation. She wonders if she's just disguising some inner pain. Being here means she's separated from her young son, Gabe. She has his picture on the wall, next to her bed; he's smiling and looks so happy. Amanda must be such a fun mum to have.

Maybe Rachel needs a distraction. Something to elevate her to the plane that Amanda floats on. Her eyes drift to the desk and the book: *Napoleon's Book of Fate,* and the sheet of paper with scribblings on it.

'What's the book?' asks Rachel.

'This is the *Book of Fate.*' She stabs her finger at its cover. 'It's an oracle. Gives answers about the future. Napoleon Bonapart relied on it to make important decisions and used it before going into battle.'

Rachel laughs. 'What happened at Waterloo? Did he misread it?'

Amanda's face drops. 'It's fate, Rachel.' She throws her hands out as if trying to explain something obvious. 'Some outcomes you just can't change.'

'Of course,' Rachel says solemnly. 'So, how does it work?'

Amanda picks up the book, flipping it open and launching into what sounds like a well-practised explanation: draw four rows of symbols, calculate a pattern, choose a question, align it the table and decode the final answer from a letter system. Rachel loses track after the first step. It sounds like numerology with extra steps, and no more scientific than astrology. She resists the urge to mock it any further.

'Can I ask a question of my own?' asks Rachel.

Amanda shakes her head. 'You have to pick one from the list.' She flips to the page and holds it up.

Rachel scans the list of questions:

Shall I gain or lose in my cause? Does the person love and regard me? Will I have a son or daughter?

Yes, she can see how Amanda would be taken in by that tatty paperback, which probably belongs in some bazaar.

'Shall I give it a go?' says Rachel.

Amanda narrows her eyes. 'You don't take this seriously.'

'Sorry, I don't mean to laugh. I just… need a bit more convincing.'

Amanda sits. 'Let me tell you about the last time I used this book for a big day.'

Amanda tells Rachel about the day she was due to accompany her CEO to an investor meeting. Her job was to present the company finances and try to land a two-million-pound investment. That morning, she consulted the book, and picked the question:

Shall I have success in my undertakings?

The book's answer: *This day will end in disappointment and disaster.*

'And?' Rachel prompts.

'It was true. I left the house in my best clobber, got to the office. Then, within thirty minutes, I caught my jacket pocket on the arm of my chair and ripped it – cost me 300 quid.'

Rachel tries not to laugh. 'Oh dear, that was a disaster.'

'No, it wasn't.' Her head drops. 'Later that day, the police came to the office and arrested me. That's why I'm here.'

Rachel's smile fades. 'I'm sorry.'

Later, they both head for the dining hall and find their usual spot among the younger women. Tanya is there, just released from segregation and buzzing about seeing her baby boy tomorrow in the mother and baby unit – a three-hour bonding visit. She swears she'll keep out of trouble – no more scraps.

Amanda, true to form, starts entertaining the table with talk of Rachel's 'fit solicitor,' and how Rachel's 'gagging for it.' A small cheer rings out. They bang trays on the table and tease Rachel about how to give him a hand job under the table without Officer Denton noticing.

Amanda is holding court, as usual. Rachel's mood has lightened, and she is going along with the hilarity. Despite everything, she doesn't dislike Amanda. In fact, she needs this – the noise, the laughter the sense of fun. It helps to drown out the silence of despair.

Back in their cell, the television is off and the mood is quieter. She and Amanda sit together at the desk, which is clear for once. Amanda opens that prophetic book – *Napoleon's Book of Fate*. Rachel takes a sheet of notepaper and follows Amanda's instructions: she draws the rows of symbols, reducing them down to a pattern:

x

xx

xx

x

Amanda nods with approval. 'Now pick your question.'

Rachel scans a list of thirty-two oracular questions. Her chest tightens as she chooses:

Will the prisoner be released?

She then traces a trembling finger across the table to find the corresponding letter: **K**. Then flips to the back of the book to find the matching answer.

The prisoner will be released.

She smiles. At least that's a happier outcome than that awful tarot card the other week. She doesn't believe in any of this, but that book seemed to draw her in, momentarily. She hugs Amanda and climbs onto her bunk. Amanda switches on the television and the cell fills with monotonous chat and laughter. Rachel closes her eyes and tries to tune out. There is only one thought in her head. How long will she get? She thinks about pleading *not guilty*. It would be a chance to walk free, reclaim her life. A life without a criminal conviction. She replays what Matthew said about building her defence. It's a bit of a long shot, and could she convince a jury she is a victim? Doubtful, because the unequivocal fact is she committed a crime *without* coercion, and as for the research files, well, how can any defence claim that wasn't premeditated? Switching to not guilty would be like bluffing at the poker table. If she loses... she would be here for a long stretch. No mitigation. No discount. Just the full weight of justice. No. She's guilty. She has to fold and accept her loss.

30

Rachel stands at the back of a line of women waiting to be let into the visiting hall. The queue bustles with restless chatter and nervous energy, some women, holding pocket mirrors, are fixing their hair and makeup. Not Rachel. She feels the usual dread settle in her stomach as she prepares for another awkward visitor moment. Her dad came last week, talking about appeals and lawyers. She tried to make him believe she was coping but facing him here only deepened her shame.

Then there was Richard. She walked into the visitors' hall, searching his face for some trace of comfort and reassurance. There was none. He looked angry. The resulting conversation became a series of banal questions with short answers and awkward silences.

'Got a court date yet?' he asked.

'How's the house?' she asked.

Then she gave him the gift he was looking for. 'I don't expect you to wait for me,' she said.

He smiled, not out of cruelty, but relief. And that was when the truth hit home. Having a wife in prison, one who had hidden so much from him, was something he couldn't cope with. She set him free, and he owes her nothing. Back in her cell, Amanda was a shoulder to cry on, reassuring her she had done the right thing. 'Relationship limbo draws out the pain,' she said. The love had already drained away, but she hadn't completely let go. Richard was still someone to cling to when she was at her most vulnerable. Now she's alone. There's been no visit from Adam yet. His radio silence probably means it's over between them. It had all started so well.

But he'll get through this and reminds herself she's strong enough to stand on her own.

Now, as the door clunks and the officer calls them forward, they march inside like uniformed schoolchildren parading into an end-of-term assembly. The hall is a mismatch of colours and furniture – hard plastic chairs, vending machines, two-toned painted walls. A Christmas tree has appeared since she was last here. It stands, drooping in the corner, overloaded with prison-made decorations.

Chairs scrape across the floor and children cry out, *'Mummy!'* Partners embrace and families bond. There are tissues, tears and strained smiles. Rachel watches Amanda rush to her visitors – her sister and six-year-old son, Gabe. They wrap themselves around each other.

Rachel spots her visitor – Ray Dunlop. He stands, ready to greet her. Her heart pounds as she recalls the last time they spoke, in his office with her incriminating laptop sitting on his desk. She next expected to see him in a courtroom. Then his handwritten letter arrived, asking to be added to her visitor list. *Why?* She showed it to Amanda, who said she should tell him to go fuck himself. But his tone was conciliatory, sentimental even. He too had lost his job and said he wanted her help with something. Rachel agreed to meet because she has an idea – a longshot, but she'll try anything. She walks towards him. *Keep your head up, girl.*

Ray offers his hand. She takes it. Her grip is firmer than expected.

'You probably shouldn't wear a suit and tie in here,' she says, attempting humour. 'My new friends might think you're a detective.'

He breaks into a smile as he loosens his tie. 'I don't want my neighbours to know I'm unemployed.'

She smiles. 'My neighbours think I'm in Yorkshire, looking after my sick mother.'

They both laugh. Their shared dark humour seems to break the ice.

He glances round the hall, nodding towards the tree with its twinkling fairy lights. 'Nice place you've got here.'

She tilts her head and smiles. 'We're expecting carol singers next week, maybe even the Salvation Army. And guess what? On Christmas day, we get a selection box – if we're good. I can't wait.'

'For what it's worth, I don't think you should take the fall for this, alone.'

She shrugs. 'Life's unfair. I'm sorry you lost your job, by the way. My fault.'

Ray shakes his head. 'I rattled the wrong cages.'

They talk briefly about their old company – friends they will miss and others they won't. The motivational speeches about gratitude, followed by outsourcing and layoffs. It feels liberating to bad-mouth her former employer without fear of reprimand. They agree that it had become more toxic over the last year. Ray might have lost his job, but he'll get another and at least he's got a home to go back to. And a wife. Rachel's lost so much more. Thoughts of Florence and Adam come to mind. Good things in her life that she's destroyed.

She shifts in her seat. 'So, you want my help?'

Ray nods. 'I do. And if I can help you in return, I will.'

He tells her about Jim Craig – the respected scientist turned whistle-blower. His ethical hotline complaint that was closed down, unsubstantiated. How Sydney and Aidan started investigating and were told to drop it. How he believes someone's falsifying clinical trial results to make the new drug look more effective than it is. Good clinical trial outcomes will boost Synaptonica's valuation and share price. A bid comes in, share prices rises even more and the directors cash out.

'I recognise his name,' she says thoughtfully. 'Yes, I accessed his account. I even read one of his reports, but I didn't really understand the science.'

Ray leans forward. 'Jim prepared the outcome reports. But he questioned the source data – too many anomalies, too many conveniently excluded results. He suspects someone is tampering with the data once it's received from the study centre and before it gets submitted for analysis. That makes the new drug look better than it actually is.'

Rachel lets this sink in, wondering if this can help her case. It doesn't sound much like mitigation, but can it undermine the prosecution case? That's a question for Matthew.

Ray continues. 'When the board saw the list of files that were accessed – the files you downloaded – they panicked. They couldn't pay the ransom quickly enough. I thought it was fear of losing their intellectual property. But maybe there was something they wanted to hide. Jim believes that if he can get hold of the files, he can confirm if someone tampered with them.'

Rachel nods. 'So the files I downloaded could be evidence of fraud?'

'We believe so.' He pulls out stapled sheets of paper and slides them across the desk, pointing to the list of Excel filenames. 'These spreadsheets all contain source data from the study centre.'

Rachel lets this sink in. If true, this would be a gigantic corporate scandal, planned and premeditated, making her crime look like opportunistic fare dodging. Maybe it can help her. A hint of excitement stirs within her. Then doubts creep in. Her life has been full of letdowns these last few weeks. Can she trust the man sitting opposite?

'How are you going to get to the files?' she asks.

Ray smiles. 'I cloned your hard disc and have recreated your laptop. I can see everything on it.'

Rachel shuffles uncomfortably. She thinks of her browsing history – fertility clinics, divorce lawyers and more. It may not matter, but still – it's private. 'There's personal stuff on there.'

Ray waves his hand. 'We're only interested in the research files. We just need the password for the encrypted folder.'

Her mouth hangs open. Yes, the folder is password protected. Aleks was desperate to get hold of it; she was equally determined to withhold it.

Her head drops. 'I can't remember it.'

Silence, then Ray leans in, voice soft. 'Did you write it down or use a password manager?'

She shakes her head.

Ray holds out his hands, as if pleading. 'Do you have common passwords? Names, dates?'

She shuts her eyes, trying to rewind her brain, taking herself back to that Friday – crisis day. She'd pulled an all-nighter. People were angry. Aleks and Izabela were threatening her. She was pre-occupied with Florence sleeping over that weekend. Too much going on. She remembers the fear she was feeling and her determination not to hand over the files. She typed out a new password, one which must have been meaningful in the moment. But she never used it after that. After the attack, she never wanted to see those files again. The memory of it has gone.

Ray slides a notepad and pen across the table. 'Try writing out some of your old passwords – it might jog your memory.'

She thinks and scrolls out six or seven old passwords, but nothing sparks a memory. She slides the notepad back to Ray, shaking her head. 'I'm sorry.'

Ray exhales slowly. 'That's a shame.' He tears a sheet from his pad and writes his phone number and slides it across the table. 'If it comes back to you, can you call me?'

She nods and blinks away the tears forming behind her eyes. For a fleeting moment, she had sight of a lifeline.

They lapse into lighter talk – potential future jobs for Ray. She asks his opinion about her employment prospects once she gets out. Ray suggests going freelance as an ethical hacker. They're never short of work and she would be good at that. Yes, she would. A fragile bond is building between them. Surprisingly, Rachel is enjoying his company.

An officer calls out, 'Five minutes.'

Ray turns to her. 'Is there anything I can do for you?'

She hesitates. 'There might be.'

She explains she is trying to build a defence based on mitigating circumstances and cooperation. Ray could support her claim of cooperation, and she asks if he could give a statement to the court telling them she opened up and explained everything she had done, truthfully.

Ray nods. 'That is the truth, so yes.'

Another thought forms in her mind. 'If we could trace Aleks and Izabela, that would give me my best possible defence.'

'And would stop them causing so much harm to other companies,' says Ray.

'My Telegram account and crypto wallet are on my laptop. I synced them with my phone. There could be something there to help trace them.'

She doesn't know what or how, but she'll try anything.

He nods. 'Let me get Sydney and Aidan on the case. If there are any clues, they'll find them.'

'And I'll really try my hardest to remember that password.'

They shake hands and say goodbye. A flicker of warmth passes between them, along with a strand of hope.

The bell rings. She watches him leave, then glances around the hall. Other prisoners embrace their loved ones. Children cry and cling to their mothers. She catches sight of Amanda, who is clutching a crayon drawing – a homemade card from her son. Rachel thinks of Florence and the card her niece gave her when she was in hospital. Children are precious. Her chest tightens. She is not giving up on that dream.

Rachel begins the slow walk back to the wing with the other women. Officer Evans is striding towards her. 'Rachel.'

She straightens instinctively. 'Yes?'

'You're needed,' says Evans, pointing at the word 'Listener' stitched onto Rachel's top. 'In another wing. A resident has asked to speak to a Listener. Are you free?'

Rachel nods. 'Of course.'

She follows, heart ticking faster with every step. This will be her first official listening client since the Samaritans training. The corridor between the wings feels longer than usual, colder. They reach the convicted prisoners' block. Evans stops outside a cell.

'Jackie.' She points to the open door. 'We'll leave you to it.'

Rachel knocks gently before stepping inside.

Jackie is curled up on the bottom bunk, knees clutched tight to her chest. Her face is reddened and blotched from crying. She looks up for half a second, then away again. She's thin. Too thin. Rachel pulls out the plastic chair, sits, leans in. 'Hi, I'm Rachel,' she says softly, placing a hand on Jackie's thin arm. 'I'm here to listen. That's all. Just talk if you want to.'

Silence.

'Take your time,' says Rachel.

'My life is shit,' she shouts. Then she slams her feet against the mattress and lets out a scream that fills the cell.

'Jackie, everyone has something good in their life—' Rachel stops herself, recalling her training. 'Would you like to tell me what's making you feel this way?'

She shakes her head. 'No one cares about me.'

Rachel glances around the cell. 'Would you like a cup of tea?'

She nods.

Rachel moves to the sink, fills the kettle, rinses two stained mugs, drops a teabag in one. There are no biscuits, no comforts.

The kettle clicks off, and she pours in the boiling water. She stirs the first cup then transfers the teabag to the second cup and stirs UHT milk into both, all the time, thinking about what she can do practically to make her feel better. She hands Jackie a steaming mug. She clutches it with a trembling hand. They sip in silence.

'How long have you been here, Jackie?'

Jackie talks and tells Rachel she's been inside for three months. Not one visitor. Her birthday was last week – no cards. For eight years, she's lived in hostels, shared houses, sofa-surfed, women's refuges. Sometimes on the streets. She's twenty-six.

Rachel thinks about her visitors – people who care. She notices the scars on Jackie's forearm, still healing. Deliberate cuts. Each one an unanswered cry for help.

'Do you have any family?'

Jackie shakes her head. She tells Rachel she lost touch with her dad years ago. Her mother lives with her new partner, and there's no room for her to stay over and never seems to have time to see her. Jackie's inside for repetitive shoplifting – sweets, chocolates and booze, which she would steal to give to her homeless friends.

'Do you have a prison job?'

'Laundry.' Jackie grimaces. 'Where's that going to get me? I've got five months left here. Then what? If I died, no one would notice I was gone. No one would come to my funeral. What's the point?'

The words hang between them like lingering smoke.

Rachel remains with her. At times, they speak. At times, they don't. She makes more tea, keeps her posture open, her voice calm, her eyes kind. She listens. That's what matters. An hour and a half pass. Rachel stands, uncertain if this is the time to leave.

'Thank you, Rachel.' Jackie's voice is low but steadier.

Rachel smiles. 'Anytime.'

Walking back, Rachel feels weighed down by emotion. Jackie is alone in the world, and not because she failed, but because the world failed her. Rachel had a home and a career, family and friends. Her lot in life was never that bad. She then played a bad hand and lost. Jackie was never even dealt a hand.

The main door to the hall buzzes open and Rachel is back on the remand wing. She walks down the hall, pushes open her cell door and freeze. The place has been trashed. Bedding and pillows strewn across the floor. Books and magazine lie scattered, pages torn. Broken coffee mugs, spilled mascara tubes and makeup brushes scattered as if flung in a fit of rage.

Amanda leaps up from the bottom bunk, eyes bloodshot. 'Where have you been?' she shouts.

Rachel steps back. 'I was doing a listening session. In another wing. Someone needed help.'

'You didn't tell me?' Amanda grabs her by her arms, gripping tight.

Rachel has never seen her like this before. Gone is the happy-go-lucky Amanda who believes the universe has a plan and everything happens for a reason. Something's happened. Something bad. 'Amanda, what's wrong?'

Amanda lets out a desperate scream, covers her face with and collapses onto the bunk, sobbing. Rachel's arms tremble. She kneels beside her and gently wraps her arms around her, unsure what to say. They sit side by side, Amanda talking in gasps and gulps until it all comes spilling out. She misses her son, Gabe. A card he made sits on her bed, the photo smudged but the message, written in red felt-tip, still clear: *I love you Mum*.

If found guilty, Amanda could face five years in prison. Five years separated from her child. Rachel realises now that Amanda has been concealing her pain. Her natural cheerfulness was no more than a fragile defence against the truth that's finally broken through.

Amanda is Rachel's best friend here. When others turned against her, Amanda had her back. When despair took hold, Amanda found a way to lift her. Now it's Rachel's turn. She can't take away the pain, but she can be here for her.

'Will you stay with me?' Amanda asks through her tears.

Rachel squeezes her hand. 'I'm going nowhere.'

Amanda talks about her sister – the one looking after him. She's taking him to his friend's birthday party, then will meet his teacher at parents' evening. All the things she should be doing. 'I can't be inside for five years,' she whispers.

Rachel holds her as she trembles and thinks of all the mothers inside – forced to say goodbye at the end of visiting hour, their children in tears, too young to understand why their mums can't come home. The pain of it settles deep in her chest.

The cell door swings open and thuds against the wall. Denton appears in the doorway.

Please, fuck off.

He surveys the wreckage and sneers. 'You two had a fight?'

'She's having a bad day,' says Rachel curtly.

He snorts. 'Not the only one. Get this place sorted before dinner.'

Rachel bites her tongue. She begins to tidy: sheets and pillows back in the beds, books stacked, broken crockery in the bin. Amanda sits on the bed, tearful and shaking.

'I'm sorry for screaming at you earlier,' says Amanda.

Rachel swallows hard, thinking about her own problems – the fear she'll never become a mother. Adam's silence. But she pushes those thoughts aside. Not tonight.

She offers to switch on the TV, but Amanda shakes her head. 'I just want to talk.'

So she talks – about Gabe, about her sister who will soon know her son better than she will. Rachel listens, letting the conversation circle and repeat, because sometimes listening is the best you can do.

Late that night, when the hall has fallen silent, Rachel lies awake on her bunk, staring at the ceiling. Amanda is snoring softly beneath her. The scent of lavender oil from her pillow hangs in the air. Rachel feels drained and her head is throbbing. She needs to decompress but her thoughts are churning like a multi-tasking computer stuck in an endless cycle as she starts to put her own crisis into perspective. Amanda's meltdown was a shock, but it's Jackie who lingers in her mind. The way she clutched her mug with both hands like it was her last precious possession. The pale scars on her arms. At least Rachel still has people in her life who care for her: Tony, her mum and dad. Jackie has no one. Jackie thanked her for listening. Rachel didn't fix anything, but for one hour and thirty-five minutes, Jackie wasn't alone. The thought stays with her.

Tonight, for the first time, she understands that she's not the only one in pain. Every woman in here is carrying their own personal crisis.

Eventually, she drifts off to sleep, the day still looping in her mind, and somewhere, beneath it all, is that password she still can't remember.

31

Ray sits at a coffee-stained table in the prison visiting hall. The room looks much as it did last week – cluttered, restless and grimly functional. The chairs don't match, and the unevenly spaced tables irk him. The lopsided Christmas tree is an almost comical attempt to create a festive atmosphere. The stench of tobacco smoke lingers, probably from the man slouched at the next table who's having a mumbled conversation with his female companion. Children rummage through a battered toy box, arguing over broken trucks, dolls with limbs missing, colouring books and felt-tip pens without lids. Ray watches them, thinking the toys look like something a charity shop would throw out.

He checks his watch and calculates that even if he stays the full hour, he should still be home before Kirsty. She doesn't know he's here. She thinks he's spending most of his time researching the job market and preparing job applications.

The door to the wing opens with a clank. Ray stands. The women walk in single file, dressed alike in their blue and grey tracksuits, moving like schoolchildren who have been told to behave. Rachel is third in line, her hair pulled back with a hairband and no makeup. She stands out because her top has the word *Listener* stitched on to it, same as last time. He gives her a half-smile. She returns it, steps forward and they shake hands – still formal, but more familiar this time. Around them, partners, families and children hug.

'You've dressed down,' says Rachel, eyeing his attire of jeans and checked shirt. 'What will your neighbours think?'

He chuckles. 'I have a change of clothes in the car.'

Rachel asks him about his job hunting and Ray ask her about her defence case. Neither has much of an update since his last visit. Ray mentions he has a second interview tomorrow. Another CISO position. Then he gently reminds her he's still investigating the data-tampering allegation.

'If you're here for the password,' says Rachel, slumping lower in her chair, 'I'm going to disappoint you. I've tried everything...' She shrugs. 'It's gone.'

Ray exhales. 'That's a shame.' His gaze drops to the scratched tabletop. 'Have you tried meditation techniques or anything like that?'

She lets out a hollow laugh. 'Let me tell you what I've tried: hypnosis, aura reading, crystal therapy, automatic writing. My cellmate, Amanda, has a list of crackpot therapies which supposedly tap into the unconscious memory. Last night, during the full moon, she had me lie flat on my bunk with a quartz crystal down my bra and rosemary oil rubbed on my temples while I repeated some stupid chant. Nothing. I can remember pointless crap like how many coffee shops I walk past in the way into work, but not that damn password.' She throws her hands up. 'Sorry.'

That word hits Ray like a door slamming shut. Without access to those files, his investigation is at a dead end. He feared it would come to this. Kirsty's been telling him to put past grudges behind him. He probably has to let this one go now.

Rachel watches him. 'Did you find any clues or leads on my laptop?'

He shakes his head, 'Not *yet*. But Aidan and Sydney are on it and are "chasing the rabbit" to use their phrase.' He explains how they accessed her Telegram account through her browser and could see the history of message exchanges with Aleks. Sydney even tried to start a chat with him. No response. Then they went on to the dark net, trying to trace his user ID. Still no joy.

He shrugs. 'We'll keep digging. Sydney is going to look at your crypto wallet next, and do some crypto transaction analysis across the ledgers, whatever that means.'

Rachel's head drops. 'Thank you.'

Ray looks at her. He still sees the confident, straight-talking Rachel he interviewed, but she looks exhausted and worn down with worry. He wishes he could give her some hope.

They sit in silence for a moment. Rachel wipes away tears.

She tells him about her latest meeting with the solicitor. He showed interest in the data-tampering allegation and said it might help her case, but he'd need to review the evidence. He still says her strongest card would be to provide information that leads them to the Ninja Magpie criminals. Law enforcement teams around the world have been hunting them for years.

Ray nods. 'They're clever. That Izabela fooled us all.'

'I watched her operate. She was good at making friends. The men in my team were bending over backwards to teach her the basics of computing. She didn't need to try too hard.' She laughs.

Ray nods. 'Sydney is kicking herself from being taken in by her fake friendship.'

'She tried to latch on to Johnathan Winstanley once. She butted into a conversation we were having during lunch.'

Ray smirks. 'Winstanley's a halfwit. He'd easily be taken in by a good-looking woman ten years his junior.'

Rachel raises an eyebrow. 'You have a low opinion of your old boss.'

Yes, he does. In fact, he can't think of anyone he dislikes more. Expense scandals, ethics complaints closed down without investigation... He's a rogue and Ray had the evidence locked in the drawer of his old office. He almost tells her but holds back. 'Sorry, I know he was your mentor.'

Rachel snorts. 'Don't be sorry, I think he's a prick.'

Ray raises an eyebrow. That's news. He always thought they were close.

Rachel slams the palms of her hands on the table. Ray jolts.

'Oh my God!' she shouts, loud enough to draw glances. An officer looks towards them.

'What is it?' says Ray.

'Pen and paper. Now.'

Ray pats his body. 'I don't have any.'

Rachel leaps up, darts to a nearby table and snatches a child's colouring book and broken crayon, then rushes back.

'I've just remembered that fucking password.'

Ray's heart jumps. A hush falls over their section of the hall as Rachel writes something out, letter by letter.

An officer reaches them, points to Rachel. 'You. Stay in your seat, and no swearing.'

She rips the page from the colouring book and hands it to Ray, like a school student handing in a prize-winning project. He takes it, hand trembling. He doesn't need to read it twice.

<u>J</u><u>W</u>-is-a-<u>P</u>rick!

Rachel grins triumphantly. 'He had been stalking me and I was hiding from him. He tried to get me to go on a date with him – never mind the fact

I was married. Then, during the crisis, he told me to go faster with laptop restores. That was the first thing I thought of as a password.' She smiles. 'What do you think?'

Ray stares at it in disbelief, eyes wide. 'Oh, that's good.'

She points. 'I've underlined the capitals.'

'You're sure?'

Her face lights up. 'One hundred per cent.'

Ray exhales. His day has suddenly got better. If this works, it's game on. Whatever happens now, he will do whatever he can to help Rachel get out of this place.

They chat more about prison life. Rachel tells him about the *Listener* programme and how it has given her a sense of purpose in what would otherwise be a mind-numbing existence. She talks about the people she's met, so many with troubled backgrounds – domestic abuse, abandonment, mothers separated from their children. Self-harm and depression are an everyday sight. She is teaching one girl to read and write and helping her fill out her canteen order. It has caused her to reflect about what she once had and lost. If nothing else, she can make a difference to some. If she gets a long stretch, as is likely, at least she will have a vocation.

Ray is growing to like Rachel more and wonders where they would be now if he had given her the job rather than Sydney. He can imagine her taking her seat at the table in the cyber ops room for the daily huddle. Ray would provoke her, and she would forthrightly argue back. If only he could have employed both Rachel and Sydney. What a team he would have had.

The five-minute warning is called, and the room starts to shift. Ray wants to leave before the bedlam starts – children screaming, tears and emotional goodbyes. He stands up. Rachel does too.

'Good luck with the job interview,' says Rachel.

Ray smiles. 'Thank you. I need it.'

She leans in and hugs him – not a clutching embrace, just a brief, trusting hold between two people who want to help each other.

He walks out, through the gates and back to the car park and climbs into his car. He doesn't really have a change of clothes here, but it seemed to humour her. He stares once again at the sheet of paper, with the orange-coloured writing. How could she not remember that password? He drives off, singing to himself.

Ray sits in his study, the glare from his widescreen monitor illuminating the dimly lit room, the only other sound the tapping of raindrops on the windowpane. The bleakness of the outside feels haunting. He breathes deeply.

He clicks on the secure folder, and it prompts for a password. One finger at a time, he types it, conscious of each tap. He presses *enter* then watches the rotating circle. Seconds later, a flicker and a list of spreadsheets and documents fill his screen. His pulse races. A quick scan of the filenames confirms everything. He has the research files. The files they paid forty-million pounds to protect. Beads of sweat form on his forehead. Was it fear of losing their intellectual property that caused them to pay or were they in a panic over the discovery of falsified clinical-trial results? Fraud still seems far-fetched. Perhaps Jim Craig is just an obsessed, disgruntled ex-employee chasing shadows.

He opens a document at random. The text is dense with medical jargon, obscure metrics and statistical tables. This is not his world. But, if Jim Craig is right, the spreadsheets are where the evidence sits: the daily test results from the clinical trials.

He opens the first spreadsheet, navigates to *File* > *Info* > *Version History*. A metadata pane appears: only one version. No edits. He opens another two. Same results.

He opens another and freezes. Two versions: one created, one modified. He lines them up, side by side. A quick compare highlights the altered values in lurid yellow. Ten records changed. He checks the metadata. Edited by *Howard Stamp*. That name means nothing. But is it fraud or a legitimate alteration? There is no way for him to tell.

He leans back, heart racing. The list of filenames blurs for a moment as his mind jumps to the image of those three men in the boardroom – Winstanley, Bristol and Chester – whispering in their own little huddle. Their game is conniving money-saving schemes with little regard for the people impacted. But would they really stoop this low? If there is fraud, and if implicated, they would face jail time. They may be chancers with no ethical boundaries, but they are not stupid. Surely, they would not take that risk. Yet he still recalls the flicker of relief on their faces when Catherine Davenport authorised the ransom payment.

His eyes return to the screen. He shouldn't have these files. If discovered, he'll be the one in the courtroom. But he's committed now. He's taken the first steps into a minefield and he's not turning back.

He grabs his mobile and makes a call.

'Dunlop?' comes the irate voice.

'Hello, Jim. Sorry to interrupt your evening. It's about those spreadsheets—'

'Have you got them?'

'I might have.'

'Don't piss me about. What do you want?'

'Does the name Howard Stamp mean anything to you?'

He snorts. 'He's in the data administration team. One of Sean Bristol's puppets. Pretends he's a scientist. Continually drops scientific terms into conversations, trying to impress others.'

'I know the type,' says Ray.

'What about him?'

Ray tells him he has the files and walks him through what he's done and what he's discovered. Jim listens in silence, then interrupts.

'Okay, Dunlop, you've done a good job. Now send them to me.'

'They're not leaving my machine,' says Ray, determined to hold his ground. 'If you want to see them, come over to mine.'

There's a pause. 'Give me your address.'

Ray does so, and Jim says he'll be there in an hour. The phone goes dead. Ray heads to the kitchen, unable to hide his smile. Kirsty is sitting on a bar stool, sipping herbal tea and scrolling her phone. He tells her his news.

She places her mug carefully on the countertop and pats the seat next to her. 'Sit down and talk to me.'

Ray sits, sensing a serious conversation ahead, something like, *drop this case and focus on job hunting*.

'Raymond, I'm worried.'

Ray nods. 'How come?'

'You have files you shouldn't have. You're about to accuse your old company of serious fraud. They have a team of lawyers who will paint you as a bitter, disgruntled ex-employee holding a grudge. Why are you getting involved, exactly?'

Retribution. 'I'm just helping someone out.'

'And how well do you know Jim Craig?'

'Not that well, but he was dismissed unfairly, like me.'

Kirsty's takes his hand. 'Play it safe. You're under non-disclosure.'

Forty minutes later, flickering headlights come to a halt at the bottom of their garden. Ray opens the door as Jim Craig strides up the path, side-stepping puddles. He enters and removes his shoes. He and Kirsty have polite introductions, then the two men make their way upstairs. They sit shoulder to shoulder in front of the monitor. Kirsty appears with two mugs of tea and Ray slides a coaster across the desk towards Jim. 'Use this.'

'Kirsty seems very nice,' he says, with what seems like a hint of surprise in his voice.

Ray shows Jim the altered files. Jim scribbles in his notebook and mumbles to himself in statistical language. Jim explains that every trial has two treatment groups: those receiving the new drug and those receiving the placebo. Patients and doctors don't know who is in what group, but people with access to the patient database can look that up. People like *Howard Stamp*, a data administrator with access to all the databases and digital vault folders. Ray mentions the possibility that someone may have stolen Howard's password and is using his account.

Jim shrugs. 'At this stage, Dunlop, I just want to prove falsification. You've done a good job, and I think we can work together. But I need these files so I can reanalyse the results.'

Ray shakes his head. 'Tell me what you're planning to do if you confirm fraud.'

Jim takes a breath. 'I'll write a detailed report to the regulators, highlighting the specific trial dates and files. They will probably do a dawn raid on our clinical research centre, demand access to the labs and these files.'

'And if they confirm fraud?'

'That would be a crime. The police will be called and arrests made. And let me tell you, Dunlop, I'll be there, standing outside, watching them squirm. I want that satisfaction,' he says, planting his fist on the desk.

Ray realises he is in the company of a man obsessed with revenge. Kirsty's warning words echo inside his head. *Why are you doing this?* In truth, it's personal. He stares at his partner, who is salivating with anticipation. Ray is uncertain now. He doesn't really understand what he's about to get involved with. More importantly, he doesn't want to work with Jim Craig. He's uncomfortable. 'Jim, let's make a deal. I give you these files, then you *never* disclose to anyone where they came from.'

Jim stares at him. 'Don't you want to be part of this? They screwed you over too.'

Ray shakes his head. 'I'm backing out.'

Jim shrugs. 'Fine by me.'

Ray copies the files to an encrypted password-protected USB stick and hands it over. Jim thanks him.

'We have Rachel to thank for this,' Ray says without thinking.

'What?'

'She gave us the password.'

Jim stiffens. 'She stole confidential research. We have nothing to thank her for. I want to see her prosecuted and imprisoned for a long time.'

Ray declines to debate with him on that point. They walk downstairs and say their goodbyes. Jim mellows as Kirsty appears to say goodbye. They let him out the front door and they stand watching as he drives off into the rain, happy. Ray hopes that is the last time he sees him.

32

A Bluetooth speaker sits on the window ledge of the recreation space, looping through a Christmas playlist of old favourites: 'All I Want for Christmas is You', 'Fairytale of New York'. One girl, strands of tinsel tied to her wrists, spins in an off-balance pirouette and improvises with a monotone rendition of 'Last Christmas'. No one complains. Even the officers are trying to keep things light. There are no jobs today. No mandatory sessions. Just the hope of keeping the mood festive and letting the goodwill flow.

Rachel chalks her pool cue, leans in, adjusts her arm positioning and lines up her shot. A stripe ball sinks cleanly into the corner pocket. Great start. Her next one hugs the cushion and rolls in.

'Good shot,' says Tanya, her partner in this doubles tournament. Normally sharp-tongued and volatile, the Christmas Day vibe seems to have mellowed her mood.

Rachel misses the third. She shrugs. At least they have two balls down. This is her third game of the morning, and they won the first two. She glances at the leaderboard. They might even win. She's enjoying this distraction. It brings back memories of Friday pub nights back home in Yorkshire, when she would take delight in beating the men and having drinks bought for her.

'Two shots,' Tanya calls out.

'What for?' snaps Kate, one of their opponents.

Tanya points to the table. 'Double hit.'

'Fuck off.'

Rachel sees it coming – Tanya and Kate face off, sleeves rolled up, cues in hand like weapons, jaws tight. Rachel steps in between them, faces Tanya, arms out, her voice low but firm.

'Let it go,' she says to Tanya. 'We'll win this one, easy.'

The cheers from the onlookers grow louder, and a guard strides towards them. Tanya steps back, and the game continues with a little more competitiveness and a lot less goodwill.

Two balls remain on the table. Tanya misses. Kate lines up her cue and takes the shot for the game, but the black ball stops an inch short of the pocket. Rachel takes a deep breath. Her turn. She crouches low, aims and sinks the last stripe ball. She needs a perfectly weighted stroke for this last shot. But it's too soft and grazes the edge of the ball. Her opponent steps up and pots the black to take the game.

Kate and her teammate Sarah high five, but there are no handshakes. Tanya curses under her breath. Rachel leaves the table and strolls back to her cell, still replaying the last shot she missed. It will be thirty minutes before her and Tanya are on again.

She climbs onto her bunk. Amanda has gone walkabout, which gives her precious solitude and time for reflection. She closes her eyes and wallows in her melancholy. She recalls last Christmas, at Richard's parents' house, which she had been dreading. Once the formalities of lunch and the rituals of present-giving were over, the drinks flowed, games started and it turned out to be a lot more fun than expected. She imagines he'll be there again this year. She pictures them at the dinner table, the mood more sombre while they ask probing questions about his wife's actions. He's likely told them that they've officially separated, and they will say how sorry they are but secretly will be relieved not to have a criminal in their family. She hasn't heard from him since his visit. Looks like he's moved on.

She thinks of her own family and what they are doing right now – her mum and dad preparing a traditional lunch, just the two of them, lamenting the fact that both their children have been in prison. Tony's got a new job in a hotel and is working all day. It sounds like a step up. She still worries. He's relapsed before. And then there's Florence. She had been so looking forward to spending time with her over Christmas – taking her to the outdoor ice rink and seeing her smiling face as she opened her presents. Sarah will never bring her here. They had just bonded and now she doesn't know when she'll even see her again. The punishment of prison runs deep at this time of year, and she's asking herself how many more Christmases she will spend inside. She'll find out soon because a date for her court appearance has come through – 12th of January. Less than three weeks' time.

She spoke to Matthew again, who's still optimistic for a reduced sentence. Remorse, cooperation and good behaviour in prison will all go in her favour, he said. Three to five years, out in two or three, under licence. That still gives her a chance of becoming a mother. Something to hope for. That's more than many of the women in here have. She thinks of Jackie, her first listening partner – young, vulnerable and abandoned by her family. It's little wonder she feels suicidal. Rachel sent her a Christmas card, just to let her know that someone cares. She wishes she could do more.

Lying on her bed are three Christmas cards. She picks up the first, a nativity-themed one from her parents, with a message full of love and prayer. The guards have photocopied it, just in case it was used to smuggle in spice. Next, a glossy Moonpig card from Tony, with a photo montage of them and Florence. She traces her niece's beaming face with her finger. On the inside, is a picture of Tony and Florence with Mum and Dad. A family reunited, at last. Her throat tightens. That's everything she was hoping for. She still feels a pang of guilt for the rift, though. In Mum and Dad's eyes, Rachel was a success story – university graduate, rising in her career. Tony the disappointment – drunk, disorderly behaviour. She didn't deserve that praise.

She picks up her last Christmas card – another photocopy – although she can imagine the original with its elegant styling and calligraphy. The front message says: *All I want for Christmas is you!* Mariah Carey. That song was playing in the hall this morning. Inside, the message reads:

Thinking of you this Christmas.

Love, Adam. xxx.

Five weeks of silence. She had written, added him to her visitor list. Nothing. She thought he'd moved on. Why wouldn't he? Then his card arrived. She holds it and thinks back to the night they spent together and how natural it had felt, and how this new relationship instantly felt so permanent. They had so much to build on and discover together. Then she went and wrecked everything.

She has ten minutes' phone credit remaining, which she was saving for her mum and dad. She climbs down from her bunk, lifts the receiver of the wall-mounted phone, taps in her PIN, pauses, then taps the phone number, reminding herself that someone may be listening in. Her heart pounds.

'Hello?' Adam's voice is soft and uncertain.

She hesitates. 'I hope this isn't a bad time,' she blurts out with a shaky laugh.

STEVE WILLIAMSON

'Oh my god.' A pause. 'Just a minute.'

She hears muffled sounds and faint chatter in the background, then it goes silent.

'I've been thinking about you,' he says.

Relief floods her body. He sounds genuinely happy and imagines he is with family – his parents and his kids, maybe. Then they talk. He tells her how much he misses her. She tells him the same, and it feels real. As if no time has passed. She asks why he hadn't replied to her letter, why he didn't visit. He tells her he tried to visit once but saw Richard in the prison waiting room. He thinks Richard may have recognised him by the way he looked at him, so turned back to avoid a confrontation.

She checks the wall clock; they only have two minutes of call time remaining. This next bit is going to be hard.

She takes a breath. 'I have my court date in three weeks.'

A pause.

'My lawyer's built a great defence, and he thinks I might escape prison.'

'Wow. That's fantastic,' he says with a hint of hesitation.

Another pause.

'Are you going to visit me?'

'Absolutely. When's the next visiting day?'

Then the line cuts out.

She replaces the receiver, slumps into the chair and sighs with relief. She still has him. But she's just lied to him. She should have told him straight that she'll be inside for at least two years and he needs to forget her and move on with his life. But his voice was like a passion-inducing spell, activating an outcome that only exists in a dream.

There's a double tap on the floor and she looks up to see Tanya in the doorway. 'We're on, Rachel.'

She holds out a cue. Rachel grabs it and the two of them head back to the pool table.

Later that day, Rachel is back in her cell, satisfied with second place in the pool tournament. Tanya is still seething from the earlier double-tap incident and Rachel had to pull her back from confrontation once again.

A sharp whistle pierces the air. Amanda bursts in, wearing a red Santa hat and a length of tinsel knotted around her waist.

'Come on, girlfriend – Christmas dinnertime.' She beams.

Rachel climbs down from her bunk. Amanda produces another Santa hat and plants it on Rachel's head. They link arms and march out, giggling like sixth formers.

The dining room is decked out with prison-made decorations – paper chains, festive paintings, balloons and a limp tinsel tree. Crackers are pulled, jokes exchanged, and a speaker belts out that same Christmas playlist they've had all morning. No one objects. They sit in a group of six, Rachel wedged between Amanda and Tanya. Dinner arrives: roast turkey with gravy, stuffing and sprouts. At least it's something different, even if it still has the canteen food taste to it.

One woman – Jo – produces a plastic bottle and furtively tips its contents into the jug of orange squash. 'Hooch,' she whispers with pride.

Rachel glances around, making sure no one has noticed. 'Where did that come from?'

Jo explains how the prison has to provide a fruit quota to ensure the prisoners get adequate nutrition. She takes the fruit, pulps it and ferments it with water, sugar and breadcrumbs. A few weeks in a warm cupboard and she has high-potency hooch.

That's why she's been collecting the plastic Coca-Cola bottles, thinks Rachel.

Amanda picks up the jug and pours. A rank, yeasty smell fills the air.

'Christmas toast,' Amanda announces, raising her cup to the centre of the table.

Everyone follows suit.

'Cheers,' they shout together.

Amanda slaps her palm on the table. 'Stop! You're not doing it right.'

The girls exchange glances, curious.

You've got to keep eye contact when you toast.'

'Is this a drinking game?' asks Tanya with a smile.

'If you break eye contact during a toast, you're cursed with seven years' bad sex,' explains Amanda.

Rachel laughs. 'Well, that becomes irrelevant if I get a full sentence.'

Amanda jabs a finger in the air. 'Again. Everyone. Properly this time.'

They raise their cups, taking care to look each other in the eye. Rachel takes a gulp. It tastes crude, as expected. It's effective, though, as she feels her shoulders loosen. Another bottle appears and cups are refilled.

After the meal, the officers give out clear goody-bags containing a Terry's Chocolate Orange, a tube of crisps and a piece of fruit. Everyone passes their fruit to Jo. Rachel clutches what she has left. She loves Chocolate Orange and will limit herself to two segments a day and keep it hidden from Amanda.

The music gets louder, the laughter freer and a Christmas quiz begins. The quiz master has to repeat each question because of heckling and the loud party atmosphere. She never imagined Christmas in prison would be so much fun. Pity there isn't a karaoke mic; Rachel would love to burst into song – an ABBA duet with Amanda. Another bottle of hooch appears under the table. It smells, and she's had enough to drink, but out of the side of her eye, notices Amanda topping up her cup. She gulps it down, then immediately regrets it. That was worse than the first lot. It must be from a bad batch. She reaches for the water and gulps down as much as she can.

Five minutes pass and the room is spinning; she feels sick and rushes to the bathroom. She stands with her head over the sink, willing herself to vomit, but nothing comes. She wants to sit down. As she tries to walk to the cubicle, she collapses, hitting the floor with a thud. Then her eyes close.

Rachel awakens to stillness and is vaguely aware it's Boxing Day morning. She's in the right cell, but the wrong bed. The bottom bunk – Amanda's bed – with a basin by her side. She sits up. Her head is throbbing and her mouth tastes of bile. She presses a hand against her cheek. It's sore. She staggers to the sink, drinks three cups of water, and crawls back to bed.

Amanda awakens. 'Aren't you the party animal?'

'What the hell happened?'

Amanda laughs, then fills in the blanks in Rachel's memory. After ten minutes, Amanda went to look for her and found her on the floor of the toilet, unable to stand. Conveniently, a fight kicked off in the hall – Tanya and Kate, arguing over the pool tournament earlier in the day. The officers were all over that, so Amanda and Jo walked her back to her cell, one on each side, taking her weight.

Amanda holds out a goody-bag. 'You're lucky this didn't get nicked.'

Rachel reaches for it. 'Thank you,' she says meekly.

She lies back down in the bed and closes her eyes. Rachel has never been so drunk as to black out like that. She now fears she will pay a price much greater than a pounding headache. She is relying on a good behaviour report for her court appearance, and she's just got paralytically drunk on bootleg booze. She could end up in the segregation unit for this.

33

The coffee shop is in a lull. That brief window after the morning rush and before the lunchtime crowd arrives. It smells of fresh ground coffee beans, fresh-baked breads and cakes.

Ray sits at a table upstairs, a pot of tea and a wedge of carrot cake in front of him. Through the tall window, he watches the world shuffle by: pedestrians with gloves, hats and scarves pulled tight around their necks. They should be here soon.

He checks his watch then pours himself a cup of perfectly brewed tea – loose leaf, steeped for five minutes – then stirs in a splash of milk. Around him, staff clear the tables. Soothing background music mingles with the clattering of stacked plates and spoons dropping on the floor. Once they leave, Ray gets up and nudges the chairs back into alignment. He wouldn't be able to concentrate otherwise.

His old office is only five minutes' walk from here – the headquarters of the company whose share price is soaring on news of a pending takeover. Ray smiles with quiet satisfaction. That rocket will implode once Jim Craig submits his report to the regulators. He would love to be a fly on the wall, observing the directors in disarray as their share-sale windfall dissolves. It will be a shock for the workforce. He knows he had a habit of rubbing people up the wrong way with his 'hostile communication style' as HR liked to call it, but there are many good people there, and he wouldn't want them to become casualties to someone else's malpractice.

He hears the familiar clumping of size-twelve boots on the staircase. He takes another sip of tea. They wanted to see him urgently, and he's intrigued. Whatever their news, it won't be as dramatic as his.

Aidan appears first, carrying a bucket-sized coffee. Sydney follows, green smoothie in one hand and laptop in the other. Ray stands, gives Sydney a hug and high-fives Aidan.

'Happy New Year,' they say to each other.

He holds back his news because they have that excited look in their eyes, like a couple of kids who went to the fair and returned with a goldfish.

Sydney flips open her laptop and powers up.

Ray picks up his fork and cuts into his cake. 'Does your boss know you're meeting up with me?'

'Winstanley told us not to talk to you again,' says Sydney

Ray smiles. His day is only getting better.

'We've done some crypto analysis. Now, wait till you see this,' says Sydney, angling her screen towards him. A schematic fills the display: nodes and lines connecting like constellations across a dark background.

'First, let me tell you how Bitcoin works.' Sydney's face is sparkling with excitement. 'Every transaction gets posted on a public ledger – the blockchain – which means anyone can read it and trace the flow of payments from one wallet to another. Once it's on the ledger, it's permanent.'

Ray nods. He knows this already, but he'll indulge her.

She continues. 'Every crypto wallet has a unique address – a random string of characters. No names. No IDs. We already knew the Ninja Magpie wallet address because that's how we paid the ransom.' She clicks, highlights a transaction line. 'This is the transfer of forty million in Bitcoin to their wallet.'

Ray tops up his cup of tea from the pot. 'We've done all this already, and it got us nowhere.'

Aidan leans forward. 'But now we've got something we didn't have back then – Rachel's wallet address.'

Ray, curiosity piqued, nods in acknowledgement.

'We found her recovery phrase on her laptop and recreated her wallet,' says Sydney.

Ray watches as Sydney clicks on individual lines on the diagram. 'Three transfers, amounting to thirty-five thousand pounds, but *not* from the main Ninja Magpie wallet.'

'They used a *different* wallet to make those payments,' says Aidan.

Sydney clicks again. 'There are multiple payments to different addresses, from this wallet. Then one big one of forty-eight Bitcoin – around four million pounds. Transferred to someone's wallet a few hours *after* we paid the ransom.'

Ray inhales. 'So, payment to someone who helped them with their extortion.'

'Exactly,' they say in unison.

'Well, it's a pity those wallets don't come with a name and address,' says Ray.

Aidan grins. 'Stay with us.'

Sydney leans in. 'Sometimes people post their wallet addresses online – fundraising sites, forums, or on X, asking for donations for a cause or a business venture. And that leaves a trail.'

Ray straightens. 'Are you telling me you have linked this wallet ID to an identity?'

They both smile. 'Found it on a tweet from a couple of years ago,' says Sydney.

'We thought maybe it was Izabela's as she was doing all the work on the inside,' says Aidan.

Sydney continues. 'We pulled the firewall logs to see if anyone accessed that X profile page from inside the company.'

'And we got a hit. Multiple logons to that X account,' says Aidan, excitement levels clearly elevated.

'The logs gave us an IP and MAC address. And it wasn't Izabela,' says Sydney.

Ray drops his fork. Looks at Sydney, then Aidan, his mind racing. Are they about to tell him there was someone else on the inside?

Sydney switches windows. The screen turns black with lines of system logs in white text – timestamps, codes and digital gobbledygook.

She points to the line at the bottom, which displays user ID and name.

'That's who got paid four million,' says Sydney.

Ray leans in and glares at the name:

» *Jude Wiseman.*

Ray draws a sharp breath, then slams his fist on the table, hard enough to rattle his teacup. He glances at Sydney then back at Aidan. He frowns as he points to the screen. 'That doesn't surprise me.'

The adrenalin surges through him. Pretty boy Jude. The expert consultant, who ingratiated himself with Catherine Davenport. He contributed little in the boardroom but chimed in with just enough insight to sound credible. Catherine deferred to him like he was an all-knowing cyber oracle. Ray remembers the way he sowed panic, subtly playing off the fear of the board. They couldn't pay the ransom quickly enough. Ray always knew there was something fake about him. Rage simmers beneath his skin.

Sydney displays a table of transactions. 'Over the last year, there have been multiple payments from Ninja Magpie to him,' says Sydney.

Ray shakes his head. 'I should have seen this.'

'You couldn't have known,' says Aidan.

Ray exhales slowly. This is big. Jude works for the NCSC. Another trusted insider, but this time, it's someone at the heart of the UK's cyber intelligence organisation. Someone with access to the latest threat intel. No wonder Ninja Magpie are so good at evading capture.

'What now?' says Aidan.

Ray lifts his eyebrows and smiles. 'We do the right thing.' He points to Sydney's laptop. 'Send me all the evidence. I'll make the phone calls.'

'I'll email it over now,' says Sydney, already tapping at her laptop.

'This is an incredible piece of detective work,' says Ray.

'Having Rachel's crypto wallet was the key. We would never have discovered this otherwise,' says Sydney.

'This is going to be big news,' says Ray. 'It even eclipses the news I was going to share with you.'

He tells them about the data-tampering investigation, about Jim Craig and his obsession with revenge against Synaptonica, in particular Sean Bristol. Any day now, the regulators are likely to make a dawn raid – not at the head office, but at their clinical study centre in Cambridge. It will send shockwaves through the company and could mean the proposed takeover is called off. He explains how he had to back off as he was getting into matters he didn't fully understand. They both nod and thank him for the heads up.

They linger a few minutes more. Their mood is still high and they make plans for their next pub night out – Sydney's turn to choose.

The coffee shop fills again, lunchtime chatter rising to a warm cacophony around them. They leave in high spirits, the uncertainty of an impending crisis at Synaptonica failing to dampen their elation at solving another cybercrime.

Ray arrives home and heads directly to his office. He takes a moment to gather his thoughts, then makes the call to his friend Jack Brady at the National Cyber Security Centre.

'Hello, Ray. How are you?' says Jack warmly.

'Couldn't be happier, Jack. You?'

He sighs. 'Same old shitstorm, Ray. Two more companies hit by ransomware this week. Looks like at least one's going to pay, otherwise they'll go bust.'

Ray sighs. 'It's becoming an epidemic.'

'You said it. We're missing you in our weekly briefings. They aren't the same without someone to agitating the discussion.'

Ray laughs. 'I miss them too.'

'What can I do for you, Ray?'

Ray takes a breath. 'Are you sitting down?'

Ray lays it out, piece by piece: the crypto analysis, the wallet trace, the link to the pseudonymous Twitter account. Jude Wiseman – one of his staff – is on Ninja Magpie's payroll. Just like an old-school bent copper.

Jack listens in silence, then speaks. 'Ray, you can't make accusations like that without evidence.'

Ray presses the send button on the email he's pre-prepared. 'I have just sent the files to you.'

Jack receives it a moment later, then opens the attachments. One by one, Ray walks him through it, meticulously, unemotionally. He describes the crypto transaction flow and the blockchain ledger which records transactions which no one can alter. Then the link to the X profile, which Jude logged in to. All the facts, all the evidence, ready for him to verify. If Ray has jumped to the wrong conclusion, Jack will tell him. But there is no counter challenge.

There is silence for a moment. 'Okay, Ray. We will take it from here.'

'Can you keep me updated?' says Ray.

'Of course.'

Ray has never felt so alive. He paces into the kitchen, makes a cup of tea he won't drink, and carries it back to his study. He sits, staring at the monitor, unable to focus on a single thing. His mind races, replaying every step that led to this moment: Rachel's crypto wallet, the public blockchain ledger, the firewall logs that exposed Jude as the owner of that X profile. The evidence had been there all along. There's always a digital fingerprint. It just needs a skilled team to find it. *His* team.

He still thinks of Aidan and Sydney that way – his team. Together they uncovered the truth.

A thrill surges through him. This is what he lives for: the chaos, the breakthrough, the moment of revelation. He reclines back in his chair, smiling to himself. He's euphoric. Yet a quiet ache lingers inside. He misses it. The hum of his old cyber operations centre. The glow or the real-time video wall, the hammering of keyboards, the rising energy levels as the hunt closes in. He misses it so badly.

Two hours pass and Ray's phone rings. He recognises the number.

He answers. 'Jack?'

'Ray, I promised you an update,' says Jack.

Ray is gripping his phone. 'Go on.'

'Your evidence checks out. We're in shock.'

Ray's shoulders drop and his body relaxes. 'So, what happens now?'

'The National Crime Agency have picked him up. They arrested him mid-meeting with a client and he's now in custody. Thank you, Ray. I can't tell you how important this is.'

'Fantastic. How else can I help?'

'You need to leave it with us now, Ray. But we owe you. Is there anything we can do for you?'

Ray thinks. One name rises in his mind – the person who provided the breadcrumbs, and this might be perfect timing. He leans back in his chair. 'Perhaps one thing, Jack.'

Ray and Kirsty sit together, chatting, without the distraction of television. Ray is walking Kirsty though his extraordinary day. He's not sure he'll get to sleep tonight as his brain is still buzzing.

He tells her he's thinking about going freelance. He has many connections in the industry and feels he can pick up work and build a client base.

'Go for it,' says Kirsty.

Ray's feels instantly relaxed. To have Kirsty give him the thumbs up is validation that he's making a good decision. He'll enjoy being his own boss.

'Rachel's court appearance is coming up in a few days. I was thinking about going to it. She's pled guilty, so it's a sentence hearing and her fate will depend on the strength of her mitigating circumstances,' he says.

Kirsty shakes her head. 'There could be someone from Synaptonica there, and that could lead to awkward questions. Best you stay away.'

Ray shrugs. 'I'm just curious.'

'Tell you what, I'll go. I'll sit discreetly in the public gallery. No one knows who I am.'

34

Rachel doesn't flinch as Officer Denton leans in and stares into her eyes.

'When you come back, your new home will be through there.' He jerks his thumb over his shoulder. 'The convicted criminals' wing.'

She shrugs. 'I'm looking forward to making new friends.'

He sneers. 'And we've lined up a lovely cellmate for you. A real welcoming type.'

She doesn't give him the reaction he wants and remains unfazed as the escorting officer fastens the handcuffs, cold metal biting into her wrists, then guides her through the security gate into the waiting white prison van. She steps into her box-like compartment and the door clanks shut behind her.

She exhales slowly. Not long now.

She is coming to terms with the weight of the likely sentence – six years, perhaps. It doesn't crush her anymore. Three inside, three on licence. She'll take that. She has a plan. She'll study. Start that psychology degree she's been thinking about. Hit the gym every day and continue her prison listener role. That is the most rewarding thing she has done since being inside. People thank her for just listening to them.

She'll be forty-one when she gets out. Still time to possibly become a mother. It's something to hope for.

The van slows as it jolts over the speed bumps on the access road. She braces herself and closes her eyes, drawing a deep, cleansing breath. Inhale. Hold. Exhale. She dreams of a non-custodial sentence, visualising herself doing graffiti removal and litter-picking on the canal towpath as community payback. But that's a longshot. Her mitigation isn't strong enough.

She's going to walk into court, accept her guilt and pay her dues.

Somewhere in the bowels of the court building, Rachel waits in a holding cell. No windows. No books. Just a plastic chair, a wooden bench, a stainless-steel toilet and a limescale-stained sink. Her prison cell feels five-star in comparison. She can't sit still and paces in a tight square and steps on the spot, as if in an exercise class. She's only there for ten minutes when the door clunks open and she sees the smiling face of Matthew, her solicitor. He's early. The hearing's still two hours away.

'Rachel.' He greets her with all the enthusiasm of a man welcoming guests to a housewarming. This is his first case. He's probably excited and wants to make a good impression with his senior.

They shake hands. 'We need to talk,' he says.

It looks like he has a new suit – navy with burgundy check. A faint purplish mark peeks above his shirt collar. A love bite. Rachel holds in a smile. She wonders if that's from a girlfriend or a one-nighter.

They climb a narrow flight of stairs, then into an echoing hallway with varnished wood panels. The building creaks and echoes with heels on wooden floorboards, creaking doors and murmuring voices. Through an archway, up a stairwell then finally into a room, with leather chairs and floor-to-ceiling bookshelves filled with thick-spined law books. A tall bay window looks out over the inner courtyard. Rachel watches two barristers in wigs and gowns crossing the stone square below, deep in conversation. She hasn't even met her barrister yet.

She sinks into the chair opposite Matthew, and without warning, the nerves hit. Her legs tremble. She grips the armrest and breathes.

Matthew straightens, lacing his fingers on the desk. 'There have been developments,' he says. 'Good ones.'

Rachel jolts upright in her chair. 'In what way?'

'One of the Ninja Magpie gang is now in police custody.'

Her mouth falls open. 'Wow. Who?'

'Jude Wiseman.'

Rachel frowns. 'I don't know anyone by that name.'

'He pocketed four million from the cyber-attack.' He taps the desk with his finger. 'And if it wasn't for you, he'd still be out there, scamming his next victim.'

She shakes her head. 'I think they've got the wrong person.'

Matthew pulls a document from a plastic wallet and reads it through, quickly nodding to himself. 'This is a statement from the National Cyber Security Centre, who have been working with the National Crime Agency. They have evidence of cryptocurrency transfers from Ninja Magpie to his crypto wallet. Some clever geeky person performed blockchain ledger analysis, whatever the hell that is, and traced multiple payments from Ninja Magpie to him over the last year – including four million from the cyber-attack on Synaptonica.' He waves the document. 'This discovery was all thanks to you.'

Rachel's head spins with confusion and excitement. She feels a sharp pulse at her temples. Ray Dunlop said he would look into her crypto wallet, but he never got back to her. And who the hell is this Jude person?

'Matthew, I can't keep up. Bottom line, what does this mean for me?'

He leans forward, eyes bright, smile wide. 'I've spoken to our barrister; she's negotiating with the prosecution now. This is our strongest mitigation, Rachel. You *might* walk free.'

Her fingers tighten around the armrest. She feels her heart pounding as she takes in Matthew's beaming face. Or is it a naïve smile? *Please don't give me false hope.*

'What is realistic?' she asks, dragging out the word.

He exhales. Pauses. 'Two years.'

Rachel nods. 'Thank you.' She still doesn't understand how all the pieces fit together but will take all the help she can get.

He launches into a run-through of court procedure: prosecution, defence, judges summary. Rachel tries to concentrate as she watches him talk, but the words wash over her. This is the best news she's had, but she's too scared to raise her hopes. Her eyes focus again on the faint mark on his neck, still visible above his collar. Perhaps his optimism is more to do with last night's sex rather than insights into the judge's likely decision.

When her time comes, Rachel is led to the elevated dock at the centre of the courtroom. Thick glass panels enclose her on all sides, as though she's an exhibit under scrutiny. She faces the judge's bench directly, in direct sight of the intimidating high-backed chair in the centre of the bench. A symbol of authority.

There are few people in court, but her eyes immediately find Tony in the public gallery. He's sitting upright, wearing a suit. She feels supported. That helps. Her little brother will stick by her, no matter what. He catches her gaze and gives a thumbs up. She nods and returns his smile. Alongside him are three student-like people, with notepads. Perhaps law students. On the back row is a solitary woman, slightly older than Rachel. Mum and Dad stayed away, just as she had asked. She doesn't want to see the hurt and despair on their faces when the judge passes sentence. No one else she knows. Not Adam and certainly not Richard.

She glances down at the long wooden table before her. Matthew is deep in discussion with her barrister, a tall, slim woman who looks no older than thirty. They seem close. She touches Matthew's arm and Rachel wonders if she's his girlfriend, then dismisses the idea. She's out of his league.

'All rise, if able,' shouts a court usher.

Everyone stands and the judge enters, her robes flowing as she takes her seat at the centre of the bench. Everyone bows in synchrony. Rachel rises too, legs trembling, heartbeat rapid. This is it. Everything that happens now is out of her hands. Her palms are sweaty. She closes her eyes. *If there is a God, I ask for forgiveness.* She glances at the main entrance door and imagines walking out with Tony by her side, then back into the mundane outside world, where she can have a coffee, ride the Tube, wear jeans and visit Florence.

She breaks out of her daydream as the prosecution opens. He seems like a seasoned barrister – tired, puffy eyes, probably close to retirement. He reads through the charges with solemn precision, pausing at key points for effect. He speaks of unauthorised acts and impairment of computer operations. He uses words like *culpability*, *intent* and *consequence*. Then, *millions in lost revenue*. It could have been a West End stage performance.

'Rachel Carter was a trusted employee, in a position of managerial responsibility. She abused that privilege for her own gain, causing material damage to the organisation,' he says as a finishing statement.

She shuts her eyes and guilt sinks in as she pictures herself back in prison. Locked in her cell, awakening to the sound of shouting and feet kicking against cell doors. The daytime boredom, trading shampoo for postage stamps, the fights and the low-grade canteen food. Denton's gloating face as he engineers the worst possible prison experience for her.

'Counsel for the defence,' says the judge.

Her barrister rises, spine straight, voice steady. She's young, articulate and assertive. Probably went to a private school.

She begins with Rachel's character: a hard-working professional entangled in circumstances far beyond her control. She speaks warmly, as if they've known one another for years.

She goes on to the mitigation circumstances and outlines the bribes and the attack, and how she refused to help the gang, even under duress. Then her eventual cooperation with the police. There is a report from the prison – remorse and rehabilitation. Her work as a listener. Then, just as Matthew had said earlier, the game changer. The arrest of a key member of the notorious Ninja Magpie cyber gang. Someone involved in multiple extortion attacks which would have continued had it not been for Mrs Carter volunteering information leading to his arrest, as supported by a statement from the National Cyber Security Centre.

'May it please the court, that concludes my submissions,' she finishes.

Rachel exhales slowly. Whatever the outcome, she knows they've fought for her. Her barrister. Matthew. Even Tony, just by showing up.

The judge begins her summary remarks. She reiterates the gravity of the offences, the economic impact, the breach of trust. Then she acknowledges the mitigation and cooperation. Rachel's legs tremble again. It feels like they are holding a gun to her head, just to draw out the distress. The judge pauses, then continues.

'Rachel Carter, I sentence you to two years' imprisonment.'

Rachel's hands fly to her face, palms covering her eyes. Her body shudders. The tears come. They're unstoppable.

'However,' she continues, 'this sentence will be suspended for two years.'

Rachel lowers her hands. Did she hear that right?

The judge continues, explaining that if she commits another offence, the sentence will automatically activate. Then there are other conditions: 200 hours of community service.

'You are free to go.'

Rachel collapses back into her chair. The tears still pour down her face, but this time the emotion is elation.

35

R achel sits alone at a table for two, taking pleasure from a barista-crafted latte, which she sips from a proper ceramic cup. They have artistically traced a heart – or is it a coffee bean? – on the micro-foam and a thin wafer biscuit sits on the edge of the saucer. The banana-and-walnut loaf was tempting. It looked moist and still warm, but four quid a slice seems indulgent for an ex-con without a job.

In the corner, a group of mothers have gathered at a bench table. One stands, gently rocking her baby while a toddler tugs at her sleeve. Another feeds her baby from a bottle and the third struggles to get her baby to sit still in a high chair. A server brings her a warmed jar of baby food and a bright plastic spoon. She catches snippets of their conversation – the cost of pre-school, playdates, sleep routines. She imagines they are stay-at-home mums with working husbands, or maybe they are enjoying maternity leave. All look about Rachel's age. A pang of envy rises within her, but she lets it soften. She has time. And five frozen eggs in the bank. Yes, something to hope for.

She glances at her watch. She's early. But sitting alone in the sunlit coffee shop is a luxury in itself. The winter sun streams through the tall windows, warming her face. Outside, the city hums to its morning routine. Office workers with briefcases stride past, students meander, glancing at their phones every few seconds, cyclists, scooters, cabs and white vans negotiate roadworks. A beanie-wearing window cleaner draws a squeegee in smooth, practised strokes on the other side of the glass. Inside, the coffee shop fills with chatter and laughter. No one gives her a second glance because no one knows who she is. That's the beauty of London; it's easy to be anonymous amongst the familiar.

She could so easily have been in prison rather than sitting here and has so many people to thank: her solicitor, her barrister, her brother. It was the combination of people, luck and circumstance that converged at the right moment in time. Amanda would likely call it karmic intervention from the cosmic universe. She smiles and makes a mental note to write to her. She'll also write to Matthew's senior, telling him what a great solicitor he is.

Rebuilding her old life is going to be tough. No, impossible. She imagines walking back into her gym, being stared at as she rejoins her regular classes. Judged. She's not ready for that. There are going to be many awkward moments. One's coming up this afternoon.

Through the sparkling window, Rachel spots a familiar figure crossing the road. He's wearing a beige overcoat and has a woollen scarf wrapped round his neck. Ray Dunlop is as pristine as ever. On time, to the minute. She waves; he nods. When he steps inside, she rises and they hug. He heads to the counter, orders a latte then joins her at the window table. She's happy he came to meet her. She doesn't understand all the twists that brought her to this point, but hopefully he can fill in the gaps.

'You look like you're off to an interview – or are you still pretending to have a job?' says Rachel.

He smiles. 'Neither. I've gone freelance. Meeting with a potential client later. I'm hoping it will be my first billing assignment.'

'Congratulations,' she says with a smirk. 'And good luck to the client.'

He laughs. 'I know I'm not the easiest person to work with.' He brushes biscuit crumbs into a neat pile at the corner of the table. 'But I have a good network to draw on. Someone will bite.'

His coffee arrives and he stirs in a sugar lump. 'How are you? It must be good to be out of that place.'

Rachel shrugs. 'Don't knock it. No bills, no rent, three meals a day and bonus phone credit for good behaviour. Now, I'm sleeping on my brother's sofa and have just enough to buy a budget shop from Lidl. Still, mustn't grumble.'

Ray offers to buy her a second coffee and a slice of cake. She accepts.

She has many questions for Ray. Who is this Jude person, and what's happening with that data-tampering investigation? Ray starts with the data tampering, describing how they discovered it from the Excel version history. Jim Craig reanalysed the data and reported his findings to the regulators. They will do their own investigation and if they confirm the fraud, then it will be one of the biggest scandals in the industry, leading to the arrest of those involved. Jim Craig is probably standing outside the office, waiting to gloat. Ray explained it was too risky for him to get involved, so he stepped back and left it to Craig.

'What do you think will happen to Synaptonica?'

'They'll survive. They have other drugs in development. But the takeover will collapse, and the share price will drop even more, which means Winstanley and the other directors will miss out on their big payday, and will probably have to resign – if they haven't already been arrested.'

Rachel smiles. 'I won't lose sleep over that.'

'Tell me about Jude,' Rachel says.

Ray tells her about the cyber consultant, Jude Wiseman. An upstart who ingratiated himself with Catherine Davenport. A flagrant con-artist, masquerading as a second-rate cyber security consultant. Ray never trusted him nor liked him, but the discovery of him being on Ninja Magpie's payroll blindsided him. Thanks to Rachel's Bitcoin wallet, Aidan and Sydney traced transactions to a X profile, then discovered he was behind it. A trusted investigator from the NCSC – beyond suspicion. He was clever, except for that one slip-up.

Rachel nods. 'Thank you. That's what got me out of jail.'

'His arrest is big news. The Americans want him extradited.'

'And Aleks and Izabela?'

He shakes his head. 'True identity and whereabouts still unknown.'

A flicker of unease passes through her. She's still looking over her shoulder, knowing what they are capable of. Then she thinks back to the lone woman in the public gallery of the courtroom. Attentive, taking notes. Who was she? Her barrister made such a performance about Rachel volunteering information which led to the arrest of Jude. Is she one of them? Are they now looking to exact revenge?

They talk for over an hour about jobs she can do. Ray mentions the website, *UpWork.com*, a marketplace for freelancers. He says, without intended irony, that she could set herself up as an ethical hacker and do bug bounty challenges. They pause their conversation when a woman server appears and clears the crockery from their table. She asks if they want to order food. They take the hint and say they're just leaving. Rachel zips up her thick walking jacket. Ray begins what seems to be a ritual: coat on, coat off, smooths it flat, then on and buttoned up. Then the scarf, wrapped, unwrapped then rewrapped until it passes his self-inspection. Rachel watches, amused. She likes Ray, but he must be a nightmare to live with.

They hug at the door.

'Take care of yourself,' he says.

'You too.'

As he steps away, Rachel has the distinct feeling their paths will cross again. It's fate, as Amanda would say.

Rachel walks a familiar path through the drizzle. The hood of her coat shields her from rain and nosey neighbours. She reaches the front door. It's been nearly three months since she last stepped inside. Feels more like three years. She reminds herself that this is still her house.

She exhales, grabs the handle, pushes open the door and steps inside. She hangs her coat on the hook, as if in autopilot.

'Hi,' she shouts, more impatient than she intended.

Richard appears at the top of the stairs, ever familiar in his navy Nike tracksuit. He descends slowly. No smile. He reaches the hallway and folds his arms. 'You must be happy.'

'Two years suspended and community payback.' She shrugs. 'Can't complain.'

There's an awkward silence.

'How are you?' asks Rachel.

'Keeping busy.'

She glances around. It's tidier than she expected. No sports kit littering the hallway or clothes draped over the banister. She wonders if he's had another woman back.

She brushes past him towards the kitchen. 'I'm having a cup of tea. Want one?'

'Okay.'

She wasn't expecting balloons or fanfare or even a hug. That's fine. She's only staying long enough to agree arrangements.

In the kitchen, the emptiness stings. Her windowsill garden has gone – the salad leaves, herbs, spring onions, carrot shoots. It looks bare without that little patch of vegetation she cared for and harvested. She shoots him a look as she fills the kettle. It wouldn't have taken much for him to keep them alive. She opens the fridge to find the basics of butter, milk, jam, bread, pizza and a few ready meals. She used to store her pre-prepared meals on the top shelf, kept fresh in Tupperware boxes. She notices a tub of Greek yoghurt, opened. He doesn't eat yoghurt. She grabs the milk and closes the door slowly. It might make things easier if he has found someone, but he shouldn't bring her back here.

She brews two mugs of tea with a single teabag and stirs in the milk, memories swirling inside her head. This kitchen was her retreat in the evenings after work, when Richard was out. This is where she baked her own bread, and she would always have a jar of Kombucha fermenting. It feels like someone else's kitchen now. She throws the teaspoon into the stainless-steel sink bowl. Her anger levels are rising and is going to say something. She pauses. Closes her eyes, takes a breath and reminds herself that the two of them need to have an adult conversation.

They move to the living room and sit opposite each other. He's slouched with his legs crossed. She notices the wall behind the sofa, once filled with photographs of their engagement, wedding and honeymoon. Now bare. Only the hooks remain. That shouldn't upset her, but it feels like her personality is being removed from the home she furnished and decorated. Maybe that's what has to happen, but she still needs a bit more time to detox, emotionally.

He takes a drink from his mug. 'What are your plans?'

'I'm staying with Tony for the next couple of nights. Then I'll be back here.'

He snorts. 'Really?'

She stares into her mug. 'We are going to have to live together, Richard. Like before, but separate. You take the spare room, I'll have the bedroom. A house-share, basically. We share bills.' She forces a smile. 'Live as friends.'

He shakes his head. 'Too many secrets and lies, Rachel.'

Rachel flinches. He's changed. It's as if he hates her. 'Well, neither of us can afford a place of our own. So, can we just try to get along?'

'And you'll still bring Tony and his daughter back here when I'm out?'

'He's my brother!' she shouts.

'And what about Adam?'

That hits her like a stone. He's worked it out or someone's told him. That would explain his surliness when he came to visit her in prison. Her grip on the mug tightens. She turns her head away.

'I think,' she says calmly, 'we need to respect that we're free to see other people. Just not here. This should be neutral ground.'

They sit in silence, both containing their own rage. This is not how she wanted the conversation to go. But she *will* move back in on Saturday and *will* reclaim her kitchen. He can play pickleball to his heart's content and Tony and Florence *can* come round when he's out. She'll stay at Adam's house some nights. With good coordination, they may hardly see each other. She needs this to work, for the short-term at least.

Upstairs, she opens the door to the bedroom. The duvet lies neatly over the bed. He has never made a bed like that in all the years she has known him. She opens her wardrobe and her drawers. Her clothes look untouched. She unzips her overnight bag and starts packing – jeans, wool jumper, socks and nice underwear. She gathers up her makeup and electric toothbrush. Overnight essentials – luxuries by prison standards. She grabs her dead iPad and charging cable.

She glances around her bedroom. A question nags her. What would he have done if she'd served two years? Would she have come back to find her clothes boxed up and another woman in the house? How much of her life would he have erased?

Outside, it's dark. Richard stands by the front door, expression unreadable.

She walks down the stairs, bag in hand. 'I'll be back Saturday.'

'I'll be out most of the day. But you can take the spare room. And I don't want your brother here unless he starts to pay back the money you gave him. That's what caused this mess.'

'Well then, you can catch-up on all those mortgage payments you've missed. Nine months, I believe.'

She shoves past him, and the door slams shut behind her. The nice guy act was brief, and his true personality is showing once more. He's always known what buttons to press and when to press them. Her inner rage lingers. That's what he does to her.

She follows the satnav to Tony's house. It's a large mid-terrace Victorian property, probably once a family home, now converted into a house of multiple occupation. What was once a front garden is now a patch of cracked concrete with weeds pushing up through the fractures. A scratched and dented blue van and an ageing Ford Fiesta sit there, side by side. The house has large bay windows, their wooden frames flaking with white paint, exposing rotten wood.

She unlocks the door with the key Tony gave her. The hallway is narrow and dim. The woodchip wallpaper, once white, is now stained with patches of grey and yellow. Two pairs of men's work shoes sit against the skirting board. They smell. She wants to put them outside but thinks they might get stolen.

She climbs the stairs and finds numbered rooms, like in a hostel, each with a digital keypad lock. She punches in the code for room 2 and steps inside. The double bed takes up most of the floor space, forcing her to climb over it just to reach the window. She opens it wide, letting in the chill, damp air. This is what he gets for £1,100 a month. On the dresser sits a framed photo of the three of them: Tony, Florence and her. She picks it up and smiles. Florence is beaming, her arms wrapped round her dad's neck. Rachel wonders when she'll see her again. Sarah refused all visits during her time inside. Fair enough. But she's out now and family is important.

It will be two hours before Tony's back, after his twelve-hour shift at the hotel. Not that long ago, he was drifting and sleeping rough. It's as if he's now found a purpose in life. His job as a chef and love for his daughter are keeping him off the booze. She'll make him dinner when he gets home. Whatever food he has in the house, she'll rustle something up.

She finds the kitchen at the back of the house, stretching into a narrow extension. She flicks a switch, and the fluorescent lights stutter before buzzing into life. The magnolia walls are bare and the counters are clear, except for a kettle, a budget microwave and a scratched toaster. Every cupboard has a combination padlock. Above the sink is a paper sign, hand-written: *UNWASHED CROCKERY WILL BE BINNED*. She opens the fridge and finds a carton of milk with Tony's name on it. She makes a cup of tea, enjoying the warmth of the mug.

Tony arrives home just after eight, carrier bag in hand.

'Leftovers from a corporate event we were hosting,' he says, lifting out a cardboard tray of sandwiches wrapped in clingfilm. 'They would have gone in the bin otherwise.'

She smiles. 'Perfect. I can't abide good food going to waste.'

He grins. 'I've got some good news for you.'

'Good news has been in short supply today,' she says, arching an eyebrow.

'I spoke to my manager. He said he'll give you a start. Tomorrow. Trial shift.'

She straightens. 'That's brilliant. Doing what?'

'Officially, front of house, but it will be a bit of everything: serving, pot washing, cleaning tables, toilets.' He grimaces. 'It's a bit of a come-down, I know—'

'Tony, I don't have any other offers and I'm skint, so I'll clean the men's urinals with a toothbrush if I have to.'

He laughs. 'The toilets are quite lavish in this place.'

She smiles. 'What time do I start?'

'Seven. But you need to be there ten minutes before.'

Later, Rachel slips into the sleeping bag Tony laid out for her on the living room sofa. The house is quiet except for the faint noise of televisions from locked rooms and the occasional creaking of floorboards as other occupants pass through. No one speaks to her. No eye contact. But that doesn't matter. It's been an exhausting day, and she's too tired for small talk with strangers.

She lies on her side, phone in hand, scrolling through her social media accounts. Her feed is full of happiness – drunk friends at New Year's parties, people on the ski slope, family gatherings. She considers posting something. Perhaps a photo with the caption, *I'm out*. Then decides against it. Low profile for now.

She scrolls through some history and finds a picture of her friend Cathy, with her arms wrapped around her man. Both smiling. They are on a beach somewhere. It is a *change of status* post. They are now engaged. She thinks back to when they last spoke – at that restaurant in Chinatown. She hopes she hasn't lost her as a friend. They have always been there for each other. Under difference circumstances, Cathy may have asked her to be maid of honour. She hesitates, then adds her congratulatory message in the comments.

The glow of her phone fades and she stares at the ceiling, listening to the sounds of the house – doors clicking shut, floorboards creaking, the boiler switching itself off and on. She's missing Amanda's irrepressible chatter. It feels quite eerie sleeping alone in a room with an unlocked door. The sleeping bag is thin and the sofa sags, but she's not chasing comfort tonight. She is thinking of the new life path she has to navigate. Richard's going to be difficult, and who knows what other curveballs will come her way. She feels secure with Tony looking out for her, and she still has Adam. They chatted briefly on FaceTime this evening. It was brief, but long enough for him to tell her he's looking forward to seeing her again. He's going to prepare dinner for her coming over tomorrow. She pictures herself back in his house, sitting on his sofa drinking Prosecco. Then in bed together, curled under his duvet, luxuriating in his sleek ensuite wet room. She's ready for that now. The perfect escape from the tribulations of a post-prison lifestyle.

36

A shrill ringtone jolts Rachel awake. She blinks repeatedly. After a few moments, she remembers where she is and what day it is. The room is dimmer now with fading light. She only intended to have a ten-minute nap but has been zonked out for forty-five. She had collapsed onto Tony's bed the minute she got back from her ten-hour shift at the hotel. It was relentless.

She rolls out of bed, peels off her tight-fitting uniform and wraps a barely adequate towel around herself. Grabbing her shampoo, she trundles to the shared bathroom at the end of the landing, steps into the cubicle and wets herself with lukewarm water trickling from the mouldy shower head.

Her legs and ankles ache most, as if she's climbed a mountain or run a marathon. Other than her twenty-minute lunch break, she hasn't sat down all day. Not like Lisa, her shift partner. Twenty-something years old and six months pregnant – by accident – giving her a perfect excuse to spend most of the day perched on a cushioned stool, folding napkins and preparing side salads, while Rachel did pot washing, serving and table clearing. All day! Prison jobs are a cushy number by comparison. There were some generous tips from the restaurant, and she wonders how they get shared out. She didn't want to ask on her first-day trial shift. She received cash-in-hand, minimum wage.

Fifty-five minutes later and she's ready. Hair blow-dried into an asymmetric bob, makeup applied with care: mascara, foundation, a sweep of lipstick and a touch of perfume. She studies her reflection. She hasn't looked or felt this much like herself in months, but still a flutter of nervousness from a mix of hope, apprehension and a fear that something is going to go wrong. It's three months since they last slept together. A month since they last saw each other, separated by a visitors' table. Then she remembers how he looked at her on the video call last night, how he joked about her turning up in a sexy, revealing hotel uniform.

She picks up her phone and summons an Uber. Four minutes until pickup then twenty minutes journey time. Hope and nerves run through her as she slips on her coat. Tonight matters. This is the start of her new life path. She messages him:

Just leaving, see you shortly, xx.

He replies instantly:

Ready and waiting :-), xx.

She picks up her overnight bag and smiles, heart drumming faster. She closes her eyes. *It's going to be fine.*

The journey time was accurate and the driver courteous, but she can't afford to give a tip. She steps out of the Uber, walks carefully up the paved drive. Her breath swirls in the cold night air. As she approaches the door, a security light clicks on, casting a golden glow across the drive. She presses the doorbell. The door swings open. Adam stands there, styled hair, trimmed beard, fitted crew neck top that hugs his toned frame. He grins.

'You're not Uber Eats,' he says.

'I can be Uber whatever you want me to be,' she replies with a laugh.

He opens his arms, and she steps inside. Her bag drops with a thud in the hallway as she sinks into his embrace and enjoys the familiar scent of aftershave. His hands cradle the back of her head as they kiss. It's a lasting kiss. Reassuring. It makes her feel wanted and safe. When they part, he helps her out of her coat and hangs it neatly on the coat stand.

Inside is just as she remembers: the record player, quirky artwork, framed pictures of his children. A scented candle flickers on the coffee table, and the dining table is carefully prepared – plates, cutlery, flutes and napkins. Unlike last time, the kitchen is showing no sign of food preparation or cooking chaos.

'Let me guess – I'm cooking?' she says.

'You're welcome to raid my fridge and surprise me with one of your culinary concoctions. Or we can wait for the takeaway man and enjoy the nice Thai meal I ordered.'

She drops onto his sofa. 'After the day I've had, I just want looking after.' She nods towards the table. 'Are those glasses part of the decor or can we do something practical with them?'

'At your service, precious one.' He opens the fridge, pulls out a bottle of Prosecco, pops the cork and pours two flutes. As he hands one over, she feels it. That flicker of happiness she feared she had lost. The doorbell goes and Adam goes to answer – it's the takeaway. As he sets down the food cartons, she looks on, and wonders if he's had another woman back here, sitting on this sofa. She wouldn't blame him. It's been three months. He must have thought about walking away. It's not as if they were in a long-term relationship. And he didn't really know if she was getting out.

Adam spreads the food cartons across the table: spring rolls, crab cakes, green curry, red curry, pak choi, noodles and more. Too much for two, which means plenty of leftovers for Rachel.

They quickly finish the Prosecco and start on the red wine and fall into catch-up conversation. Rachel tells him about her plan to go freelance, setting herself up as a security tester – an ethical hacker, as it's known in the trade. She opens up about her less-than-ideal living arrangements with Richard, who's determined to get the best deal – the main bedroom and more house space. It's going to be a continuous points-scoring game.

'Sounds like *War of the Roses*,' says Adam.

She raises her eyebrows. 'What's that?'

'A book that was made into a film. Bit of a dark comedy. A self-destructive battle of wills between an estranged couple – the Roses – cohabiting in their marital home while attempting to divide living space and possessions. The original film starred Michael Douglas and Kathleen Turner.' He sips more wine. 'On second thought, best you don't watch it. It didn't end well.'

Adam talks about a job interview he has coming up – a step up and a higher salary. He needs it because his ex-wife is demanding more maintenance. She's relentless. He wants to take his kids on holiday over Easter, but she's demanding he redirects that money to her. She works full time but overstretched herself on a mortgage and is constantly demanding more. The arguments are getting unpleasant.

Bitching about each other's ex-partners isn't quite the romantic night-in conversation Rachel was envisioning, but it's honest and it's bringing them closer. When she was a prison listener, she learned everyone had some sort of background crisis. She's learning it's the same in the outside world. Perhaps behind every perfect persona is a big bag of life stresses.

A sudden thought crosses her mind. Maybe she could go on holiday with him and his kids.

When dinner is over, she gestures to the cartons with a grin. 'Want to keep the leftovers?'

He shakes his head. 'My kids are here tomorrow, so it'll be pizza or burgers.'

'Perfect. I'll take them. Bonus meals.'

He wanders over to his record player. 'Any requests?'

'Surprise me,' she says, stretching out on the sofa.

He selects an album, removes the record from its sleeve and drops it onto the turntable. Sting's voice fills the room. He sits beside her, drapes his arm across her shoulder. She leans into him.

'Let me show you pictures of my niece.' Rachel pulls out her phone and flips through the pictures. Finds one of the two of them in the house, with Rachel crouched down next to her.

He looks at the picture for a moment. He smiles. 'She's cute.' He hands the phone back. 'It must be great being an aunty. You can have all the fun then hand them back afterwards.'

Rachel smiles. That's not how she sees it.

Morning light pushes through the curtains. Rachel sits propped up in bed while Adam makes coffee in the kitchen. The afterglow of their night together lingers - the warmth of his touch, the ease of their laughter. She feels radiant.

A touch of sadness creeps in as she checks the time. The ex-wife is due to drop off his kids in an hour. She would like to meet them, but perhaps it's still too soon, and she doesn't want to appear pushy. There's something else pressing on her mind. A question she's rehearsed in her head a dozen times, each version having different degrees of desperation. Maybe she can test the water with something casual, like: *aren't children so rewarding or I've always wanted to be a mum.* No, that's too forward.

Adam returns with two mugs of coffee. He hands her one, slips off his robe and slides back under the duvet beside her. Their legs brush. He leans over and kisses her softly. 'I wish you didn't have to go,' he murmurs.

She grins. 'Tell you what, let me stay. Then when your ex- turns up and asks why you've got a big smile on your face, I'll jump out from behind the door, still in my negligee, and say hi.'

He laughs. 'You're so funny.'

'You'll get used to me,' she says, tracing her fingers down his thigh.

He hesitates, then smiles. 'If you're comfortable, maybe... come round tomorrow? For lunch. Meet the kids. I think they'll like you.'

A feeling of warmth passes through her. The doubts that have hovered all week dissolve. She nods, 'Okay'.

They sit in a comfortable silence, sipping their coffees. *This feels like a good moment.* 'There's something I want to ask you,' she says, setting down her mug.

He raises an eyebrow. 'Go on'

She opens her mouth, then falters. Her pulse quickens. 'Don't read too much into this,' she says, forcing a smile. 'I'm just... curious. Would you ever consider having more children?'

For a moment he looks taken aback. Not a question he was expecting. He shakes his head. 'No. I have my children. I love them but don't want any more.'

His words hit her like a punch. So definite. No hesitation. No, shrug of the shoulders to say, *maybe someday.*

He exhales. 'That's why I had a vasectomy. I'm forty-six. I've done the family stuff.'

She stares at him, scrambling for something to hold on to as the future she imagined evaporates like the steam from her coffee. Only last night, they said they loved each other, for the first time. She swallows. 'The thing is ... I do want children... Not right away, but eventually. It's something I've always wanted. More than anything.'

He doesn't answer. Just watches her, his expression soft but unyielding.

She tells him about her vision of family life, with a loving partner, sharing the pleasures of parenthood. About the five frozen eggs, waiting in a freezer - her insurance policy against time. She isn't asking for promises, only a glimpse of possibility.

Adam's voice is gentle. 'I am so sorry. Truly, I would love to share my life with you. But raising another child... I can't do that.'

Her eyes sting. She forces herself to nod as she holds back the tears. Five minutes ago, she was glowing, cocooned in happiness. Now, her dream has come to an abrupt end and the warm glow replaced with a cold reality.

They lie in silence, staring at the ceiling, realising they are on different life paths, which will never converge.

37

Three months later

The prison visiting area has changed little since Rachel was here last. Same scuffed floors and grubby, painted walls. Only the new family area stands out: a small cluster of multi-coloured child-sized tables and chairs. A recent donation from some women's charity, apparently. It seems out of place, like a floral clock in an acre of weeded wasteland.

She sits, sipping familiar lukewarm tea from a plastic cup. The sound of the heavy door clanking open sends a jolt through her. For a moment, she's back inside, coping with the lock-up routines and the uncertainty of what the next day will bring. She's been out for three months now, but it doesn't take much to trigger the memories.

She glances around the room – husbands, families and restless children climbing on chairs that are too big for them. She's the only volunteer visitor here, as far as she can tell.

The women file in. Some faces she recognises, others she doesn't. The room fills with chatter, laughter and a bit of sobbing. Rachel waits, scanning the line. Jackie is last to appear. Their eyes meet. Rachel waves and Jackie gives a slight nod before shuffling over and sitting down. She's still too thin. Tracy – Officer Evans – had told Rachel she was still on suicide watch. She reaches her hand across the table; Jackie takes it with her own cold hand. Her grip is as light as a feather.

'How are you, Jackie?'

Jackie shrugs. 'Getting out next week.'

'Do you have somewhere to go?'

She stares at the floor. 'A shared house, somewhere in South London.'

Rachel pictures it, a house just like Tony's. Borderline functional. The sort of place where you keep your door shut. Not somewhere to call home.

'Are you still working in the laundry?'

She shakes her head. 'I couldn't cope with it. Just stay in my cell now.'

Rachel searches for something practical to say. There are jobs out there for ex-prisoners, but they aren't easy to find, especially for someone like Jackie. She's fragile and will need help.

They continue talking about life inside, her favourite television programmes, the nicer prison officers. Her voice stays flat, but there is a flicker of presence there. When the hour is almost up, she talks more and becomes interested in Rachel: Where does she live? Does she see her family? Does she work? All awkward questions. She can't reveal too much about herself, but maybe that's a good sign. Perhaps Jackie imagines a future for herself on the outside.

They say goodbye. Rachel tells her to stay strong and eat more.

Rachel waits in the visitors' reception. After five minutes, Tracy appears. 'We appreciate you giving up your time to do this, Rachel,' she says.

'I wish there was more I could do.'

'There is, actually. Someone new came in last week. Young woman. Vulnerable.'

'In what way?'

'She hasn't spoken to a single person since arriving. Mostly stays in her cell. Just lies under her blanket.' She grimaces. 'We're out of options.'

Rachel straightens. 'Sounds like she needs medical help.'

'She's on medication, but...' She shakes her head. 'I was just thinking that someone like you might help her open up.'

Rachel nods. 'I'm free again next Tuesday. Put me down for a visit.'

'Thank you, Rachel. It may not be obvious, but people like you really make a difference.'

They shake hands, showing mutual respect. It feels strange, calling her by her first name. In a different life, they may have been friends.

Rachel boards the bus for the journey back home, feeling appreciated and grateful for what she has. She has life stresses, but at least she's not lonely. She pulls out her phone and notices a new message on WhatsApp. It's from Amanda. Her trial was last week. Rachel wanted to attend but couldn't because of her shifts at the hotel. The work is still casual, and she needs to take all the shifts available. Amanda's trial ran for four days, and the jury found her not guilty. What a result. She thought she was facing a five-year stretch. How did she pull that one off? Rachel smiles. Perhaps an intervention from some supernatural force. Her message says she'll be round at eight o'clock, after reading Gabe his bedtime story.

She taps open her freelancing app to find a message from someone who wants her to perform a security test on their new website. She reads through the details and estimates it to be at least twenty hours' work, but they are only offering £100. She declines. That's worse than the hotel. Her freelancing career is proving to be a slow burn. There is a big demand for security testers, but she's competing against people with hundreds of five-star reviews. She needs to build up her profile. Ray Dunlop has passed a couple of jobs her way, which has helped. She's also enrolled on some bug bounty programmes and recently earned £250 for finding a security flaw in one of Google's apps. She was proud of that. She is now working on two other apps from different software companies. It's a pay-by-the-bug gig, so for the meantime, she still needs her hotel job.

Shortly before eight, the doorbell rings. Rachel hurries to answer it and pulls open the door to find Amanda standing there, arms already outstretched.

'Darling.' She wraps her arms tightly around Rachel. 'I've missed you.'

'Well, congratulations, innocent person,' says Rachel.

'Tonight, we are celebrating freedom.'

She steps inside, unzips her overnight bag and hands Rachel a bottle of red wine and a small, gift-wrapped box.

'It's a seven-crystal feng shui tree,' she explains, 'for balance, healing and good vibes.'

Rachel feels immediately uplifted. She's looking forward to having a good chat and a laugh. She's been working non-stop, can't afford to go out and is tired of her own company in the evening. A fun night in, a few drinks and Amanda's irrepressible energy is exactly what she needs. They head to the kitchen.

'How's your living arrangement with Richard working out?' asks Amanda.

'We avoid each other most of the time. Works surprisingly well.'

'He won't mind me crashing on the sofa, then?'

Rachel laughs. 'He'll hate it. All the more reason for you to stay.'

They pour two generous glasses of wine and settle into the living room. Amanda launches into her stories. She is so happy to have little Gabe back in her life and making him breakfast in the morning. Then there's her sister's wedding in two weeks at a posh country estate. Over 100 guests and she wants Rachel to be her plus one.

Rachel listens patiently, smiling at Amanda's whirlwind updates, going from one topic to the next, hardly pausing for breath.

'So, Rachel. What about you?'

Rachel tells her about the hotel job, and how she's building up her freelance work. She's also doing one day a week in a charity shop for her community service. Best of all, she is seeing Florence again, with her dad.

'What about the love life?' asks Amanda.

Rachel hesitates. 'It's... complicated.'

Amanda rolls her eyes. 'Men aren't complicated. Come on, spit it out.'

So Rachel does. She tells her about Adam. The emotional reunion. The night he said he loved her. How for a brief, perfect moment, she pictured their lives together. Then the bombshell – his absolute certainty he did not want children. An irreconcilable difference that means they don't have a future together. She was heartbroken.

Amanda listened with uncharacteristic silence, then reached out to touch her hand. 'That's so sad.'

Rachel shrugs. 'Life can be crap sometimes.'

Amanda swirls her wine. 'So, are you back on the market?'

'Well, the trouble is, we're still seeing each other.'

Amanda's mouth falls open. 'My God. Is the sex that good?'

Rachel continues her story. They agreed to go their separate ways and remain friends, but within two weeks, they were back in bed together. She stays at his place every second weekend. They sort of exist in their own love bubble that refuses to pop.

'So, more than a fuck buddy but not really a proper relationship?'

Rachel swallows some wine. 'We both know it's temporary. One day, we'll have to move on, but...' She shrugs.

'Unless one of you changes your mind about family.'

Rachel shakes her head. 'Not going to happen.'

They are silent for a moment. The wine bottle is empty so Rachel fetches another and refills both glasses.

Amanda taps the rim of her glass. 'It's time to move on, Rachel. You need a distraction. Someone else to take your mind off him,' says Amanda.

Rachel smirks. 'I agree.'

Amanda grins. 'And I have an idea.'

Rachel sighs. 'Please don't suggest online dating. I've tried that. Disaster. One didn't turn up. Another was ten years older than his picture. Everyone else just wants a hookup. Some even send me dick pics.'

'Rachel, you are beautiful, funny and can hold an intelligent conversation. You deserve better than that.'

'Thank you.'

Amanda leans in. 'So, I am going to set you up on *sugardaddy.com*.'

Rachel's jaw drops. 'Tell me that's a joke.'

Amanda holds out her hand. 'Phone.'

Twenty minutes later, Rachel's *Sugar Babe* profile is live. They shaved six years off her age and applied filtering to a few photos. They scroll through the Sugar Daddy profiles. Most are in their fifties or sixties. Rachel suspects they are married. They close the app with a laugh and agree to check messages in the morning.

The front door opens, Richard comes in and sticks his head in. 'Hello,' he says, glancing at the two of them. He looks like he wants to say something. Probably something snide, like *Are you a friend from prison?* He'd have both of them to contend with if he does. He disappears upstairs without further interaction. He still has the main bedroom. That's a battle for another day.

Amanda dives back into wedding talk. Her sister's gown is a bit tight, so she'll have to drop a few pounds. Her mum's bought two new outfits. The groom is Scottish, so many of the men will be in kilts, which means legs on display. Her dad's almost guaranteed to make a smutty speech. There'll be single men there – well, divorced. A live band, Uncle Jimmy will probably get drunk; her cousins are a bit rough and might start fighting. But she and Rachel can dance until the early hours and have a great time.

'Perfect. Just what I need,' says Rachel.

Rachel's phone pings. She ignores it as she suspects it's a *Sugar Daddy* alert. As soon as Amanda leaves in the morning, she will remove her *Sugar Babe* profile. It was briefly funny, but adding a sixty-something non-committal man to her life is a distraction she can do without.

38

Rachel reads the message one last time. It must be a scam, but a quick glance at her PayPal wallet confirms the credit: £1,000. Her biggest bug bounty payment yet. She'd slogged for two days on that website, working through the night, attempting every abnormal input until she hacked it. It belongs to one of those city firms she could never work for now thanks to her conviction. But they outsource their security testing to an agency who farm it out to freelancers like her. She never imagined she would be thankful for big corporate outsourcing. The bug was an old-school SQL injection flaw, missed by the code scanners. She's getting better at finding security flaws and bugs, but this is the gig economy and there's no way to predict when the next job will come or how much it'll pay.

She steps into her bedroom and slips into her outfit – a blue, off-the-shoulder fitted dress with matching jacket. Thanks to her community service shifts in the charity shop, she picked it up for thirty pounds. It's had little wear and would cost over two hundred new. She turns sideways to the mirror, smoothing the fabric over her hips. Perfect fit for her body shape.

The Uber glides up the gravel driveway and pulls to a stop at the front entrance to a stone-built country house. She steps out of the car with her overnight bag, checks in to her room, then comes straight back outside. The guests cluster in small groups in the patio area, sipping their pre-wedding Pimm's and chatting. The men stand out with their kilts and dress jackets, all coordinated with green and blue tartan, lace-up brogues, waistcoats and blue heather buttonholes. The women wear fascinators or hats and are holding clutch bags and drinks. Amanda must be with her sister, helping her to get ready.

She is immediately conscious of how alone she is. She's normally comfortable starting conversations with strangers but this is different. She feels exposed. Many of these people probably know her background and will be talking about her. 'She's the guilty one,' she imagines them saying. Perhaps it wasn't such a good idea to come.

A young waiter approaches with a tray. 'Pimm's or orange juice?'

She smiles. 'Silly question.' She plucks a glass of Pimm's from the tray.

She walks a few steps to the edge of the lawn, pretending to admire the sculpted trees and manicured flowerbeds. The vast garden looks like something that would feature in *Country Life* magazine. She imagines people playing croquet on the expertly mowed lawn with its faint tramlines.

'You must be Rachel,' comes a voice from behind.

She turns, startled. A balding man approaches with a friendly smile. His wife follows just behind.

'I'm Andy,' he says, holding out his hand.

'And I'm Margaret,' adds the woman.

Relief spreads through Rachel like a sudden burst of sunlight. She shakes their hands.

'Amanda told us to look out for you,' says Andy. 'Come, let me introduce you to a few people.'

'I love your dress,' says Margaret as they walk. 'That colour really suits you.'

They lead her to a group of men and women around her own age. Andy makes the introductions. They shake hands, kiss cheeks. Rachel instantly forgets their names, except for one man. Ben. Tall, clean-shaven, and with the physique of a gym regular. His soft brown eyes meet hers just long enough to spark something. He smiles. So does she. A blonde woman edges close to him, touches his arm and starts talking. Phones come out for random group pictures and selfies.

'Can the guests please make their way to the ceremony room,' comes the booming voice of the master of ceremonies, who's decked out in red tails and a chain of office. Guests drain the remains of their drinks and file inside.

In the ceremony room, Rachel sits halfway down on the left, with Andy and Margaret beside her. Sitting next to her on the other side are a young couple who are talking about the beautiful venue – the flowers, the wall-hanging tapestries and the chandeliers hanging in the staircase. Probably thinking ahead to their own wedding, Rachel imagines. Across the aisle, she spots Ben sitting with two other male guests. The blonde is three rows ahead. Not his girlfriend, then.

String quartet music plays from the speakers. First down the aisle come little Gabe and his girl cousin. They're the same age as Florence. Then Amanda, radiant in a powder blue dress. Finally, the bride, in an elegant ivory gown, walking arm-in-arm with her proud father.

Rachel watches. She's never even spoken to the happy couple but still feels emotional. Her wedding was something like this. She would like to get married again, someday.

After the official photos, the guests drift towards the reception room for the wedding breakfast. Rachel's had at least three drinks in the last hour and hasn't paid for a single one. She spoke to strangers, chatted with little Gabe and made friends with Amanda's uncle Jimmy, who slipped her a double gin and tonic.

She finds her seat, marked with a handwritten name-card. It's a circular table for ten guests, alternating boy/girl. To her right are a married couple who must have fallen out as they are not smiling and don't seem to be speaking to one another. To her left is someone named Jason, who looks like he'll pop a few waistcoat buttons before the day is out. Ben sits at ten o'clock, two seats away. Next to him is the clingy blonde woman she met outside, who she now knows as Lucy.

As the waiter fills wine glasses, Jason waves him away. He's already cradling a large dram of whisky.

'I'll stick with my twelve-year-old Macallan,' he announces. 'I'm all-in Scottish today.' He pats his leg. 'First time I've ever worn a kilt.'

Rachel nods at him. 'I hope you're wearing it properly?'

'Absolutely.'

'Evidence!' Lucy shouts across the table.

He laughs. 'Two women have already checked.'

The table bursts into laughter. The wine flows, the noise rises, and Rachel feels completely at ease. Jason turns out to be the table's main entertainer, Ben the quiet one. She's not the outsider anymore. The jokes are flying and the vibe is warm, and every so often, she and Ben catch each other's eyes across the table. They hold their gaze a little longer this time. She smiles.

Then Lucy strikes. 'So, Rachel. How do you know Amanda?'

She asks with casual curiosity and underlying malevolence. She's chosen her moment well. Rachel didn't expect that. The table quietens. Lucy is still smiling.

Think of something, quickly. Rachel lifts her wine glass and swirls it. 'We met in a pub. I was on a hen-do, she was with her friends. We were both pissed. It was karaoke night, and we were the only two brave enough to sing. We hammered out a couple of ABBA songs and have been friends ever since.'

Jason roars. 'That is *so* Amanda.'

The table erupts in laughter again, the moment broken. Lucy narrows her eyes and says nothing. Rachel smiles. That was a punch below the belt, but she deflected it and is back in the game. Now she knows what she's dealing with.

The rest of the day hums with good-natured noise. Conversations get louder, jokes get ruder. The French windows swing open, allowing excitable children to run between inside and out. The band strikes up with a repertoire of familiar upbeat party hits. Night falls, the room darkens, and the multi-coloured disco lights pulsate to the music. Rachel has switched to sparkling water. She's not quite drunk, but one more cocktail might just raise her confidence enough to start a confrontation with Lucy, playing right into her manipulative hands.

Amanda appears by her side and takes her hand. 'Dance with me, darling.' They manoeuvre themselves onto the middle of the crowded dance floor. Amanda takes her hand, and spins her in an underarm turn, does a neat sidestep and places Rachel face-to-face with Ben, then shuffles away. *Nice move, Amanda.* Ben, looking pleasantly surprised, takes her hand and they dance. He leans in towards her and says something. She can't hear because the music's too loud, so she kisses him on the lips. She can tell he liked that, and they continue dancing, her hands on his shoulder, his around her waist. After a few more songs, they leave the dancefloor, hand in hand, and head to the lounge area with its plush sofas, soft lighting and a subdued ambiance, quiet enough to talk.

He's separated. No children and works as a self-employed kitchen fitter with a flat less than ten miles from Rachel. She likes the way he talks. He's open and uncomplicated. Ben's friend Jason strolls past behind her. She glances at him in the mirror and notices him nod to Ben and give a thumbs up. She smiles.

They wander outside together, with the excuse of needing fresh air. A smokers' group congregate by the main entrance, so they walk towards the side of the building. The music from inside fades as Uncle Jimmy gets hold of the mic and gives a slurred and rambling speech. There's cheering and a roar of laughter. But Rachel and Ben are elsewhere now. They stand in the shadow of a country house, holding hands, with the faint sound of garden wildlife in the background. He comes in close and they kiss, longer and deeper this time. It heals the sting of Lucy's jab and dissolves all of her life stresses – past and present.

It's dark by the time Rachel gets home from her late shift at the hotel on Sunday. She twists off her shoes, unbuttons her uniform and slips into soft cotton pyjamas. The kettle boils while she checks on her kitchen garden. She's still glowing from the wedding last night. She and Ben have been messaging each other, and he's taking her out for dinner on Tuesday. She asked where; he said he'll surprise her. She likes that.

She carries her tea to the desk and switches on her computer, which whirs to life with the usual flicker of light. She takes a sip and thinks back to last night – Amanda's spinning hand, Ben's body close to hers as they slow kissed outside. Maybe this is it. The turning point. Her new life path. *Please God, no more bad news.*

She opens her freelancing dashboard and notices a new message. It's from the client who paid her £1,000 pounds for discovering the SQL injection flaw. Maybe they've got another website for her to test. She really needs the money. She clicks on the message:

Hi Rachel,

I hope all is well with you, and you have received payment. We have utilised that SQL injection on our latest campaign. The company are in a panic, and we expect them to cough up soon.

I have a proposition for you. You have a talent for discovering security flaws and we need someone like you. Just to sit in the background, discovering those hard-to-find security bugs. We'll do the rest.

The money's good and you'll always get a fair share of the ransom payment. I would really like to work with you again.

Best wishes,
Aleks.

The air leaves her lungs. She freezes as she stares at the message and the blinking cursor. Her mind races. Suddenly, she's not at her desk anymore but back in the courtroom, standing in the dock, facing the judge, whose words come to her as if on playback:

If you commit another offence during the suspension period, the suspended sentence will be activated, and you will serve that time in prison.

She collapses to the floor, head in her hands, terrified of what might come next.

THE END

Epilogue

Rachel, Ray and Amanda embark on their new lifepath. Find out what that involves in a bonus chapter on my website:

www.stevewilliamsonauthor.co.uk

Facebook page: **No Crime Intended**

Acknowledgements

My deepest thanks go to my writing mentor and editor, **Thalia Suzuma**, who has been guiding me from the very beginning. From plotting and character development to pacing and structure, Thalia was always there to steer me in the right direction. A big thank you to my copyeditor, **Gary Jukes** and my cover designer, **Finn Dean** who skill and attention to detail helped make this book the best it could be.

Thank you to my colleague and friend, **Teri Petree**, for lending scientific credibility to a key scene, and to Ramandeep (Ram) Singh, another valued colleague and friend, for helping me capture the authentic atmosphere of a Security Operations Centre.

Thank you to my son **Darren**, whose stories of life in a women's prison inspired many of the scenes and characters, and to my daughter **Natasha**, a nurse who has often come to the aid of people in moments of crisis.

Thank you also to my fellow novelists from Jericho Writers. I always look forward to *Feedback Friday* and have learned much from the weekly exercises and constructive feedback of other authors.

Afterword

I have always wanted to write a cybercrime thriller. The idea lived in my head for many years, but a good story needed more than technical induced tension – It needs human depth. That's why I created Rachel: a woman under everyday pressure, making choices that many might make if pushed far enough. Ray was there from the start too: gruff, meticulous and unexpectedly endearing. As for Amanda, she simply appeared on the page one day and refused to leave. A few characters were subtly shaped by people I've known.

Synaptonica is an entirely fictional company, as are its people. The only real setting is the iconic British Museum. Ninja Magpie, and their methods, however, are rooted in reality. Social engineering, credential theft and double-extortion are not the invention of novelists but the tactics, techniques and procedures – the TTP's – commonly used by digital adversaries. Even companies with robust cyber defences can fall victim. It only takes one click, one lapse of concentration or one vulnerability to kick-start the cyber kill chain.

I wrote this story in 2025, a year when companies like Jaguar Land Rover and Marks & Spencer were hit by devastating ransomware attacks from a group known as *Scattered Spider*. Cyber extortion continues to grow in scale and sophistication and is now the biggest risk that many enterprises have to manage. Law enforcement agencies, including the UK National Crime Agency pursue the perpetrators relentlessly and some major figures have been caught and jailed. But the rewards remain high and the odds of prosecution are still vanishingly small – estimated at less than one per cent.

Cybercrime shows no sign of slowing. Don't be surprised if this theme resurfaces, in one form or another, in my future novels because behind every breach, is a human story waiting to be told.

Trust no one
Steve Williamson

Also by Steve Williamson

Latte Dreams

In *Latte Dreams: My one shot at coffee shop ownership*, Steve Williamson takes readers on a charming journey through his over-year-long venture into small business ownership.

A witty, relatable and insightful look into the realities of small business ownership, told through the voice of a novice entrepreneur.

About the author

Steve Williamson studied Computer Science at university and has built his professional career in the cyber security industry, helping large organisations defend themselves against digital adversaries, such as organised e-crime groups and nation state threat actors. A lifelong writer, his work has ranged from travel blogs to magazine features, but it is the creativity of fiction writing that truly motivates him. His twin passions of technology and storytelling often blur at the edges, inspiring stories with the edge of a psychological thriller, grounded in the realities of the digital age. For Steve, most mornings begin at the gym, a ritual that brings calm and clarity ahead of the workday. Originally from Falkirk, Scotland, Steve now lives in Northamptonshire with his wife, Sharon.

www.ingramcontent.com/pod-product-compliance
Lightning Source LLC
Chambersburg PA
CBHW030523120726
47904CB00005B/1599